# CHARLOTTE E. BASSETT

## you are here

estd 2025

**SHINE BRIGHT**
press

*For My Family*

*To Hali – my brave first love. You teach me strength every
single day. Shine bright, beautiful girl!
To Hannah – my fierce heart. You remind me every day that love
is the bravest thing we carry. Keep loving fiercely!
To Charlie – my shining muse. Your creativity is the spark
that keeps me reaching higher. Never stop imagining!
To Katie – my laughter and light. Your laughter is my
favorite song. Keep laughing loudly!
To Coban – my anchor and my home. Thank goodness for you!*

# Acknowledgments

The dedication and time required to write a novel are never carried alone. They are made possible by the love, encouragement, and patience of those who surround the author and make space for the work. I could not have written *You Are Here* without that kind of support.

To my family — thank you for being my constant source of strength, laughter, and love. You gave me the courage to tell this story and the foundation to finish it.

To my alpha reader, Hali Orizabal — your early encouragement and thoughtful feedback were invaluable, and I am deeply grateful for the light you brought into this process.

To my beta readers, Hannah Bassett, Lisa Misson, and Ayva McComas — thank you for your honesty, your insights, and your belief in this story. You each made this book stronger, and I could not have asked for a better team to walk alongside me.

And finally, to every reader who opens these pages — thank you. Stories come alive only when they are read, and I am honored that you chose to spend your time with mine.

# 1

## the arrival

AMELIA ANN LANE doesn't wear dresses. Not really. Not ever. She avoids them for work, skips them at brunch, and even steers clear at weddings—unless she's persuaded and tempted with cake.

So why had she, in a moment of uncharacteristic panic about meeting Nate Carter, woken up and zipped herself into this dress—a fitted navy-blue number that looked great on a hanger and betrayed her body with every step—was a mystery.

Now she stood in the middle of the Crawford Hotel lobby, tugging at the hem like it owed her an apology.

The fabric clung to her hips when she walked, bunched at the waist when she stood still, and shifted just enough at the neckline to make her worry she might flash someone if she breathed too deeply.

And don't even get her started on the shoes. Stylish, yes. Sensible? Only if you consider concrete stilettos sensible.

A blister was already blooming on her right heel—an angry, burning promise of regret. What had she been thinking?

Her palms were clammy, her mascara was probably melting, and her stomach did an anxious somersault every time the lobby doors opened.

In one hand, she clutched her phone a little too tightly. In the other, a neatly labeled folder—creased now, edges bent from her grip, but still a tangible attempt at control.

She hoped she looked composed. Or busy. Or invisible.

Just a fundraiser. Just a Hollywood star. Just... Nate Carter.

*Crap.*

* * *

THE LOBBY OF the Crawford Hotel in downtown Denver was a hive of activity. Tourists began their mornings with mimosas, staff in sharp uniforms navigated the space efficiently, and a toddler cried near the elevators. In the midst of all this commotion, Amelia stood motionless, feeling out of place and filled with anxiety.

She was here to welcome Nate Carter, the superhero actor, to Denver for the Grace Wells Foundation's third annual hospital fundraiser. Much to her surprise, he'd agreed to a meet-and-greet, family visits, and a gala appearance over the next two days. He wasn't quite a household name. Not the kind you'd hear in the Marvel or DC universes. But among fans of the genre, Nate Carter was a rising star. Cult-favorite turned breakout lead, especially since landing the role of Captain Orion.

She'd written the itinerary by heart, from the heart. It was a big weekend for the hospital—a bigger one for her, which was already off to a questionable start.

Her phone buzzed in her hand. A text from Ronnie lit up the screen:

> *"Breathe, Lane. Don't freak out. It's only THE Nate Carter.*
> *No big deal!*
> *Love you, see you later today!"*

Amelia blinked, exhaling through her nose as she reread it.

Ronnie, her best friend since grade school, always called her Lane now. It started right after the divorce. "You took it back," Ronnie had told her. "I'm proud of you."

Lane was Amelia's maiden name. It had been a quiet reclaiming, an act of survival as much as defiance. But somehow, hearing it from Ronnie made it sacred. Lane *was* hers.

She started typing a reply—something sarcastic and flippant, anything to slow her racing thoughts—when a sticky blur collided with her legs.

A chocolate-covered toddler slammed into her, arms outstretched like a sugar-fueled missile. Amelia stumbled back a step, catching herself, but not before a streak of brown smeared across the navy fabric of her dress.

*Of course, this would happen today.*

On any other day, she would have knelt down, pulled a funny face, perhaps inquired about the snack still gripped in the toddler's other hand. She adored children. Truly, she did. But today was not that day.

Today, she despised this dress. Today, she had a tight schedule. Today, she needed to appear polished and professional, like someone fit to host a glamorous guest—a charming Hollywood star.

The mother rushed over, wide-eyed and apologizing, before she even reached them. "Oh my gosh, I'm so sorry—he's usually not like this—here, please."

She shoved a handful of baby wipes toward Amelia with an outstretched hand.

Amelia accepted them with a forced smile and knelt to dab at the chocolate blot that now bloomed across her dress. The wipes did little but smear it around, making the spot darker and wetter than before. *Fantastic.*

"Don't worry," she managed to say to the flustered mom. "I have... a thing for accessorizing with chocolate. It's very in this season."

The mom gave a tired laugh and herded the toddler away, still offering a stream of apologies. Amelia stood, clutching the damp wipes and wondering if she could strategically angle her purse to cover the stain.

She adjusted the strap on her shoulder, fidgeting with the zipper out of habit, then scanned the lobby—part nerves, part distraction.

Her eyes landed on a woman near the windows. Phone pressed to one ear, iced coffee in the other hand, leather tote slung effortlessly from one shoulder—*that* was Cassidy Mercer. After weeks of curt emails and conversations that read as business transactions wrapped in barbed wire, Amelia could've picked her out of a lineup.

Sleek, polished, professional in that intimidating "I don't even own sweatpants" kind of way. Cassidy didn't look like she'd traveled from Los Angeles. She looked like she *was* Los Angeles.

Amelia took a breath, smoothed her dress regretfully, and approached her with the polite sort of smile she usually reserved for HOA meetings and dentist appointments.

Cassidy didn't acknowledge her at first. She held up one perfectly manicured finger, the universal symbol for *not now*, before ending the call with a single tap. No goodbye, no softening. Only immediate eye contact and a blink that somehow conveyed both disapproval and impatience.

"Cassie Mercer?" Amelia asked, extending a forced smile and a nervous hand.

"It's Cassidy Mercer," the woman corrected without hesitation, ignoring the offered handshake entirely.

Amelia swallowed. "Right. Sorry. Nice to meet you, I'm Amelia Lane."

Cassidy gave her a slow once-over—a look that made Amelia painfully aware of her not-designer shoes, the way her dress bunched at the waist, and the faint stain she hadn't entirely scrubbed away. Cassidy didn't need to say a word—her cheekbones did all the heavy lifting.

"Ms. Lane," Cassidy said briskly, "let's go over the itinerary for today."

It wasn't a request. It was a statement delivered with the resigned energy of someone who expected incompetence.

Amelia rifled through the folder in her arms and pulled out the itinerary—again. She'd sent this itinerary to Cassidy more times than she cared to count, clearly outlined, bolded, underlined, and stamped with enough confirmation emails to start a paper trail. But sure. Let's go over it.

She was about to point out the morning's first meet and greet when the energy in the lobby shifted as the air itself leaned forward.

Conversations quieted. A few heads turned.

And then she saw him.

Nate Carter.

He was taller than she'd expected. Six-foot-two at least, with shoulders that filled the doorway without trying. Lean but solid, like a distance runner who could also lift you over his head. His dark brown hair caught the light—espresso in the shadows, amber where the sun hit those loose curls that flopped just so over his forehead. The stubble along his jaw wasn't the patchy kind that screamed "I forgot to shave," but the deliberate five o'clock shadow that belonged in cologne advertisements, framing lips that looked soft despite the angular cut of his cheekbones.

He wore dark-wash jeans that fit him like they'd been measured to the millimeter, paired with a crisp white button-up rolled precisely to mid-forearm, revealing tanned wrists. *Since when did wrists become sexy?* An outfit that whispered rather than shouted, but somehow made the Italian marble and crystal chandeliers of the lobby seem suddenly ordinary.

And then there was that smile—not the practiced red-carpet flash of teeth, but something that started in his eyes, crinkling the corners before it reached his mouth, revealing a slight asymmetry in the way his lips curved upward on the left side.

She tried not to gape as he strolled toward them—toward her—but her brain briefly forgot how eyes worked. Why had her eyes frozen? Had she blinked recently? *Was blinking still a thing?*

Cassidy cleared her throat, loud enough to startle a deaf dog.

The sound jolted Amelia back to Earth in time to watch Cassidy step directly into Nate's path with the warmth of a seasoned publicist. "Good morning, Mr. Carter."

*Who is this woman, and where has she been hiding?* Amelia thought. *Do I need to download an app and subscribe to access this version of Cassidy Mercer?*

After a brief, scripted hello with Cassidy, Nate shifted his attention toward Amelia, a brighter expression now in his eyes.

"You must be the Amelia Lane I've heard so much about," Nate said.

She didn't offer a hand. She couldn't remember if she was supposed to. Did people shake hands anymore?

His voice was smooth and friendly. When Amelia turned to look at him, he was smiling at her with an openness so disarming that it was as if she'd met him before. In a dream, maybe.

"Yes," she said, a little too quickly. "That's me. Amelia Lane."

Cassidy's eyes snapped toward her like a missile locking on target.

She flipped through the itinerary and held up a page. Her fingers were still and deliberate, as if building a case against Amelia. "Ms. Lane," she said, her tone tightening, "this says *two* days." She tapped the paper twice for emphasis, her perfectly lacquered nail clicking like a gavel. "Mr. Carter is only booked for today."

Amelia's stomach tumbled. But Nate didn't flinch. He didn't even glance at the paper. He was still looking at Amelia with a smile. *That smile.*

"Cassidy," he said calmly, "could I have a word for a second?"

Cassidy blinked, but nodded tightly. "Of course."

Nate glanced back at Amelia. "Would you mind meeting us outside in a few minutes?"

Amelia nodded. Probably too eagerly. "Sure. Yes. Outside. Absolutely." Great, *now one-word answers. Nice, Amelia. Speak much?*

Before he turned, he reached out and lightly touched her arm—a gentle brush of his fingers against the fabric near her elbow. "Nice to meet you," he said, warm and sincere. "I'm Nate."

Then he was gone, following Cassidy toward the elevator corridor, her heels striking the floor like punctuation in a scathing email.

Amelia stood frozen, her heart thudding, scrambling to catch up. She touched the place on her arm where his fingers had brushed, a phantom ache blooming beneath her skin. It rooted her to the polished floor, still clutching her folder as if it were the only thing tethering her to the room.

And now Cassidy was saying he was only here for the day. Just today. Not tomorrow. Not the next day. Just—today.

Was Nate already upset? Was he planning to leave? Had she already blown it?

She took a breath. Squared her shoulders. Cool. Calm. Collected.

Or at least, a decent impersonation.

* * *

AMELIA EMERGED FROM the hotel's main entrance, the brisk morning air gently rousing her. The Colorado climate was distinctively crisp, with the sun shining brightly, yet the chill was biting at her skin. Clutching the folder closer to her chest, she paced back and forth in front of the valet stand, her heels making a sharp clicking sound on the concrete.

She tried to slow her breathing, but her thoughts moved too fast—cataloging every way this day could fall apart. What if Cassidy had already convinced Nate to leave? What if he decided this wasn't worth the press risk? What if she had blown the most critical weekend of the year before it even began?

Looking down at her watch, it was now 10:17 a.m. Eleven minutes since they disappeared toward the elevator corridor. Not that she was counting.

Amelia could feel a fresh layer of sweat forming behind her knees, despite the chill. She shifted her weight, adjusted her purse strap, and wiped her clammy palm against the side of her leg.

Then—"Thanks for waiting," came his voice, steady and warm.

Amelia turned around, startled but trying not to show it.

Nate stood just a few feet away, the morning sun softening the sharp lines of his face, turning him almost golden. He looked impossibly at ease—hands tucked into the pockets of his coat, that same half-smile playing on his lips, completely unrattled. Not by Cassidy. Not by LA. Not by awkward first meetings.

Somehow, the chaos in her chest eased—still here, but no longer screaming.

"No problem," she replied, and for the first time that morning, she almost believed it.

"I spoke with Cassidy," he said calmly. "I'm all yours for the next two days."

The words hit harder than they should have. *I'm all yours.* God, that sounded nice—dangerously nice. Like a wish whispered into the universe, or something you weren't supposed to want but did, anyway.

Her brain scrambled to remember this was professional—that he didn't mean it that way. Of course, he didn't. But her heart? Yeah, it wasn't listening. Neither was her stomach, because it flipped so fast she nearly laughed out loud.

"Really?" she managed, her voice smaller than she meant it to be.

"I wouldn't miss it," he replied with a wink that hit her squarely in the gut, sending her thoughts spiraling into places they had no business going this early in the day.

Cassidy appeared beside him, expression tightly composed, a smile pasted on like a reluctant emoji. Her heels clicked against the concrete as she came to a stop, her posture still immaculate, her tone clipped.

"We'll make it work," she said flatly, one hand adjusting the strap on her sleek black bag, searching for something—anything—to control.

Amelia opened her mouth to thank her, but barely got a breath in before Cassidy briskly continued, "Well, we should get moving. Where's the car?"

Her heart sank.

"Oh no," she blurted, wincing as she heard herself. "I forgot to arrange one. I—I'm so sorry. I have my car."

Cassidy's expression twitched. One more strike and she'd be out.

But Nate didn't miss a beat. He smiled, easy and unbothered.

"Perfect. Let's go."

* * *

THEY WALKED THROUGH the small parking lot, and Amelia guided them to her dusty green Subaru Forester. It wasn't flashy, but it was reliable—much like the person she aimed to be today.

Determined to make up for not arranging transportation ahead of time, Amelia walked quickly to the passenger side and opened the door for Nate, playing the part of a makeshift chauffeur.

*Cassidy could open her own damn door.*

As she pulled it open, a few empty granola bar wrappers fluttered out onto the pavement like confetti.

She gasped. "Oh, no—sorry! Road trip snacks." She bent to gather them, her cheeks burning.

Nate leaned against the open door, watching her with an amused glint in his eye. "Someone enjoys chocolate," he said, nodding to both the wrappers and the faint stain near her hip. "Good choice, though. Chocolate chip peanut butter?"

She smiled as she tucked the wrappers into the door pocket. "My best friend's favorite," she said lightly, trying not to let the ache creep into her voice.

Ronnie had eaten five in one night on the trip, and neither of them ever talked about it. Amelia could still picture her in the passenger seat, grinning through a mouthful of granola, swearing they'd survive the mountain roads—and Ronnie's broken heart—or die trying.

This was not the time for that story. Not with Cassidy in the back seat.

Once inside, the car was oddly quiet. Cassidy perched in the backseat, scrolling through her phone with the intensity of someone trying to manifest Wi-Fi through sheer willpower.

Nate sat beside Amelia, his long legs awkwardly folded into the passenger seat—as if they didn't build her Subaru to accommodate six-foot-tall movie stars.

"Are you always this prepared?" he asked with a teasing smile.

She glanced sideways. "Only when I forget to be."

"Is this your full-time gig? The foundation?" he asks, keeping the mood light.

Still focusing on driving, avoiding curbs, and processing the guest beside her, it took a minute for his question to sink in.

"Yeah. After... well, after everything, it has become my entire world."

He nods slowly, understanding written all over him. And somehow, she feels seen.

They rode in silence for a moment, the kind that felt full instead of awkward. Amelia kept her eyes on the road, but stole another glance when she could, thankful for every red light that let her look a little longer.

As he reached forward to shift the air vent, the edge of his T-shirt lifted—revealing part of a tattoo: two dark lines crossing at a sharp angle, curved slightly at the ends.

Baseball bats? Swords?

Above the upper line, she caught sight of something rounded. A loop? A ring? A halo?

Her eyes lingered, brow furrowed. Curious.

But before she could piece it together—

"Light's green," Cassidy announced dryly from the back seat.

Amelia startled, foot jerking to the gas as if it had remembered its job.

Her cheeks flared. "Right. Yes. Sorry."

"You OK over there?" Nate asked, voice smooth and too amused.

"Fine," she said, voice strangled. "Thinking."

"About my air vent technique or my tattoo?" he asked, flashing a grin so quick and wicked it nearly unraveled her seatbelt.

Amelia coughed. Or tried to. She might've choked on her tongue.

She fumbled with the steering wheel, eyes definitely on the road now, and not at all on the warm stretch of skin or the smirk beside her. Her brain short-circuited. Had she forgotten how legs worked? Was posture always this hard? Since when was oxygen optional?

Nate leaned back again, clearly enjoying her flustered silence. "So..." he said after a beat, "granola wrappers your version of backseat snacks, or is this your personal filing system?"

Amelia laughed—actually laughed—and shook her head. "You know what? I'm not even going to defend myself."

"Probably wise," he said, grinning. And then, with that same effortless charm, he winked at her.

And somehow, in the middle of all of it, she was glad she'd forgotten to schedule a car.

# 2

# room 316

T HE SCENT IN the hospital atrium was strong, dominated by the crisp aroma of lemon-scented sanitizer blending with the chemical odor from the freshly polished floors. Beneath these layers, a subtle hint of cafeteria mashed potatoes lingered, unmistakably marking the space as a hospital lobby.

Amelia knew the smell too well—it had seeped into her bones, stitched itself into the fabric of who she was. It was the scent of waiting rooms and whispered updates, of holding tiny hands and praying for miracles. Familiar. Heartbreaking. Yet, for Amelia, it was comforting, in a strange way.

She walked in ahead of the others, nodding to the security desk, waving the badge she already had in hand.

Nate and Cassidy followed, taking in the bright murals and quiet energy of the place.

"This is Denver's Children's Hospital," Amelia said, her voice softer now. "We will get your guest badges before heading up to the third floor."

They stopped briefly at the front desk, where Amelia gave a quick wave to Janice, the volunteer coordinator, who was already reaching for the visitor's badges.

The woman's eyes widened the moment she realized who was standing in front of her. "Oh, my—are you...?" Janice asked, holding the badge midair.

Nate smiled, easy and warm. "That's me. Just here, hoping to make a few new friends today.”

Janice recovered quickly, her expression softening with genuine delight. “Well, you’ve certainly made my morning. These kids are going to be over the moon.” She handed over the badges with a small laugh. “And for what it’s worth… I think I’ve seen your movie about four times now, courtesy of my grandkids.”

“That makes you the real superhero,” Nate said with a grin.

Janice beamed at that. “Welcome to our hospital, Mr. Carter.”

“Call me Nate,” he said, his tone easy, familiar. “Mr. Carter makes me sound like my dad.”

Janice laughed. “Noted. Welcome, Nate.”

With a nod of thanks, Nate and Cassidy followed Amelia past the desk and into the large central lobby, where butterflies and inspirational quotes in looping fonts sketched across the walls. Soft light bathed the space, colors bright and welcoming, but the silence settled differently than it had in the entryway. Heavier.

“This way,” Amelia said, her steps slowing slightly as they approached the elevator.

Nate caught up to her side. “So... what’s on the third floor?”

Amelia didn’t answer right away. She pressed the elevator button and stared up as the numbers ticked down. She wanted to say ‘*my everything.*’ But that wasn’t true anymore.

She cleared the pit from her throat. “The third floor is long-term pediatric care,” she said finally. “These are the kids who’ve been here for weeks, some for months or longer. Some are waiting for transplants or chemotherapy. Some are recovering from surgeries or in the middle of treatment plans that feel never-ending.”

Nate nodded, his expression shifting. “Got it.”

Cassidy, still scrolling through her phone, barely looked up.

The elevator doors opened with a soft chime, and the three of them shuffled inside.

Amelia’s fingers tightened around the folder in her arms. She’d taken this elevator hundreds of times. But today, the memories were loud. Hallway 3B,

Room 316. She didn't need to look; she could feel it.

Paper cranes lined the walls and dangled from the ceiling, greeting them the moment they stepped off the elevator.

The third floor wasn't somber, exactly, but it held a weight the other levels didn't. A child's laugh echoed from down the hall—sweet, unexpected, softening everything for a moment.

"Wow," Nate said quietly, scanning the hallway. "It doesn't feel like a hospital at all."

"They sure try," Amelia said. "These kids deserve more than machines and missed birthdays."

To her surprise, Amelia caught the faintest whisper behind her–Cassidy, barely audible, murmuring. "Beautiful."

Amelia didn't turn around, but the comment lingered—thin and surprising, a strand of warmth she hadn't expected from Cassidy Mercer.

A young boy spotted them from a doorway, his eyes going wide. "Mom! That's Captain Orion!"

Nate grinned, "You found me."

In an instant, the energy shifted, and the day officially started. Kids peeked from doorways, nurses whispered excitedly, and a small group of parents began moving toward them, gratitude written across their faces.

Without hesitating, Nate took off toward the boy. He crouched to the boy's level, gave him a high-five, and embraced him.

"He has been talking about your new movie all week," the young boy's mom said.

"You must be a Captain Orion fan," Nate replied.

Both the boy and his mom shook their heads quickly, vibrating with pure joy.

Cassidy stepped forward, her usual icy composure thawing for the first time today. She held out an 8x10 glossy of Captain Orion—so much for being immune to celebrity charm. "Would you like a signed photo from Captain Orion himself?" she asked, and–unless Amelia was imagining it–Cassidy smiled.

It thrilled Amelia to see the photos, a touch she hadn't thought of.

She exhaled a quiet breath she hadn't realized she'd been holding. Thank God. He didn't need coaching. He wasn't hesitating.

"He's jumping right in," one nurse whispered to Amelia as she passed.

Amelia smiled. "He sure is."

* * *

NATE VISITED EACH room one by one, ensuring he met every child eager to see him. He autographed casts and pillowcases, posed for photos, and attentively listened to long tales about beloved movies, snacks, and the pets they missed at home. Everyone received his full attention, and no one was hurried or ignored.

Parents hovered near the doors, offering hesitant smiles that grew more genuine as the morning stretched on. Nurses leaned quietly in doorways, watching from a respectful distance but unable to hide their gratitude. Even the walls — papered with crayon-colored rainbows and hopeful sayings — seemed to soften beneath the ripple of laughter and whispers of "Captain Orion."

Cassidy stayed close, practically flinging the portraits as if she were hosting a game show. You get a picture! You get a picture! Everyone gets a picture! By the fifth autograph, she had even slipped off her blazer, revealing a softer side beneath her usual armor of black and silk. In Amelia's book, this practically counted as a personality.

Maybe Cassidy wasn't here to manage only a schedule. Maybe, quietly, she needed to feel something too.

And Amelia? She stood back, watching it all unfold — her hospital, her mission, the place she had shaped from grief into something that looked a little like hope — and for the first time in a long time, she felt something loosen in her chest.

It wasn't just that Nate was good at this. It was the way he crouched to their level, the way he listened, the way he made each child feel important and seen. There was no doubt this moment wasn't for publicity or press, but simply for them.

In one room, he lingered a little longer with a boy recovering from surgery and his younger sister, who sat perched at the foot of the hospital bed, eyeing Nate with suspicion.

"You don't look that tall in real life," the girl said, arms crossed.

Nate grinned. "That's because I left my superhero boots at home. They add at least three inches."

The girl narrowed her eyes, clearly unconvinced. "Do they light up?"

"Only when I'm running late," Nate said, leaning in with a mock-conspiratorial whisper. "But don't tell anyone. That's classified."

That earned him a giggle, and her brother — pale but smiling — gave Nate a thumbs-up from beneath his blanket.

"You're funny," the boy said.

"Don't let that get around. I've got a reputation to uphold," Nate replied, signing a photo and handing it over with a wink.

Before they left the room, Nate took a few photos with the boy and his sister, crouching between them like they were old friends. The boy's mother hovered nearby, her hand pressed over her heart, eyes fixed on her children, as if watching them might slow time.

"Thank you," she said as she pulled Nate into a quick, grateful hug. "You don't know what this means—to him, to all of us."

Nate smiled, gently and sincerely. "I think I do."

The mom laughed softly, wiping at her eyes as she stepped back. "Well... thank you, anyway. For today."

With a final wave to the kids, Nate stepped into the hallway again, looking around for the next room.

Amelia caught Cassidy's eye as they watched him, something unspoken passing between them. Admiration, maybe. Gratitude. Or simply the quiet acknowledgment that not everyone would have handled this day with that much heart.

Only a few more rooms remained on the third floor.

Amelia glanced down the hall — Room 316 was next.

She touched the simple silver necklace at her collarbone—a nervous habit she hadn't shaken.

It had been four years since she walked into that room, and yet, even now, the thought of doing it again felt impossible.

Her pulse quickened. Her chest tightened. She could see the pale blue door from here, the paper crane taped beside it still faded from time. A door, it's just a door… but not to her. Never to her.

"Let's circle back to this one," she said, already pivoting toward the next door before anyone could notice her hesitation.

Cassidy didn't question it.

A few steps ahead, Nate had stopped where a teenage boy had wheeled himself halfway out into the hallway, IV pole trailing behind him. His hospital gown hung loose at the neck, and his shaved head bore the faint shadow of recent stitches.

"You're really him?" the boy asked, eyeing Nate with a blend of skepticism and awe only a teenager could manage.

Nate crouched to meet his eye level, leisurely and unhurried. "Depends who you ask," he said with a grin. "But yeah, I'm him. No costume today, though. Didn't want to outshine the staff."

The boy snorted, shaking his head. "My sister's gonna freak when she hears this."

"That's why we need evidence," Nate said, reaching for the glossy poster Cassidy handed him. "Autograph? Photo? Bragging rights? Let's make it official."

"Definitely all three," the boy said, grinning now.

Nate signed the poster with a dramatic flourish, posed for a quick picture with the boy's phone, and ended with a pretend-serious fist bump that had the boy laughing by the time they said goodbye.

"Oh, could you sign one for my sister, too?" the boy asked as Nate stood. "Her name's Lucy. She's obsessed with you, but she couldn't come today. She had, like… dance or something."

"Well, we can't let Lucy miss out," Nate said.

He took another photo from Cassidy, scrawled a quick signature across the bottom, and added: *To Lucy — Keep dancing. Stay brave. — Captain Orion.*

He handed it back with a wink. "Tell her I say hello."

"Thanks," the boy said, his grin wide and earnest now. "I'm Ryan, by the way."

"Good to meet you, Ryan." Nate gave a final nod. "Tell Lucy Captain Orion's got her back."

Ryan laughed again, shaking his head as he rolled back toward his room, the newly signed treasures secured in his lap.

Amelia checked the clock without realizing it. Somehow, the hours had slipped past without her noticing.

The morning had passed in a breeze. She almost forgot about Room 316.

Almost.

# 3

# my new friend

THE FOURTH FLOOR exuded a unique tranquility, marked by a noticeable quiet. There were fewer machines and fewer visitors, yet the courage remained unchanged.

Nate walked beside Amelia as they stepped off the elevator, moving easily through the corridor lined with IV pumps and crash carts.

Older children filled the rooms, some hunched over math worksheets with pencils gripped in IV-taped hands, others lost in the glow of Nintendo Switches or carefully painting ceramic figurines. Polaroids and school portraits lined the mint-green walls in mismatched frames—smiling faces from before diagnoses and treatment plans. Patchwork quilts from grandmothers and tie-dyed fleece blankets from summer camps softened the rigid hospital beds with their mechanical rails. Threadbare teddy bears with matted fur and one-eyed stuffed rabbits kept faithful watch from the window ledges; these guardians of childhood brought small, defiant echoes of home into the antiseptic, fluorescent-lit space.

Amelia led the way, her finger occasionally lifting toward framed artwork and handwritten cards that lined the corridor walls. She caught Nate pausing before a child's watercolor painting, his steps slowing to a reverent halt, his expression softening the way people's faces do in cathedrals or before masterpieces. No explanation needed—he understood what these walls held.

Sensing Amelia's heavy heart, he moved closer to her. "Are you okay?" he asked softly.

Amelia nodded. "Yeah. This floor feels different. It's less about distraction and more about resilience."

Nate looked down the hallway thoughtfully. "Yeah," he replied softly. "I get it."

The energy in the air had subtly changed—not drastically, but enough to be noticed. There was now room to breathe, to listen, to linger without the pressure of a schedule looming over them.

Somewhere between taking the elevator and standing in this hallway, something had relaxed. In him. In her. In the space between them.

They wandered leisurely from one room to the next. Nate greeted each child with the same genuine warmth he had shown on the floor below, but there was a deeper quality to these interactions. Conversations extended, questions hung in the air, and laughter emerged more slowly and authentically. Parents sat by the bedsides with coffee in hand and weary smiles, their gratitude softer yet equally sincere. These encounters weren't brief; they were constant reminders that connections remained important in this place.

In one room, Nate paused. Baseball posters covered the walls, a faded jersey draped over the back of a chair, a glove resting on the windowsill as if it had been waiting for someone to notice it. The boy in the bed couldn't have been over sixteen—tall, but thinner than he should've been. An Atlanta Braves cap sat low on his shaved head. His parents sat nearby, worn at the edges in a way Amelia recognized too well.

"Are you a Braves fan?" Nate asked, nodding toward the hat.

The boy—Caleb, according to the chart—grinned faintly. "Since forever."

"Respect. I grew up on West Coast baseball, but I've got no beef with Atlanta." Nate leaned against the doorframe like he had nowhere else to be. "What position?"

"Catcher. Or... I was." Caleb tapped his fingers against the blanket. "Hard to squat when I'm always hooked up to IV poles."

Nate didn't flinch. Instead, he offered a gentle smile. "Catcher's the toughest job on the field. You know that, right? The whole game runs through you."

Caleb gave a half-shrug. "Doesn't feel like it right now."

"Maybe not today," Nate said. "But trust me—once a catcher, always a catcher. It's a mindset. Tough. Stubborn. Strategic. Sounds like you're already built for a comeback story."

The boy's mom blinked hard. His dad gave Nate a quiet nod—the kind of nod men gave when words got stuck behind emotion.

"Mind if I sign something for you?" Nate asked. "For the next chapter, whenever it starts."

Caleb nodded, more certain now. Nate's gaze shifted to the glove on the windowsill—worn-in and familiar in a way that pulled at something unspoken.

"This feels right?" he asked, lifting it gently and already reaching for a Sharpie. "Feels like the right call."

Caleb grinned. "Perfect."

Nate signed the leather just above the webbing, writing in bold strokes: *To Caleb — Keep calling the plays. See you back on the field.*

He set the glove back on the windowsill with quiet care, as if it belonged there until Caleb was ready to take it home again.

Before departing, Nate faced Caleb's father, shook his hand with a firm, steady grip, and then embraced him in a short, friendly hug. The father patted Nate's shoulder, his gratitude beyond words.

Next, Nate embraced Caleb's mom, taking his time in a more extended hug. He whispered something inaudible to Amelia, yet whatever he said made her weary eyes soften, brighten, and finally fill with tears.

Amelia leaned against the doorframe, something catching in her chest. Nate had taken more time here than anywhere else. Not just with Caleb—but with his parents, too.

She didn't know why this room mattered more. But it did.

When they stepped back into the hallway, Nate gave her a small, unreadable smile—something held back behind it. She didn't press.

But as he rubbed the back of his neck, Amelia thought—maybe—she caught the faintest trace of tears rising in his eyes. Not full. Not obvious. Just the edge of something held too long.

He cleared his throat. "Mind if I find a restroom real quick?"

She nodded, saying nothing, watching him disappear down the hall with a stride more steady than his expression.

When he returned a few minutes later, his face had settled. Whatever weight he carried, he'd folded it back under the surface—neatly tucked beneath the practiced smile of someone who'd learned to compartmentalize.

She recognized it. She had lived it.

Whatever had stirred in that room... it meant something—more than he was saying.

At the nurses' station, the atmosphere changed once more. Word had spread among the staff that Captain Orion was making his rounds. A group of nurses gathered, phones in hand and smiles on their faces. Nate, exuding effortless charm, leaned in to snap photos, sign badges, and even strike a dramatic pose next to a crash cart as if it were part of a film set.

Amelia observed how he transformed into this different persona—lighthearted, magnetic, and playful. Yet, the memory of that moment in the hallway lingered with her.

This wasn't just another photo opportunity.

Not for him.

Not today.

"You're officially the best thing to happen to this floor all week," one nurse said, laughing as she tucked her phone away.

"I'll take that," Nate replied with a grin and a salute. "But you're the real heroes. I'm just the guy in a costume with decent lighting."

He took his time with every thank you—not for cameras or press, but because he meant it.

Because kindness mattered.

And saying it out loud seemed to matter even more.

* * *

AS THE LAUGHTER faded and they moved forward, Amelia realized Cassidy had disappeared. No clicking heels behind them, no schedule updates, no hovering presence—just absence where the publicist had been. The question of where she'd gone flickered briefly in Amelia's mind, then dissolved. She glanced at Nate walking beside her, his profile relaxed in the hallway's gentle light.

Whatever had happened to Cassidy could wait. This moment—just the two of them moving through the quiet corridor—felt too precious to interrupt with questions.

They turned the corner and stepped into room 412.

A teenage girl looked up from her sketchpad, brown eyes cautious beneath a rainbow-colored beanie. Polaroid snapshots covered the walls, sketchbook drawings spilled across the desk, and Taylor Swift claimed every spare surface—from posters to vinyls.

"Hi there," Nate said, stepping in with an easy smile. "I'm Nate."

The girl sat up straighter, caught between shyness and awe. Her pencil hovered mid-sketch.

"Mm, hi. I'm Emily," she said.

Nate gestured around the room. "Nice to meet you, Emily. Are these all yours?"

She nodded, instinctively tucking a strand of hair that wasn't there anymore beneath her beanie. "Yeah. Drawing helps me when I'm stuck here. Gives me something to do."

"These are amazing," Nate said, stepping closer to one of the wall sketches—a moody charcoal portrait of a horse mid-gallop. "You've got real talent."

Emily's smile brightened her whole face, then faltered slightly. She glanced down at her sketchpad. "After they told me you were visiting, I... I sketched Captain Orion," she admitted, fingers fidgeting with the corner of the page.

"You're kidding," Nate said, his eyes lighting up. The grin that followed was pure delight. "Can I see it?"

Emily hesitated, then reached for the sketchpad propped against her pillow. She flipped through several pages before turning the book around.

The artwork leapt off the page—Captain Orion stood with legs braced wide, cosmic energy crackling from his outstretched fingers toward a sky filled with impossible stars. Behind him loomed the silhouette of the Nebula Voyager, its angular hull catching phantom light. Emily had captured the tiny scar above his left eyebrow that most fan art missed and rendered his uniform not in the film's glossy blue but in midnight tones that seemed to absorb the light around them. Her charcoal strokes were confident, almost aggressive in places, yet delicate where a shadow met light across the contours of his face.

Nate stared at it, his smile growing. "This is incredible. You totally nailed the eyebrows."

Emily laughed, covering her mouth with her hand.

"You can have it if you want it," she said, her cheeks flushing again.

"Are you serious?" Nate blinked. "Are you sure?"

The look on his face said it all. He wanted it. And he knew what it meant.

"Yes, of course," she said. "You can have it. I mean—it's yours."

Nate placed a hand over his heart. "I'll treasure it forever. But only if I can trade you something."

He gently pulled a blank page from the back of her sketchpad and smoothed it across the tray table, as if this had been the plan all along.

"Autograph for an artist," he said, scrawling his name in bold ink. "And we need some selfies. You know, for my socials. Gotta show everyone my new artist friend."

Emily's face lit up. "Okay!"

They snapped a handful of photos—one serious, one goofy, one with Nate proudly holding his new portrait.

"Tag me," Nate said with a wink. "Deal?"

"Deal," Emily replied, eyes glowing.

Then Nate turned to Amelia, who had been standing quietly, admiration softening her features.

"Oh," he said, "Have you met my friend Amelia?"

Emily looked up from her phone and froze. "You're Amelia? The lady who runs the Grace Wells Foundation?"

Amelia smiled and stepped forward. "That's me."

"I've seen you in the halls," Emily said. "You're kind of a legend."

Amelia laughed, a blush creeping into her cheeks. "Well, that's a new one."

Emily nodded, her expression turning more earnest. "No... It's true. My mom believes you're the reason this place has changed. It's warmer, better. You help people feel remembered here."

Amelia's throat tightened. She didn't know what to say—so she simply smiled and squeezed Emily's hand before they said goodbye.

As they stepped into the hallway, Amelia walked a little closer to Nate. The space between them had changed. It felt shared now. Steady.

"Are you hungry?" she asked as they reached the end of the corridor.

Nate looked over, a look of exaggerated gravity written on his face. "Starving. I didn't want to be the one to break the spell and admit it first."

Amelia smiled broadly. "Great. I always organize a lunch for staff and volunteers the day before the gala. It's kind of a tradition. You're already invited."

"Perfect," Nate said, the smile back in his voice. "Lead the way."

# 4

# my best friend

THE CONFERENCE PAVILION on the first floor no longer resembled a typical hospital space. Instead, it radiated a welcoming warmth. Soft, golden light cascaded over tables draped in elegant linen, casting gentle shadows that danced across the room. Buffet trays emitted fragrant, curling wisps of steam, each holding a delightful array of comfort foods that beckoned with the promise of home-cooked satisfaction. Mason jars, filled to the brim with a vibrant assortment of wildflowers, added bursts of color and life to the scene. The staff had quietly transformed one of the smaller rooms, not into the grandeur of a formal gala, but into something gentler. It was an atmosphere of intimacy, radiating a human touch. This was a celebration dedicated to the individuals who had brought everything to fruition, a heartfelt acknowledgment of their hard work and dedication.

The air was thick with the scent of roasted vegetables, baked ziti, and warm bread.

Amelia walked in with Nate just behind her. This was her space. Her people.

It wasn't the gala, but this was the heartbeat of the whole thing—the staff, the volunteers, the ones who kept the lights on and the families cared for when no one else was watching.

The room was already filling. Volunteers and hospital staff chatted over sweet tea and cheesecake, laughter bubbling beneath the hum of conversation. Everyone looked up when she entered, and a few clapped.

"She's here!" someone called out.

Amelia laughed, shaking her head. "I told them no applause," she murmured to Nate.

"They didn't listen," he replied, grinning.

A woman from the child life team wrapped Amelia in a quick hug. "You're a miracle worker; you know that? This place looks amazing. And these centerpieces!"

"Thank Pinterest," Amelia said with a wink, then gestured toward the spread of food. "Let's eat before anyone asks me to make a speech."

They joined the short buffet line, Nate grabbing a plate behind her. He leaned in, voice low. "Is there a competition for the best pasta plate? Because I'm going to win."

Before she could reply, a voice cut through the noise.

"Lane, I have missed you!"

Amelia turned just in time to be engulfed in a one-armed hug and a swirl of vanilla perfume.

"Ronnie, you just saw me," she said, voice lifting with affection. "Thanks for making it."

"I always make it, plus, if I had known they were serving pasta, I would have skipped my last meeting. The new rotation is eating me alive. But for you, I would skip my wedding." Ronnie replied, pulling back to look her over. "You look good. Tired, but good. And—wait—is that a dress? Are we okay?"

Amelia laughed, rolling her eyes. "Don't start, Ronnie."

"I'm just saying," Ronnie teased, nudging her side. "Last time you wore a dress to work, I think Obama was still in office."

"It's for the fundraiser," Amelia said, smoothing the fabric like it needed defending.

"Mm-hmm," Ronnie replied, clearly unconvinced, but grinning. "Well, you clean up nicely."

Amelia nudged her with her elbow. "Let's go back to this wedding you just mentioned. You have planned nuptials I haven't been aware of yet?"

Ronnie snorted. "Please. As you know, my mom's been on me for years, convinced I'm going to die alone with a bunch of cats. Meanwhile, I can't even commit to a new pair of scrubs."

Amelia laughed, though something warm settled in her chest. Ronnie always deflected with humor, but Amelia knew it was more than jokes.

For a moment, surrounded by laughter and clinking glasses, Amelia let herself breathe. Ronnie was here, carrying her own load, yet still finding room to hold Amelia's too.

She studied her friend; exhaustion etched faintly on her face. Ronnie's scrubs were a stark contrast to Amelia's meticulously selected attire. Her scrubs were dark green, crisp, and eminently practical, adorned with trauma scissors, hemostats, and a Sharpie neatly clipped to every available pocket, each tool ready for immediate use. A hospital badge dangled from her chest, swaying gently as she moved, prominently displaying ER LEAD RN in bold letters beneath her name, a testament to her authority and expertise in the bustling emergency room.

If anyone in this hospital needed something done quickly and correctly, they called Veronica Wells.

If they needed it done with a side of sarcasm and black coffee, they called her twice.

"How's work?" Amelia asked, smoothly changing the subject.

"Busy," Ronnie replied, her grin suggesting it was more a compliment than a complaint. "Just how I like it. But I told them I was taking a lunch break today, no arguments. Besides..." — she added, glancing toward Nate—"I heard Captain Orion was making an appearance."

Nate, still holding a heaping plate of pasta and *clearly* not eavesdropping, raised a brow. "Is that me?"

Ronnie turned and extended a hand, all confidence and mischief. The trauma shears clipped to her waistband caught the light.

"You must be the famous Nate Carter. I'm Veronica Wells—Ronnie to people I like."

"Nate. Or Nathan to people who like me," he said, shaking her hand with an easy smile. "Big fan of the name Veronica, by the way. Totally underused."

Ronnie tilted her head, sizing him up. "You're smoother than I expected."

"Give me time," Nate said, grinning. "I'm pacing myself."

Ronnie snorted. "Emergency room people don't trust anyone until we've seen them under pressure."

"That's fair," Nate said. "Lunch lines count, right?"

Amelia was about to chime in, amused, when a volunteer coordinator waved her over to the Silent Auction table.

They found an open table near the windows, and Amelia set her plate down beside Nate's before straightening with a sigh.

"Back in a minute," she told them, handing her plate to Nate. "Don't let Ronnie scare you."

"I make no promises," Ronnie called after her.

Amelia smiled as she walked away.

Ronnie had a way of pulling her into trouble—the harmless kind, usually, but trouble all the same. She doubted Nate would be the exception.

She probably shouldn't leave the two of them alone.

* * *

WHEN AMELIA CAME back, she found Ronnie had left, and Nate sat at the round table with two vacant chairs. As she neared, he pushed her plate in her direction, a slight smile appearing on his lips as she sat down.

"Where'd Ronnie go?" Amelia asked, unfolding her napkin and grabbing her fork.

"She got called back to work," Nate said. "But she told me to tell you that if the dessert's good, she expects leftovers."

"Sounds like her," she said, almost to herself. "To know Ronnie is to love her."

"Well then," Nate said without missing a beat, "I love her."

Amelia laughed, nearly choking on her drink. The words hit unexpectedly— easy, unforced, and oddly comforting. Not romantic. Not performative. Just true.

"We've been best friends since the first grade," she added, a trace of joy in her tone. "She punched a boy in the lunch line for calling me weird because I brought a tuna sandwich and a Nancy Drew book to school."

Nate raised an eyebrow, amused. "Defender of justice from the beginning, huh?"

"Always," Amelia nodded. "She's the reason I survived middle school, heartbreak, college, loss... everything. She's loud and loyal and bossy as hell, but there's no one I'd rather have in my corner."

Nate leaned back slightly, watching her. "You're lucky. Working in the same place as your best friend... that's pretty rare. Makes it feel like less of a job, doesn't it?"

Amelia smiled. "Most days, yes. Other days, she makes fun of my outfits and steals my coffee."

"Still worth it," Nate said, picking up his fork. "Not everyone gets that."

Nate's eyes didn't leave hers. "That kind of friend doesn't come around often."

She nodded, her throat suddenly tight.

"I forgot to ask," Amelia said, setting her glass back down, letting the moment lighten. "Where's Cassidy?"

"She went back to the hotel."

"Oh."

Amelia paused. She wasn't sure what answer she expected, but not that.

"She didn't say goodbye," she added, more to herself than to him.

"No," he said, voice even, "she didn't."

He wiped his mouth and hands with his napkin before pressing it back into his lap. "Right before we left the third floor, she pulled me aside and said she needed to get some work done and was going to get an Uber to the hotel. She sent me a message a little while ago saying she was going to catch a flight back to L.A. tonight and start working on my next press run."

"Wow. That's... unexpected," Amelia nodded slowly.

"She never really loves being on these things," Nate said. "But this time felt different."

"Different how?"

He hesitated. "She didn't say. But she mentioned she thought I'd be fine here."

He said it with the casual certainty of someone used to Cassidy disappearing. Amelia couldn't tell if it was exhaustion talking or if he really thought it didn't matter.

Amelia chewed on the thought before slowly nodding and filing it away. Maybe it didn't matter. But perhaps it did.

Cassidy Mercer didn't strike her as someone who would disappear midday without saying something. At the very least, a quick goodbye.

It felt... off.

Amelia glanced around the room, then at her plate, and finally at Nate. A reflective tone colored her words. "It's nice to have a moment alone with you."

The instant she spoke, she felt a blush creeping up her cheeks.

Nate's smile was unhurried and sincere. "I was just thinking that, too."

They continued their lunch in a comfortable silence, the room's buzz diminishing as tables cleared and conversations turned into soft background noise.

By the time they got up to leave, most of the volunteers and staff had already departed, their farewells leaving a gentle trace in the room. Amelia took one last look at the door, half-expecting to spot Cassidy waiting in the corridor. But she wasn't there.

Truly gone.

She watched Nate, wondering if he'd check his phone. Send a message. Make a call.

But he didn't.

He just kept moving—like someone who'd learned how to live with people leaving.

A faint ache settled in her chest. Not grief exactly. Just a space where a question lived, unanswered.

She considered asking and pushing for more.

But instead, she slipped her purse over her shoulder and let the silence stay.

Nate didn't fill it. He walked beside her as they made their way outside, the rhythm of their steps steady in the quiet.

The answers would come later. Right now, she just needed this—someone who knew how to walk beside her in silence.

5

# a place for you

T HE DAY SLOWLY came to a close, with no dramatic goodbyes, just a gradual easing into the evening. Amelia was grateful for this, as she had been feeling emotionally overwhelmed throughout the day.

The elevator ride down to the parking garage was enveloped in a hushed silence, broken only by the soft whir of machinery. The walk across the dimly lit concrete expanse to her car was equally quiet, their footsteps echoing slightly in the stillness. As they slid into her vehicle, there was a palpable sense of relief, as if they collectively exhaled and let the tension of the day dissipate. The day had been both weighty and fulfilling, leaving them with a sense of accomplishment mingled with fatigue.

With the engine humming and the city stretching beyond the windshield, Amelia drove Nate back to The Crawford. The drive wasn't long—maybe ten minutes—but it stretched in a way that felt bigger, like time itself was offering them room to breathe.

A soft indie song played on the radio—one she usually turned up when she was alone. She hadn't noticed it was on until now.

This time, she left the volume alone.

Nate settled next to her, at ease, his arm draped over the passenger door as though he had occupied that spot countless times. He didn't appear exhausted, not really, but there was a calmness about him that mirrored her own. It seemed as if they were both silently reflecting on the day's events, perfectly in tune, with no need to speak.

The steady rhythm of the road filled the space between them. Amelia's grip tightened on the wheel, her thumb brushing the stitched leather as her thoughts finally caught up.

*Was this what it felt like to want something again? To not rush toward or away from it, but to sit in it?*

She glanced sideways at Nate, catching the easy curve of his jaw, the softness in his eyes as he looked out the window. Part of her wanted to pull over and memorize this version of him—quiet, present, without the weight of the world pressing in.

*Maybe I don't want this day to end after all.*

As they neared the Crawford, she exhaled slowly, a reluctant tug in her chest.

She eased the car under the front awning of the Crawfords' front door and put it in park.

Nate slowly relaxed his arms into his lap and looked over, warm-eyed. "Would you like to come in? Grab some dinner?"

Her fingers tightened around the steering wheel instinctively, her pulse kicking up as though she'd crested the first hill on a roller coaster. The question was casual—easy—but her reaction was not. She could feel it in the flush climbing up her neck, the way her body had gone suddenly, traitorously alert.

Amelia's hands stayed on the wheel. She hadn't realized how tightly she had clung to it until now.

He smiled, unrushed. "It's only food. No Cassidy. No cameras. No expectations."

She bit the inside of her cheek, puzzled by the sudden dryness in her throat. It was just dinner, nothing more. Yet, the straightforward invitation seemed to lead to a path she was uncertain about exploring. Was dinner truly just that, or was it the beginning of something she was hesitant to acknowledge she desired? She chuckled, keeping her gaze fixed on the dashboard, unwilling to glance at him now.

It was probably nothing—a friendly gesture. But her pulse had picked up, anyway. She hated that.

"Come on," he added, voice low and inviting. "You've been taking care of everything all day. Let me take care of dinner tonight."

His invitation hung in the air between them, weightless yet somehow anchoring her to the seat. The ease in his voice made it sound simple—just dinner, just tonight—and her heart leaned toward it like a plant to sunlight. But her lips remained still, as if they'd forgotten how to shape themselves around the word "yes."

She wished she could explain that it wasn't his fault—it was her own feelings. Everything felt too fresh and delicate, like she was holding a fragile glass ornament that could break with the slightest pressure.

He made it all seem so simple, and perhaps if she didn't feel that tightness in her chest whenever he gazed at her, she would have agreed.

But she released her hands and slowly shook her head. "I can't tonight."

Her voice was steady, but it didn't feel believable. She was afraid of wanting more. Fearful of how quickly she'd say yes to the next thing, and the next.

Nate didn't press. His nod was simple, steady—no disappointment, no pressure. "All right. Another time, maybe."

Silence filled the car like a third passenger, gentle and undemanding.

"So... rain check?" she asked, surprising herself. She wanted to know if he meant what he said. If she said no now, would she still get the chance to say yes later?

His smile widened a fraction, soft and sure. "The offer stands. Whenever you're ready."

Her chest constricted once more, but this time, the pain felt almost pleasant. It had been ages since anyone had said that. No one had truly waited for her before.

"Okay," she said, the word coming out as a whisper. A little more honest than she intended.

He opened his door, then paused, resting his arm on the open window. "Thanks for today, Amelia."

She smiled, "Thank you."

"I can't wait for tomorrow," he replied with a slight wink as he turned on his heels.

She almost called him back. The words caught in her throat—*Maybe I could stay, just for one drink.* But the moment passed, and the door clicked shut.

She watched his silhouette blur behind the frosted glass of the Crawfords' entrance, fingers still wrapped around the steering wheel long after his figure had disappeared completely.

The moment stretched on. Longer than Amelia cared to acknowledge.

* * *

THE DRIVE HOME to Longmont unfolded beneath a vast Colorado sky, painted in shades of lavender and deep blue, with the majestic mountains anchored at the edge of the Earth, like a promise steadfastly fulfilled. As she merged onto I-25, the Denver skyline gradually dissolved behind her, melting into the soft hues of dusk and the embrace of distance, replaced by the gentle, rhythmic pulse of the Front Range.

This stretch of highway was a familiar companion — long and open, skimming past bustling suburbs that buzzed with life and sprawling farmland where the fence lines seemed to blur seamlessly with the endless horizon. The further north she drove, the more the landscape relaxed and unfurled into a tranquil expanse. Houses dwindled, fields broadened, and the crisp air seemed to expand, filling her lungs with a refreshing sense of depth. In the distance, the jagged silhouette of Longs Peak stood tall against the deepening twilight, a constant presence akin to the steady gaze of an old friend.

Longmont was a world apart from Denver. Slower, more intimately woven. A place adorned with mountain views and vibrant community murals, dotted with quaint local bakeries and winding bike trails, where families remembered your name with warmth. It was a town where neighbors still shoveled each other's driveways, where coffee shops proudly displayed children's art in their windows, and where grief moved through the streets not as a solitary burden but with a shared, gentle understanding. It was not something to be hidden away, but rather something to be embraced by the community.

Here, Amelia felt a profound sense of belonging.  She passed the cozy little paint-your-own studio where countless rainy afternoons had been spent, its shelves still brimming with hand-painted mugs and charmingly crooked trinket dishes.  The park where she walked on the hardest days, tracing the familiar loops in her well-worn sneakers beneath the weight of cherished memories.  The corner store where the clerk always greeted her with a friendly wave, where the freezer hummed steadily beneath the flickering glow of fluorescent lights.

By the time she pulled into the Old Town neighborhood, the sun had dipped low behind the rooftops, leaving the quiet streets aglow under the amber wash of streetlights.  Porch lights blinked on in scattered rows, families winding down behind curtained windows, and the first stars stitched themselves across the sky.

She parked in her driveway as the stillness settled in fully, the weight of the day pressing gently at her temples. Her thoughts had run in circles the whole way home.

Amelia immersed herself in her familiar habits, trying to create a sense of normalcy. She put on pajamas and made tea she wouldn't drink. She lingered in the kitchen longer than needed, tidying a drawer that was already neat and wiping a spotless counter.

When she finally made it to bed, her body felt heavy, but her mind refused to follow.

She lay back against the neat sheets, replaying the day's moments like beads on a rosary. The way Nate smiled—the sound of his laugh. The warmth of his hand brushing hers in that easy, familiar way, as though they'd known each other longer than time should allow.

God help her, his smell — clean and masculine like fresh-cut cedarwood, with notes of sun-warmed cotton that had spent the afternoon drying on a line somewhere in the mountains, edged with something faintly worn in that reminded her of leather-bound books and expensive whiskey. His tattoo, too, half-glimpsed beneath his sleeve when he'd leaned forward to sign that glove, the dark ink curling like midnight waves across the tanned terrain of his forearm, disappearing tantalizingly beneath crisp fabric. Just a fragment visible — was it words? A date? Some meaningful symbol? — leaving her imagination to trace what lay hidden. She wondered what it was. She wondered what else she didn't know about him, what other secrets his body carried beneath tailored clothes and careful smiles.

Her thoughts tumbled from there, picking up speed the way they always did when the house was too quiet and her guard too low.

Did Nate Carter ask her out? Did she decline the offer? Or was it all just a figment of her imagination?

She laughed once, startled by it, then groaned and pulled the blankets over her head. What was wrong with her?

The pillow was cool; her cheeks were not.

His voice played on a loop in her head — kind, hopeful, a little teasing, a little vulnerable. The way he said her name. The way he looked at her made her wonder if maybe, just maybe, she was something worth waiting for.

He made it hard to say no. She hoped the chance would come again — and that next time, she'd take it.

But as her thoughts dragged on, looping back over every moment until they blurred together, she realized she probably would not sleep at all tonight.

* * *

THE ALARM BUZZED—loud and jarring—at exactly 5:12 a.m.

Of course it did.

She barely blinked.

She sat up, heart pounding already, a familiar churn of excitement and dread setting in. Today was the day she had planned for all year.

She was glad she'd laid out her outfit weeks ago. There would be no dress sabotaging her confidence today.

*Not today, Satan.*

The sleek black jumpsuit hugged her frame with its clean lines and subtle satin sheen, making a statement without having to shout. She slipped into low block heels—comfortable enough to stand in all night yet still refined. Around her neck, the silver 'G' pendant caught the light as she fastened it, while her fingers absently traced the familiar bracelet she hadn't removed in years. Standing before the mirror, she nodded at her reflection. Not someone who typically navigated glamorous waters, but today, no one would question whether she belonged at the gala she had meticulously crafted from nothing.

In front of the mirror, she paused longer than usual. The makeup bag sat open beside her, spilling its contents with a quiet dare. Foundation, blush, highlighter — the occasional purchases of a woman who sometimes imagined being someone who used them.

Most mornings, they stayed tucked away while she swiped on mascara and called it good enough.

But today... Maybe a little more wouldn't hurt.

A touch of foundation. A sweep of blush. Delicate and almost invisible, but it gave her the illusion of trying—of looking like she had it together.

She gave herself one last glance in the mirror, smoothing her hands down the front of her jumpsuit before heading downstairs.

Her feet moved on instinct through the familiar turns of her house, her thoughts already skipping ahead to the schedule waiting for her.

She reached for the coffeepot with muscle memory, the ritual as much a part of her morning as breathing. Most days, she'd pair it with yogurt in a halfhearted nod to nutrition. Not today. Today she needed something more substantial than food—something dark and bitter that would match her mood and sharpen her edges.

She stared down at her to-do list like it might blink first.

She wasn't running late — not yet—but her nerves never trusted a clock on important days.

Checking her reflection in the small mirror by the front door, she grabbed her keys and headed out, sure that she was as ready as she'd ever be.

She could have driven to Denver blindfolded by now. Her hands knew precisely when to signal for the turn onto Highway 119 east, when to merge onto I-25 south, her foot easing off the gas at precisely the right moment before each bend in the road. The city's jagged silhouette rose through her windshield—a skyline that represented both paycheck and purpose. On any other gala day, her mind would race through checklists: unclaimed

RSVPs, donation projections, the thousand tiny threads that could unravel everything if tugged the wrong way.

That familiar weight was still there, pressing in under her ribs. However, today, there was something else as well.

A quiver beneath her nerves. A new buzz. Nate Carter.

She despised how effortlessly his name had already woven itself into her mind.

*I just met him,* she thought.

It wasn't just the success of the gala weighing on her shoulders now, nor the speeches, centerpieces, or ensuring the silent auction went smoothly. Nate was present. In her city. In her sphere. And despite her efforts to maintain professionalism, she couldn't deny that he had stirred something within her.

She wasn't accustomed to feeling restless, curious, or hopeful.

Her fingers tapped rhythmically on the steering wheel as she joined the flow of traffic, allowing the sound of tires on the road to occupy the space usually taken up by her overthinking.

What exactly was she even doing?

Organizing a gala was one thing, but getting involved in the life of a movie star? That was never part of the plan.

The miles slipped by. Concrete barriers. Exit signs. The slow reveal of Denver's skyline pulling itself into focus ahead, rising out of the haze like it always did — sturdy and familiar and indifferent to whatever was unraveling inside her.

As she exited the interstate and approached The Crawford, her stomach knotted. It wasn't the gala that unsettled her—she had that under control—but something more intricate lurking beneath the surface.

At first, she thought maybe a wedding or some big event was starting early. A small swarm of people crowded near the hotel's entrance, pressed close behind metal barricades.

Then she caught the gleam of camera lenses, their polished surfaces glinting sharply in the morning sunlight. Flashes erupted in the already bright morning light—pointless, yet unyielding in their persistence.

Paparazzi.

*Of course.*

Her fingers wrapped tightly around the wheel, knuckles whitening as she eased past, projecting an air of feigned calm. Naturally, Nate Carter would draw attention, even here, at a hospital fundraiser. Yet somehow, a small, naïve part of her hadn't expected this—the possibility that those cameras might capture her as she stepped out of her car, oblivious to the thought that they'd care at all about her identity.

She circled the block, her heart pounding more insistently than it should. She found a quieter spot to park along the side of the building, away from the prying lenses and eager photographers. No one lingered there, cameras poised, ready to capture every moment.

She sat with her fingers resting on the keys, willing her nerves to calm. It wasn't about her. No one was there for her. Yet, when she finally stepped out, she smoothed her hair, adjusted the fabric of her jumpsuit, and lifted her chin—as if, perhaps, it might matter after all.

* * *

AS SOON AS she approached the hotel's sliding glass doors, the camera flashes erupted—intense and blinding.

"It's her! Miss Lane."

Flash.

"Is Nate inside?"

Flash.

"Are you staying with him?"

Flash.

"Is this a serious relationship?"

More flashes followed.

The questions bombarded her like a relentless hailstorm. Flashes fired off in rapid succession. She navigated through the crowd, slightly hunched, shielding her eyes with one hand. Panic rose in her throat—metallic and chilling. It felt like moving through a thunderstorm, blind folded.

Each flash, each question, further destabilized her. The voices melded into a cacophony—overwhelming, inescapable, too close to avoid.

*Where is Cassidy when you need her?* Amelia thought. She would have cleared this crowd with a single glance, her voice slicing through the chaos like a scalpel. But Cassidy wasn't here. The realization settled cold in Amelia's stomach as another camera flash burned against her retinas. She was on her own.

Across the lobby, the front desk clerk from yesterday caught her eye. Recognition flashed across his face as he abandoned his post, rushing toward her.

"This way," he said, positioning himself between her and the commotion, his body a barrier against the chaos.

He turned toward the doors, voice sharp with authority. "No cameras in the lobby! You need to clear out!"

Nate materialized at her side, his body radiating heat that crashed into her like a wave. Relief flooded her veins, but died in her throat when she finally looked up. His jaw was clenched so tight she could see the muscle twitching beneath his skin, his eyes dark with something primal—rage or protection, she couldn't tell which.

"Are you hurt?" he demanded, voice barely audible yet somehow cutting through the chaos like a blade.

She managed a brittle smile that felt like glass breaking across her face. "I'm okay. Just... blindsided."

His fingers found her elbow, gripping with an urgency that sent a shiver of electricity up her arm.

"Goddammit," he whispered, his voice rough with fury. His eyes searched her face. "I never thought they'd target you. I should have been there. I should have known better."

The words died in her throat as a uniformed valet appeared at Nate's elbow. "Sir, your vehicle is waiting at the side entrance," he said, voice low but urgent.

"Thank you," Nate said to the driver, his shoulders visibly relaxing.

He turned to Amelia, leaning close enough that she caught the faint scent of his cologne. "I've got a car waiting for us. The driver will take us straight to the hospital."

Amelia's lips parted, the words "But my Subaru" forming silently before she swallowed them back. Her eyes followed his hand as he motioned toward the service corridor behind the reception desk.

His hand brushed the small of her back as they moved, five warm points of pressure guiding her protectively through the side exit. The heat from his palm radiated through the thin silk of her jumpsuit, lingering like a sunspot on her skin.

*It was instinct*; she told herself, staring at the exit sign's red glow—pure Hollywood chivalry. Don't read into it. It means nothing.

But something in her chest had already flickered to life—a tiny pilot light she thought had gone permanently cold.

They stepped into the crisp Colorado morning where aspen leaves trembled silver-green against the cloudless blue sky. A black SUV with tinted windows waited behind the hotel's side entrance, engine purring almost silently.

He slid in beside her on the buttery leather seats, his thigh aligned with hers, his hand brushing her knee before settling there—warm, solid, deliberate.

With a shared exhale of relief that fogged the cool air between them, the feeling was akin to survivors emerging from a storm shelter.

She noticed his hand was still there, his thumb tracing an absent half-circle on the fabric. When he squeezed gently, just once, she looked up into eyes the exact color of mountain lakes in September.

"I am truly sorry about that," Nate repeated, his voice gentler this time, imbued with genuine regret. "The cameras. You shouldn't have had to deal with that. Not like this." His gaze was earnest, reflecting the sincerity of his apology.

She shook her head slowly, her expression a mix of surprise and understanding. "It's okay," she murmured, though her voice carried a hint of disbelief. "It's... unexpected."

Her eyes flickered with the weight of the situation. "Still," he continued, a deep frown creasing his brow, "I hate it happened." His frustration was palpable, an undercurrent of tension in his otherwise calm demeanor.

He let the apology linger for a beat longer before clearing his throat and shifting the conversation.

"While I'm batting a thousand over here…," he added with a dry, self-deprecating smile. "About yesterday," Nate cleared his throat again, "I didn't mean to spring that invitation on you."

"It wasn't a bad thing. Just wasn't expecting that, either."

He squeezed again. "I'm glad I tried, though."

She smiled, her gaze dropping briefly to where his hand rested against her knee. "Me too."

Nate let out a breath, softer than before. "I wasn't sure if it was too soon. Or too much."

Her smile tilted. "You're not exactly subtle, Carter."

That pulled a quiet laugh from him. "Fair. Subtlety's never really been my strong suit."

She looked at him then, properly. "But you're not making it complicated."

He nodded, thumb tracing a slow circle against the fabric. "Good. I'm trying not to."

The warmth between them lingered, quieter now but still there, humming beneath the surface.

"I'm also terrible at small talk when I'm… distracted," he added, a half-grin curving his mouth.

"That's reassuring," she said lightly, "because I'm not exactly great at it either."

Their eyes met, something unspoken but effortlessly passing between them.

As his hand slid off her knee and into the space between them, the SUV came to a slow stop—time to face the world again.

Amelia prepared herself, anticipating a barrage of flashing lights, and shouted questions as the door swung open. Instead, she was met with emptiness. No cameras, no throngs of people—just the typical smooth murmur of the hospital starting its day.

She scanned the hospital entrance, shoulders tensed for another assault of camera flashes that never came. The vultures had lost their scent—still circling the hotel's main doors, no doubt, while their prey slipped quietly through another exit. The tightness in her chest unwound.

They entered the hospital with no fanfare. A few nurses waved. The mood was peaceful.

Janice scampered to them before they could reach her desk. "Mr. Carter, I mean Nate, nice seeing you again," she exclaimed. Unashamed of her excitement, she handed him his guest badge and gave him a once-over.

"Janice, I couldn't miss my chance to see you again," Nate quipped.

"Now I know you're full of it," she replied, looking over at Amelia and giving a quick wink.

"Amelia, I peeked in the ballroom this morning. Once again, you have done an amazing job."

"That's so nice of you, Janice, but you know I don't do all that." Amelia lightheartedly replies. "The event staff works so hard to make it possible."

"It wouldn't happen without you, Amelia. Without... Grace."

Amelia's fingers instinctively reached for the pendant around her neck, outlining the letter G.

"Thank you, Janice," she murmured, her voice filled with pride and confidence.

She sensed Nate watching her, his gaze steady and grounding. His presence always seemed to stabilize her.

As they turned toward the elevators, Nate caught Janice's hand between both of his. "Don't forget about me tonight," he said with a wink. "I'm counting on that dance." Janice's cheeks flushed pink as she pressed her free hand to her heart, momentarily speechless.

Amelia couldn't stop smiling. With one gesture, Nate had cut through the ache, letting something lighter in—like sunlight finding its way through storm clouds. She clenched the pendant between her thumb and forefinger; the metal heated from her skin, and looked up—straight into those blue eyes, the color of a Colorado summer sky.

She remembered to breathe, her lungs filling with air that somehow tasted sweeter today, tinged with antiseptic.

The hospital corridors, usually washed in fluorescent pallor, seemed to glow with a different energy. Not louder or more hectic—but brighter, as if someone had adjusted the contrast on a faded photograph. Word had rippled through the pediatric floor like a current. Captain Orion—the real one in the flesh—was here.

They made their way through the halls, room to room, his presence transforming the sterile spaces. In 405, Nate performed an impromptu lightsaber battle with a seven-year-old using rolled-up get-well cards. In 511, he sat cross-legged on the floor beside a toddler's bed while Amelia squeezed the mother's trembling hand. Laughter—that rarest of hospital sounds—echoed against the tile floors, replacing the usual hushed conversations and beeping monitors. Smiles spread from face to face like a contagion worth catching.

At one point, Nate leaned casually against a doorframe, observing her as she engaged in conversation with a young boy and his parents.

His expression halted her mid-sentence. There was pride etched across his features, a sense of wonder, and perhaps something even more profound. She cast a glance in his direction, and his smile softened, becoming more tender.

The realization struck her with unexpected force, right in the center of her chest. For an instant, the bustling hallway faded away, and the usual cacophony of hospital sounds became muted.

She was ensnared in the tranquility of that gaze—as though he could see her entirely, every facet of who she was, and he didn't look away. She returned his smile, feeling a tightness in her throat.

A moment later, he pushed off the wall, his grin becoming easy and carefree once more, as if the moment hadn't just stolen her breath away.

Yet something had undeniably shifted within her. And she was acutely aware of it.

* * *

THE MORNING SEAMLESSLY melted into the afternoon, slipping away so swiftly that Amelia barely noticed the passage of time. It wasn't until they stood together, gazing through the grand double doors into the ballroom that Janice had praised so highly, that she realized how quickly the hours had flown by.

The space had undergone a breathtaking transformation. White linen-draped tables created a sea of elegance, each adorned with towering arrangements of soft white flowers intertwined with the gentle touch of pale green eucalyptus leaves. The flickering candlelight cast a warm glow across the room, even though the sun still hung high in the sky. At the far end, the stage lay beneath a majestic arch of delicate, twinkling lights, and above it, in graceful, soft gold lettering, the words "A Night of Grace" shimmered serenely.

Servers moved gracefully between the tables, like dancers on a stage, meticulously straightening chairs and adjusting the centerpieces to perfection. A sound technician, clipboard in hand, crossed the stage with an air of quiet concentration. Though the final touches were still being applied, the essence of the evening was already palpable, unfolding in gentle curves and a serene, tranquil light.

Amelia stood beside Nate with her arms folded loosely across her chest, allowing herself to absorb the scene before her. The transformation wasn't just in the elegant room—it was in her, too—a journey measured in small victories and silent tears.

The space felt authentic rather than performative, like coming home after a long absence.

"This is why we do it," she whispered, more to herself than to him. Not for the glittering chandeliers or the perfect table settings, but for the feeling that swelled in her chest when she remembered the faces of the children who would benefit.

Her fingers found the back of a nearby chair, cool fabric beneath her palm grounding her at the moment. She drew in a steadying breath and turned to share the thought with Nate—only to discover the space where he had been standing was empty.

Her eyes swept the room, quickly spotting him. At the kitchen doorway, a small group of catering staff surrounded Nate, laughing at something one of them had said. He leaned in with his relaxed stance, sleeves rolled casually to his elbows, his smile naturally putting everyone at ease. One of the younger servers squealed—not out of fear, but sheer joy—and Nate just chuckled, shook his head, and said something that earned him a chorus of smiles.

He was clearly in his element. Kind. Straightforward. Naturally great with people.

Amelia allowed herself to watch longer than she should have. Then, refocusing on her duties, she did what she excelled at. She tiptoed through the space, double-checking details with practiced accuracy—centerpieces in place, gift bags arranged on the check-in table. She straightened the Guest Book at the entrance, gave a quick nod of approval, and exhaled—it was almost time to prepare.

Her eyes moved to the nametags already set out on the tables, and years of experience had taught her how to arrange a room like this: thoughtfully and strategically, in ways that made guests feel welcome, comfortable, and connected. The NICU nurses had already taken their seats near the front— exactly where they should be, where everyone could see and celebrate them.

And there, at their table, sat the little white card: **Nate Carter.**

Months ago, before Cassidy had even confirmed he would come, she'd slotted Nate in with little thought. A neutral placement. Safe. Appropriate. Before yesterday. Before this morning in the car. Before, everything shifted in ways she hadn't expected.

Her hand hovered over his name, hesitating.

The same slow burn from last night returned, low and undeniable. Her fingers moved, almost of their own accord, sliding his card free from its neat little place. With quiet precision, she carried it to the head table and placed it beside her own.

A small, ordinary thing. Ink on paper. A name in a new place. But it felt like something else entirely. A choice. A quiet defiance against distance.

She could leave it where it was. Keep things simple. Keep space between them where it might be safer. But she didn't want space. Not tonight. Not anymore.

She wanted him beside her.

And tonight, maybe that was enough.

No one would know—no one but her.

Her fingertips lingered on the edge of his name card for a moment longer before she let it go.  A small smile tugged at the corner of her mouth, surprising her with how easy it felt.

Then she straightened, smoothing the linen with the flat of her palm, as if arranging a nameplate could settle the flutter beneath her ribs.

Across the room, Nate caught her eye again and smiled — wide, genuine, as if privy to her small rebellion. A flush crept up her neck. *Impossible.* He couldn't have seen her move the card. Yet the heat lingering beneath her collarbone suggested otherwise, a warmth that refused to cool even as she turned away.

# 6

# a night of grace

THE WAITING WAS over.

Music drifted through the air like a promise, soft and slow, winding between flickering candles and the gentle clink of glassware. Guests had arrived, their voices a quiet swell against the elegance of the space she knew by heart but now saw through new eyes.

At the head table, Amelia sat still, letting the moment settle around her.

This wasn't a rehearsal anymore. It was real.

Everything she and her team had built—every silent hour, every late-night decision, every impossible hope—had led here.

To this.

She smoothed her hand over the edge of the linen-draped table, anchoring herself in the calm before her name would be called.

To her right sat Ronnie, radiant in dark green and already whispering something that made the volunteer across from her laugh.

To her left—Nate.

Same navy suit, the same rolled sleeves, but now impossibly closer. His presence next to her was intentional. Her own doing. Her choice.

Amelia glanced at the name card she'd moved not an hour ago and smiled to herself. She had told no one, hadn't needed to.

Nate was precisely where she wanted him to be.

The chatter dwindled to a gentle murmur, then to silence as Dr. Winters, the silver-haired hospital president, approached the podium with measured steps. His voice, warm and authoritative, filled the ballroom as he welcomed the guests in his familiar baritone. When he finally introduced Amelia, the room erupted in a wave of polite applause that rippled across the sea of round tables—except for Ronnie, who shot up from her chair, fingers in her mouth for a piercing whistle before cupping her hands around her mouth to whoop and holler as if she were front row at a sold-out Madison Square Garden concert.

Amelia's cheeks bloomed crimson beneath her carefully applied blush, and she laughed, a genuine sound that crinkled the corners of her eyes. Half embarrassed at the spectacle her best friend was making and half grateful for the momentary shield it provided against the weight of three hundred expectant gazes.

She stepped up to the microphone, her soft jumpsuit whispering against her legs, immediately noticing the spotlight's heat on her already flushed face like a physical touch. The crystal chandeliers above dimmed to pinpricks of light. "Good evening," she began, her voice flowing out steadier than the trembling in her fingertips suggested it would be. "Thank you all for being here tonight."

"The Grace Wells Foundation is honored to stand with Denver's Children's Hospital this evening as we celebrate every one of you."

"Three years ago, in this very ballroom, we hosted our first A Night of Grace Gala—an earnest gathering with fewer than half the guests, plastic tablecloths that fluttered at the edges of each table, and store-bought cupcakes perched on paper plates. Look how far we've come in such a short time."

Behind her, a wide projection screen glowed to life, casting dancing light across the room as photographs cycled gently.

"As many of you know, my daughter Grace Wells was a patient here for almost two years," Amelia said, her voice softening as she lifted her gaze to the images overhead. The photos loomed large: a carousel bathed in pastel light with Grace and her mother riding side by side; Grace in bright yellow rainboots splashing through puddles under a gray sky; a half-smashed birthday cake smeared over her tiny, bald head; a quiet, tender moment with Ronnie, who cradled Grace on her lap, tubes trailing from her chest like delicate vines.

Her voice caught on the next words. "It's been four years since I last held Grace," she whispered, "and not a single moment has passed when she hasn't been alive inside me."

She raised her arm toward the photo of Grace nestled in Ronnie's arms. "The Grace Wells Foundation exists because of her. Some of you knew Grace, some did not—but her spirit has touched every person in this room. Through patient grants that lift burdens, art therapy programs that ignite hope, and the promise that no child walks these hallways alone, you have kept her legacy—and the legacies of countless children—vibrant and alive."

From the stage, Amelia could not see Nate's face; the bright spotlight blurred every gaze. A sudden realization struck her—she had never truly shared Grace's story with him. Was it the first time he understood who Grace was?

"Tonight," she continued, "we also honor you: the nurses, doctors, staff, and volunteers who pour their hearts into each day. And to the families and children joining us, this is for you above all. You are why we gather. You are why we persevere."

Her throat tightened, but she pressed on. "We are here to raise vital funds and awareness for the small miracles that happen within these walls every day. I would be remiss if I did not thank our sponsors and donors, who are seated here with us tonight." She turned left, offering applause to a row of tables draped in elegant fabrics and occupied by well-dressed patrons. These were the champions of their cause.

"I'm delighted to welcome someone who has given his time and his heart to be here with us this week. You've probably seen him already—or heard stories of someone who has." A ripple of polite laughter spread through the crowd as guests straightened their posture, smoothing gowns and adjusting ties.

"Nate Car—" Amelia paused, grinning as the audience leapt in. The applause swelled, filling the room with warmth. Finally, she announced,

"Nate Carter is here with us tonight!"

The applause started before she could finish speaking, swelling quickly.

"He is going to speak a little later this evening, so hold your excitement, folks," Amelia joked.

"Thank you again for being here tonight and believing in this mission. Please enjoy your dinner, the music, the silent auction... and, of course, the dancing. You've earned it."

She stepped down to a standing ovation–one that stunned her into stillness. Then came the hugs—the handshakes. A woman from the NICU team hugged her so tightly she thought she might break. A donor thanked her for her strength.

Ronnie rose to embrace her, arms full and wet-cheeked. "She would be so proud," she whispered.

Amelia blinked hard, tears running down her face.

As she turned around, Nate was there, his eyes fixed on hers. There was an unmistakable presence—a mix of sadness and familiarity.

With no need to discuss it, she instinctively leaned toward him. He opened his arms, and she stepped into his embrace. Her head fit perfectly beneath his chin, as though it belonged there.

For a few moments, everything else faded away. All she could focus on was his scent—amber and leather, with a hint of citrus. It was mesmerizing.

When he pulled away, she did the same, abruptly, as if awakening from a dream.

"I'm so sorry for your loss," he said, voice low and reverent, his warm breath brushing against her ear like a secret. His piercing blue eyes, flecked with gold under the ballroom lights, held hers with an intensity that made her chest tighten. "And you... You're incredible, Amelia."

She barely heard it through the rushing in her ears, the words floating past like distant music. "It's okay," she murmured reflexively.

He closed the space between them, his nearness drawing her palm instinctively to his chest, where she felt the steady rhythm beneath her fingertips. "No, listen to me. You're incredible." Each word landed with deliberate weight, as if he were pressing them into her skin.

This time, she looked at him, really looked—at the earnest curve of his mouth, the slight furrow between his brow, the vulnerability beneath his movie-star confidence. "Thank you. I'm... happy you're here," is all she could mutter, her voice catching on the last word like fabric on a thorn.

* * *

AS CONVERSATIONS HUSHED and chairs quietly moved into position, the room transitioned into a calm that signaled something significant was on the horizon. The sound of clinking silverware began, accompanied by a blend of shared stories filled with excitement, hope, and sorrow.

The rich aroma of the gourmet dishes being served was the only thing that could pierce the emotionally charged atmosphere. Above, twinkling string lights adorned the far wall, where the silent auction attracted a constant flow of visitors after the entrée dishes were cleared away.

Volunteers circulated among the guests, highlighting last-minute treasures such as artwork from local artists, signed jerseys from Colorado sports stars, private hiking excursions, and weekend retreats.

Ronnie returned to the table victoriously, grinning and waving a small yellow auction slip in the air.

"Guess who's going to a couple's hiking retreat near Emerald Lake Trail in a couple of months?"

Amelia raised a brow. "Is there a couple I should know about?"

"There might be by then," Ronnie smirked, "otherwise I'm dragging you with me. Hiking boots optional."

They both burst into laughter, and Amelia mentally saved the moment—Ronnie, with her hopeful grin and semi-playful courage, inviting happiness to come her way. *May she find the happy ending she deserves.* If anyone was worthy of joy, it was Ronnie.

Ronnie leaned over the table, fingers skimming through the floral centerpiece until she found two perfect magnolia blooms. With a grin, she tucked one behind her ear, then turned to Amelia.

"Grace's favorite," she said softly, eyes gleaming.

Amelia stood perfectly still, letting Ronnie's fingers settle the second flower behind her ear, light as a memory.

"They are," Amelia whispered, then paused. "They were."

Ronnie didn't flinch. "Still as beautiful as her."

Amelia nodded, pressing her lips together as a single tear threatened to fall.

"Just like her Aunt Ronnie," Amelia sputtered before her tears silently took over.

* * *

GUESTS DRIFTED FROM their tables, drinks in hand, glancing at clipboards, whispering about which items were still up for grabs at the auction table.

As the final bell chimed and the last bids came in, the lights in the ballroom dimmed slightly, casting a golden warmth over the tables. A string quartet began playing over the speakers. The song was soft and dreamy, an acoustic version of a classic pop ballad.

True to his word and needing no invitation, Nate crossed the room, straight toward Janice. Amelia watched from her table, smiling as he bowed slightly and extended his hand.

Janice had transformed from volunteer coordinator to ballroom vision—her utilitarian badge and navy blazer replaced by a floor-length black dress that caught the light with each movement, its subtle sequins winking like distant stars. Her silver-streaked hair, usually practical and pulled back, now swept upward in an elegant twist secured with pearl pins. The smile that stretched across her face wasn't just wide—it was decades-young, erasing the fine lines around her eyes that normally mapped her years of dedication to the hospital.

She laughed with such unrestrained delight that heads turned three tables deep, the sound bubbling up and spilling over like champagne. When she placed her hand in Nate's, her fingers trembled slightly—the gesture both theatrical and touchingly genuine, as if she'd rehearsed this moment in her mind since the day they announced his visit. They moved together across the floor—not with practiced precision but with the gentle, imperfect rhythm of two people simply enjoying each other's company, his celebrity and her position momentarily forgotten. Their simple joy rippled outward, drawing first applause, then cheers, then couples rising from their seats like flowers turning toward the sun.

Watching them, Amelia felt something unfurl beneath her ribs—a tender ache, like muscles remembering how to stretch after too long at rest.

The orchestra's brass blare softened, the final triumphant trumpets of Janice's showpiece fading into a velvety hush. In their place drifted a slow, familiar refrain—Etta James's honeyed voice weaving through the air, "*A Sunday Kind of Love*" gliding from the speakers like satin. It was a melody meant for gentle turns and whispered secrets, the kind that made satin gowns rustle and stiletto heels tap-tap on polished wood. One by one, more couples rose, smoothing skirts and straightening jackets before drifting onto the dance floor, fingertips brushing, smiles shy in the dim chandelier glow.

Amelia's gaze wandered toward the towering double doors at the ballroom's edge. She barely registered the moment—then she saw Nate striding toward her. The easy sparkle had vanished from his eyes, replaced by a steady intensity that caught her breath mid–heartbeat. His shoulders squared, chin lifted, every step measured with purpose. The soft curls of his hair caught the light as he moved, haloed by lamplight.

By the time he reached her, Amelia's pulse was a quickening drum. He didn't pause to search for words. Instead, he leaned close, his warm breath brushing her ear, and brushed a callused hand across the small of her back.

"Dance with me."

His voice was a low murmur, the kind only she could hear through the swell of violins. He added, even softer, "Not for show. Just for us."

Her throat went dry. She nodded before doubt could creep in, cheeks tingling. "Okay."

He offered his hand—strong, confident—and guided her onto the polished floor as though they were the only two in the room. His suit jacket whispered against her arm. Lanterns overhead cast halos of golden light on their faces, and a gentle hush seemed to settle around them.

As they reached the center, Nate unfurled her arm and placed his hand at the small of her back, fingers splayed like a promise. He guided her other hand to rest on his shoulder. Their bodies nestled close, breath mingling, each step measured but effortless. The melody seeped into their bones, and suddenly the noise of laughter and clinking glasses felt miles away.

Nate leaned in again, voice threaded through the music. "You know, I think this is the best part of the night."

Amelia tilted her head, a playful glint in her eyes. "The dancing? Or that I finally said yes?"

He smiled, a gentle curve that softened his strong features. "No. Watching you. Seeing what you've built. What you've survived to build."

A soft gasp escaped her. The candles flickered on the surrounding tables, shadows dancing across her face. "I wanted to create something that mattered," she whispered. "Something that told Grace's story—not in words, but in action. I wanted other families, other kids... to feel seen. To know they weren't alone."

Nate's hand tightened around hers, steadying. The warmth of his palm seeped into her skin. "You've done that. More than you know. You are extraordinary, Amelia Lane."

Heat bloomed beneath her collarbone. It wasn't embarrassment—more like a lighthouse beam of gratitude and something daringly close to hope. She pressed her hand to his chest, feeling the steady thrum of his heartbeat.

"Thank you," she breathed. "That means more than I can explain." They swayed in silence, the song winding down, and for a moment, the world beyond the dance floor ceased to exist.

Neither of them moved to step away. Instead, Nate's hand slid a little closer to her back, his thumb tracing slow, absent circles against the fabric. The song shifted — something equally soft, equally slow — but neither of them let go. If anything, he pulled her closer. Without thinking, Amelia rested her head lightly against his chest, her hand smoothing instinctively over his shoulder. His breath warmed the crown of her hair as they moved together — quiet, steady, the rest of the room continuing to fade away.

The second song wrapped itself around them — a quiet tide, easy and unnoticed. Amelia realized how far her mind had wandered when the final notes faded. For a moment, it felt as if she were waking from some place softer, quieter. As if it had carried her into him, into this, into the feeling of being chosen again.

She lifted her head slightly, catching the way a few eyes around the room lingered — not with judgment or surprise, but with warmth. Smiles that held something close to happiness. The kind that understood—without question—that no explanation was needed. Other couples still circled the floor, but somehow, the world felt like it had been watching her — quietly cheering her on.

Nate gave her hand a short squeeze, his smile easing back into something playful. "Come on," he said, stepping aside so the group could move freely. "I think we've been properly admired."

The DJ transitioned to a crowd-pleaser, and bodies rose from chairs before conscious decisions were made. The opening beats of *The Cupid Shuffle* pulsed through the ballroom, transforming the atmosphere in seconds. White coats abandoned tables, donors loosened ties, and nurses kicked off heels as they formed lines across the floor—everyone suddenly equal in their slightly off-rhythm movements, mouths open in laughter as they shouted "now walk it by yourself" over the speakers.

Her laughter mingled with the music as they wove between couples, his fingers still laced through hers, guiding her from the center of the floor back toward the edge of the crowd.

Amelia caught the eye of a silver-haired man at table seven, his polite smile tinged with expectation. "Duty calls," she whispered, nodding toward the investors. "Can't have them thinking I've forgotten who signs the checks."

Nate's fingers lingered against hers for one heartbeat longer before releasing. "Tactical retreat," he murmured, eyes crinkling at the corners. "You charm the suits. I'll handle the rest."

A rush of gratitude warmed her chest as she watched him step away.

They moved through the ballroom like dancers in separate orbits, yet somehow in perfect sync—Nate's laugh carrying across the space as Amelia bent to hear a donor's whispered compliment. Hands extended, shoulders touched, glasses clinked. Two separate paths carving one shared purpose through the glittering crowd.

For once, Amelia didn't feel the weight of obligation pressing down. Tonight, every handshake felt like giving a gift rather than paying a debt.

Everywhere she turned, the room seemed to mirror her feelings—the warmth, the brightness, the persistent beat of hope filling the space that grief had occupied for far too long. Children danced between the tables, parents moved slowly in gentle circles, and volunteers, along with nurses, kicked off their shoes, swaying together, carefree and exhilarated.

It was chaotic, lovely, and just right. A room once molded by sorrow now shone with a gentler, more vibrant energy. Amelia's gaze met Nate's from across the room, and he lifted his glass in a quiet, personal toast to her.

She pointed lightly toward the stage and then to him, a silent exchange that made his grin tilt a little wider. He gave her a wink and a slight nod; he was already ready for whatever came next. That easy confidence of his — like none of this ever rattled him — settled something steady beneath her ribs.

And then Amelia rose and headed to the stage.

"If everyone could find their seats... yes, even you, Dr. Perez. I see you trying to sneak one more dance over there." A wave of chuckles rolled across the ballroom as the pediatric surgeon grinned and threw his hands up in surrender. "Don't worry, there's more music to come. You'll have your moment, I promise."

"I hope everyone enjoyed dinner. Thank you to Rocky Mountain Catering Company for donating the delicious meal," she said into the mic.

"Thank you to all the businesses who were generous with their time and money," she continued, "and for their considerable silent auction donations."

"And to our dancers tonight," she said, her voice warm with genuine delight, "I've never seen such enthusiasm on a hospital dance floor—especially from our orthopedic department!"

This got the crowd excited again, and hooting ensued. Amelia stood flooded by the light, her smile beaming from ear to ear.

"Alright, alright," she continued, "it's the time you have all been waiting for."

"Tonight," she said, leaning closer to the mic, her voice softening with unexpected sincerity, "I have the honor of introducing someone whose talent may have brought him to our attention, but whose heart truly deserves our applause."

"Please welcome my new friend, and yours, Nate Carter."

# 7

## more than words

BEFORE THE APPLAUSE had entirely faded, Nate emerged from the shadows at the back of the ballroom. As he moved through the crowd, he paused briefly—a warm smile here, a firm handshake there—navigating the sea of black ties and evening gowns with practiced grace. When he caught Ronnie's gaze, one eyebrow lifted in silent conspiracy, prompting her to shake her head in that way that said she wasn't fooled for a second. Reaching the stage, he ascended the steps with an effortless confidence that sent a flutter through Amelia's chest, which she wasn't prepared to acknowledge.

The spotlight didn't faze him. If anything, it softened against him.

Only when Amelia had made her way down the steps and settled back at her table did Nate approach the podium, his eyes following her path through the crowd for just a moment longer than necessary.

He repositioned the microphone, and the room fell quiet.

"Hi, I'm Nate," he began, voice low and calm. "Some of you know me from the screen... or maybe that little superhero movie I'm in."

The crowd's laughter rose and fell like a gentle tide, washing away the last traces of formality in the ballroom.

"But that's not the reason I've come here this evening," he went on, his voice growing more composed. "I'm here tonight because, like many of you, I understand the transformative power of a hospital. Not just any facility, but one like this—a children's hospital that mends the ill, comforts the afflicted, and supports families when their world crumbles."

He paused, letting his eyes sweep across the audience—the nurses, the doctors, the parents who intimately understood the challenge of maintaining hope in the presence of fear.

"In the short time I've been here, I've witnessed the significance of this place for many. I've encountered families that remind me why this work is important, and I've seen people quietly and humbly share their truths, not because it's easy, but because it helps others feel less alone."

He rested his hand gently on the podium's edge. "In my world of entertainment, it's easy to get lost in telling stories that aren't ours— pretending and performing. But the reason I agreed to be here tonight, to support this foundation, is because it's not about acting. It's about speaking the truth, transforming pain into something positive, and creating something with your own hands to ensure nobody has to navigate the darkness alone."

He didn't mention her name, but he didn't need to. His words resonated deeply with the woman who had crafted this evening from her grief, love, and determination to turn her daughter's story into a new beginning rather than an end.

Amelia adjusted her posture, leaning in with her fingers gently resting on the linen tablecloth. She was aware he had a speech ready, but chose not to preview it in advance. She expected a few delightful remarks, perhaps a mention of the foundation, or a playful joke about the paparazzi outside. However, what he delivered was completely unexpected.

"When I was fourteen," Nate began, his voice catching, "my older brother Noah was seventeen, finishing high school as the Captain of the baseball team. Everyone admired Noah, but none more than I did. He embodied everything I aspired to be—intelligent, compassionate, and far cooler than I ever was."

She clutched the linen more tightly, her heart still bracing for what was to come.

"One evening, we got a call. Noah had been in a car accident, hit by a distracted driver on his way back from visiting friends. I recall my mom dropping the phone, and my dad trying to ask questions, but nothing was clear to us."

He paused, the microphone capturing his slight breath.

"We immediately drove to the children's hospital, where they had taken Noah. Three days. Three days of tubes and machines, waiting rooms, and hoping for a miracle. I didn't sleep. I couldn't cry, at least at first. I sat there, next to him, trying to memorize everything about his face in case... in case."

Amelia's throat ached with the familiar tightness that came before tears, a physical memory of all the times she'd tried to swallow her grief rather than let it spill over in public.

"And in the middle of all that," Nate continued, a small smile appearing, "there were nurses. There was a doctor who sat on the floor next to me when I couldn't breathe. A woman from the front desk brought us coffee and warm blankets. A night shift tech who let me play music for Noah through my headphones when I swore he could still hear it."

He looked out at the room, letting the silence stretch.

"We lost Noah on the third day." A long breath. "But we didn't walk out of that hospital alone. And I never forgot that."

His voice softened as he continued. "Losing Noah changed the shape of our family. It changed the shape of me. I used to pray I'd grow up to be exactly like him—Captain of the team, the guy everyone looked up to. But when he was gone, I had to figure out who I was without him. For a long time, I didn't know."

Tears quietly streamed down Amelia's face.

"I understand now," Nate remarked. "The reason I felt compelled to come here tonight, to be involved in this, is because Noah is still with me. In every story told, every laugh shared, every chair I occupy—he's present."

He paused, steady but emotional. "And I want to honor that."

Nate reached into his jacket pocket and unfolded a small card, glancing briefly at the table where Amelia sat.

"I haven't spoken to the Foundation yet, but I am going to pledge fifty thousand dollars to the Grace Wells Foundation," he said, voice even but filled with something deeply personal. "I want the funds to help families staying at the hospital—families like mine, like yours. So they can have warm meals, places to sleep, maybe even the small things that remind them they're not alone."

A quiet buzz spread gently across the room. Nate allowed the silence to linger.

"I'm so grateful to be here with all of you tonight," he said, steadying his breath. "To support this foundation. To support all of you. And to honor Noah, who I know would have loved it here."

Ronnie gently touched Amelia's trembling hand. She exhaled deeply and squeezed back, wiping her cheek and pretending it was the story, grief recognizing grief.

But part of her knew it was something else, too. The way he spoke, the way he looked at her after...

*Don't fall for a man just because he understands loss*, she warned herself. *That's not the same as knowing you.*

He cleared his throat gently, stepping back from the mic slightly. "Thank you."

A wave of applause rose through the ballroom, gentle yet powerful, like water breaking against stone. Chairs scraped back as guests stood one by one, dabbing at damp cheeks with cocktail napkins and sleeve cuffs, their faces shining with something more meaningful than mere sympathy.

Amelia rose with the others, clapping through the tears she didn't bother to hide.

When Nate came back to the table, she remained silent, simply gazing at him, understanding that words were insufficient. He gazed back with glazed eyes and a faint smile, giving a single nod.

It shifted—whatever had been holding still between them.

Sorrow encountered sorrow, and a sense of recognition emerged.

But understanding wasn't the same as safety. It wasn't the same as trust.

And yet, even as the applause faded around her, even as the room settled back into quiet conversation, Amelia felt something loosen—something she had kept tightly guarded for a long time.

A door she hadn't dared approach in years now stood slightly ajar.

Nate lingered beside her chair as the room slowly returned to its soft chatter. "You okay?" he asked, his voice quiet enough for only her.

She glanced up at him, her throat tight. "I didn't expect you to say all that."

He smiled softly. "Yeah, me neither. But this place, and you, well... it feels like the place where you should tell the truth."

Her lips parted, but no words came.

"Would you like some air?" he asked.

She nodded. "You read my mind."

As they made their way toward the terrace doors, they caught the familiar voice of the hospital president rising above the soft music. "Thank you again to everyone who made tonight possible — our volunteers, our donors, our staff, and the families who inspire us. We'll close out the night with dancing, so please, enjoy yourselves."

They slipped out of the ballroom onto the adjacent terrace, the cool night air washing over her skin, calming but not enough to still the flutter in her chest.

The city stretched out below them, lights twinkling, distant but alive.

"I rarely tell that story," he said, leaning against the railing, watching the reflections of string lights dancing faintly in the ballroom's tall windows, laughter and music still spilling faintly from inside.

"That's the first time I've told that story to a room full of strangers," he said, leaning against the railing. Behind them, string lights reflected in the ballroom's tall windows while muffled laughter and music drifted through the glass.

"I understand," she whispered, joining him at the railing. "I only share mine once a year, on nights like this."

Nate watched as her fingers found the small pendant at her neck. "Your daughter?" he asked softly.

She nodded, thumb brushing over the engraved surface. "Grace."

They stood in silence, the weight of their stories settling between them in the cool air.

It wasn't heavy, though. It wasn't suffocating. It was... understood.

When Nate finally turned toward her, his smile was gentle, tinged with a hint of sadness. His eyes held a depth that seemed to convey unspoken emotions. "Thank you for letting me be part of this tonight. It's one of the most genuine nights I've had in a long time," he confessed, his voice a soft murmur in the cool evening air.

Her chest tightened at the sincerity in his words, a warmth spreading through her. "Me too," she replied, her voice barely above a whisper, as if speaking too loudly might shatter the delicate moment they were sharing.

They stood together a while longer, sharing the silence like a secret. Amelia felt the space between them—not empty, but filled with something unspoken.

She wasn't ready to fall, not yet, but she tilted toward him anyway, like a building slowly surrendering to gravity. The thought struck her suddenly— here she was, exhausted and raw-nerved, swaying dangerously close to someone she barely knew—a sleep-deprived skyscraper with structural concerns. The absurdity of the image tugged at her lips, pulling them into an unexpected smile.

Nate noticed. "What?" he asked, his voice warm, quiet.

She shook her head, letting the grin linger. "Nothing. Just... thanks for being here."

He didn't press, just gave a soft nod and reached for the door, holding it open for her.

The sounds of the ballroom met them instantly—music, laughter, the gentle murmur of voices floating up like steam. The evening was winding down, but not yet over—still time for goodbyes.

Amelia stopped briefly to hug Ronnie, catching her outside the staff doors.

"You survived," Ronnie teased, pulling back to look her over. "And you looked good doing it."

Amelia smiled. "Thank you for coming down today. For everything. I mean it."

Ronnie's expression softened, the teasing fading slightly. "Always. You know where to find me if you need me."

They hugged once more, tighter this time, and then Amelia let go.

"Get some sleep, Lane," Ronnie said, stepping back with a knowing look. "You've earned it."

"You too," Amelia replied, her smile soft but tired. "I'll text you when I get home safely."

"You better, love you, babe."

Ronnie squeezed her arm once more before disappearing through the staff doors. Amelia lingered in the emptying ballroom, watching volunteers collect abandoned champagne flutes and fold tablecloths over their arms. The overhead lights had dimmed to a gentle glow, casting long shadows across the floor.

She turned and found Nate leaning against the wall. His posture was relaxed, hands in pockets, as if time were something he had plenty of. His eyes met hers without demand.

* * *

BEFORE SHE COULD close the distance, Nate pushed off the wall and gently took her hand, as if it naturally belonged there. His touch was warm and familiar, igniting a gentle spark beneath her skin.

"Come on," he said, his voice low and reassuring, carrying a promise of something better. "I found us a better way out."

She allowed him to lead her, feeling the comforting warmth of his fingers as they entwined with hers.

"A better way?" she inquired, raising an eyebrow in curiosity.

He flashed a mischievous grin. "Out of the terrace doors. More scenic. Feels... less like goodbye."

Instead of walking through the bustling lobby, he guided her down a quieter side hall. They passed the darkened gift shop, its windows displaying shadows of forgotten trinkets, and moved beyond the elevators where staff badges emitted soft beeps, a quiet rhythm in the night's stillness. Ahead, the terrace doors awaited, their glass panes misted over from the evening's warmth and the press of bodies within. Beyond the doors, a vast expanse of cool air and tranquil quietness beckoned — a gentler way to conclude the night, offering a serene escape before the world resumed its slumber.

As she spotted the black SUV waiting in the same spot as the morning, she smiled. "Were you trying to escape?"

He grinned. "Always."

The driver must have seen them coming because he was already stepping out from behind the wheel to open the back passenger door with practiced ease.

"Good evening, Mr. Carter."

Nate motioned for Amelia to go first. "Thank you, sir."

Amelia slipped inside, smoothing her pant legs beneath her as she settled in. Nate followed, pulling the door shut behind him with a soft click.

For a long moment, neither of them spoke. The quiet between them wasn't awkward or empty—it was a respite, like the stillness after a storm.

Denver glittered through the tinted windows. The lights of the city felt blurry and distant now, tempered not by glass but by everything that had happened in the hours since they had arrived. She leaned her head lightly against the seat, trying not to let her thoughts spiral too fast or too far.

Nate turned slightly toward her, his voice low. "Thank you, Amelia." He paused, searching for the right words. "Tonight... it felt like the closest thing to home I've had in a long time. Even if it's not mine."

He smiled, soft but certain. "Thanks for letting me be a part of it. All of it."

She turned to him, keeping her head slightly tilted back. "It meant a lot that you were there."

"I meant it all," he said. "Every word."

She believed him. She wanted to speak, but a lump in her throat stopped her.

They didn't fill the silence after that. There was nothing else to be said. The car moved steadily through the night, headlights pulling them back toward the hotel. Outside, the streets blurred by in soft streaks of light, and inside, it was just the two of them — a shared quiet, comfortable, and unspoken.

* * *

AS THE SUV pulled up to the Crawford, the familiar valet awning came into view, softly lit against the dark Denver sky. But it wasn't the building that Amelia noticed first.

It was her car. Parked in the same place it had been that morning. Half in shadow, the small sedan sat waiting like a tether to the real world. Her life. Her schedule. Her exit strategy.

The sight of it hit her harder than she expected—suddenly, it felt like a lifeboat waiting in case she needed to escape.

Instead of relief, however, she felt something else. A tiny pang of sadness, maybe. That the symbol of her safety had also become the symbol of something ending. A quiet sign that this night, this connection was temporary.

She couldn't believe what she was thinking, but *she didn't want this to end. Not yet, at least.*

The luxury vehicle came to a gentle stop under the portico, and the driver rounded to open their door.

Nate stepped out first, then offered his hand to her. Amelia followed, heels clicking against the stone, her mind a mess of possibility and nerves.

They stood side by side in the entrance's glow, guests still trickling in and out, laughter echoing from the nearby bar, a late-night hush blanketing everything in velvet.

The chaos of the morning was gone, leaving a space for something more still, something waiting.

Nate turned slightly toward her; one hand tucked in his pocket while the other held his jacket over his shoulder.

"I know the night is technically over, but... I've got the best view in Denver upstairs."

Amelia looked up at him, trying to read his tone, the line between casual and intentional. But he was smiling gently—no pressure, no assumption.

"And unless I missed it, you skipped dessert," he added with a smirk. "Which, in my book, is a crime."

She laughed gently, surprised by how much she liked the sound of his voice when it was just for her.

"The Crawford is allegedly famous for its dessert cart," he said, voice playful. "Would you consider that coercion?"

Her heart fluttered, not with fear, but with the strange electricity of something beginning.

She hesitated—not because she didn't want to go, but because the last time someone looked at her the way Nate had, she was wearing a white dress.

That had been a lifetime ago.

And this... this felt different.

Amelia looked once more toward her car. Then back at Nate.

"Okay," she said. "You had me at dessert cart."

He didn't cheer or grin broadly. He simply nodded, almost as if he'd expected she'd say yes, and stepped toward the doors. She followed him toward the elevator, their footsteps soft against the polished floors.

The ride up to the penthouse was silent, the only sound the soft vibration of the elevator. Her palms were slightly damp, and her heart fluttered with a mix of excitement and nerves. She concentrated on the illuminated numbers climbing steadily higher, their faint reflections glimmering in the polished, gold-lined walls like tiny, distant stars.

When the elevator doors slid open at the top floor, she stepped into a scene straight out of a designer magazine. The penthouse was breathtaking, with floor-to-ceiling glass windows that framed a sweeping view of the Denver skyline. Beyond the windows lay a vast terrace, nearly matching the size of the interior space, inviting thoughts of open-air gatherings and quiet moments under the stars.

The main living area exuded a modern elegance, its design striking a delicate balance between sophistication and warmth. Rich, earthy tones complemented the plush, inviting textures of the furniture, creating a space that felt both stylish and welcoming. A long dining table stretched along the windowed wall, ready for lively dinner parties or intimate meals with a view. Just beyond it, a hallway to the right subtly beckoned, hinting at other luxuries hidden within the penthouse—spacious bedrooms, luxurious bathrooms, perhaps even a private study. She resisted the urge to explore further, her eyes lingering only briefly in that direction.

In the far corner, a sleek, modern fireplace cast a gentle glow, its flickering flames dancing beneath a large painting. The artwork was just obscure enough in the dim light to intrigue her, its colors and shapes suggesting a story she couldn't quite decipher.

"This place is unreal," she said, her voice barely above a whisper.

Amelia walked over to the terrace door, slowly approaching the glass. She wrapped her arms around herself and stared out. She wasn't sure if it was the altitude or the moment, but her breath felt shallow in her chest.

"And this view," she muttered.

"You okay?" Nate asked from behind her.

She nodded, still facing the window. "I've never been this high in the city before," she said. "It's beautiful."

"It is," he agreed. "But it is better with company."

"I have a confession," he continued.

"Oh?"

"I love... dessert. And you seem like the kind of person who might understand that."

She laughed. "Depends on the dessert."

"I'll let you be the judge, then," he said, grabbing the hotel room phone. "They've got this warm cinnamon bread pudding with bourbon sauce. And a Boston crème pie that has ruined me."

Her stomach rumbled — traitorously. "You've clearly done your research."

"Guilty," he grinned. "I take dessert seriously."

"Apparently."

He leaned back, smirking. "In my defense, I ordered half the dessert cart last night after you turned me down. Had to eat my feelings before I could sleep."

Amelia widened her eyes in exaggerated concern. "Are you okay now? Emotionally stabilized?"

"Jury's still out," he said. "Might need more pudding for confirmation."

"Should I be worried? Is this how you cope with all your deep emotional wounds?"

"Trust me—you won't regret it," he quipped, raising an eyebrow. "And yes, dessert is always a great way to cope with anything."

Amelia laughed again, a softer, more open sound now. "I'm trusting you with a lot tonight."

"I know," he said, his tone shifting, more serious than before. "And I don't take that lightly."

She felt her heartbeat shift again, a slow thrum beneath her ribs.

They sat for a moment, the quiet settling comfortably between them. Nate gave a short nod, as if they'd just agreed on something without saying a word.

Nate reached for the side table and placed their dessert order, confirming to the person on the other end that, yes, he did, in fact, want the same thing he'd ordered the night before. Again.

He hung up, turning back to her with a grin. "Pretty sure the guy on the phone is concerned I'm going through something. Or he's impressed by my consistency."

He leaned in, his voice dipping lower, a secret folded into the space between them. "What can I say? Some people self-soothe with yoga. But I go for bread pudding and Boston crème."

"I'm happy you came up," he said, voice low but certain.

Amelia nodded, still standing near the edge of the terrace door. "Me too."

She wasn't used to this kind of stillness with a man—certainly not since… well, not in years.

The view outside beckoned again. She drifted back toward the windows, looking out at the vast sweep of the city. Somewhere out there was her car. Her exit. Her before.

Behind her stood Nate. And everything she hadn't expected from this night. Everything that might still happen.

And for the first time in a long time, she wasn't scared of it.

"Mind if I use your restroom?" she asked, breaking the quiet.

Nate smiled easily. "Down the hall. First door on the left. You'll know it when you see it — it's the dark, slightly creepy hallway. Very horror-movie chic."

Amelia laughed under her breath and made her way down the hall. He wasn't kidding about the lighting. It was dim and dramatic in a way that felt designed for mood, not function.

Inside the bathroom, she handled the essentials quickly — though she couldn't help rolling her eyes as she peeled down the top half of her jumpsuit, sitting there half-naked in Nate Carter's bathroom. Of course, she'd worn the one outfit with no easy exit strategy.

She washed her hands, splashed a little cool water on her cheeks, and leaned into the mirror with a quiet sigh. Tired. That was the headline.

Her gaze drifted. A few things on the counter caught her eye — shaving cream, aftershave, a frosted bottle of Armani Acqua di Giò. Of course. Mystery solved. The scent that had been following her for days now had a name.

She straightened, smoothed her hair, and pulled herself together.

When she stepped back into the living room, she found Nate exactly as she should have expected: barefoot, stretched out on the couch like it belonged to him, a white t-shirt clinging soft and comfortable, black lounge pants hanging low on his hips.

*Shit*, she thought. He is not making this easy.

She paused at the end of the hallway, watching him for a moment too long.

She knew she should have some thoughts. Something sensible. Something self-preserving.

But right now, she couldn't seem to think of anything except the way his abs flexed when he shifted, the faint trail of skin visible where his shirt had ridden up enough to be distracting.

This wasn't helping. Not at all.

Nate didn't even look over. "How long are you planning to stand there staring at me?" His voice was casual, but the grin pulling at the corner of his mouth gave him away.

She stepped forward, heat creeping up her neck. "I'm... collecting myself."

"Take your time," he said, finally turning to look at her. "I changed. Figured I'd be more comfortable. You looked like you might need me to set the tone."

He patted the space beside him. "You gonna sit? Or are you just here to admire from a distance?"

Amelia crossed the room, trying to ignore the fact that every step made her more aware of how close she was about to be to Nate Carter's lounge pants. She lowered herself carefully onto the couch, keeping an ample space between them to pretend she wasn't thinking about how close was *too close.*

She'd barely settled when the doorbell chimed, the sound cutting through the charged silence between them.

Nate groaned but pushed up from the couch with a lazy stretch that pulled his t-shirt taut across his shoulders. "That'll be the pudding."

She was, in that moment, deeply thankful for the distance between them. She needed air. Space. Maybe prayer, or a cold shower, or both simultaneously.

And then he stood, the black lounge pants riding dangerously low on his hips, revealing a sliver of tanned skin and the faint lines of muscle disappearing beneath the waistband.

The pants clung just enough as he stretched his arms overhead, fabric pulling across his backside in a way that made her mouth go dry.

She watched, mesmerized, as he padded across the plush carpet toward the door, his shoulders rolling with an easy confidence that made her grip the edge of the couch cushion.

Had a man's back always been this fascinating? The subtle shift of muscle beneath cotton, the way his waist tapered, the curve where his lower back met—

She didn't realize she liked butts.

Did she like butts?

She knew nothing anymore.

# 8

# edge of staying

THE DESSERT WAS dangerous.

Warm cinnamon bread pudding with a bourbon glaze, served with fresh whipped cream—a miniature Boston crème pie with glossy chocolate ganache that shimmered under the gold lighting. Nate hadn't exaggerated—it was unfairly good. And Amelia, nerves and all, had eaten far more than she meant to.

"I didn't know one person could eat this much dessert and still be nervous," she muttered, pressing a hand gently to her stomach.

Nate grinned, lounging comfortably on the large sectional. "You've officially made it through step one of my patented anxiety-reduction method: sugar overload."

She smiled, genuinely this time, letting the richness of the dessert soothe the frayed edges of her thoughts. "Well, it's working."

"You're doing great," he said, quieter now.

Amelia paused, twirling her fork lightly over her plate. "By the way... thank you, Nate. For your donation offer tonight. It was incredibly generous."

He shrugged as if it was nothing, but his eyes softened. "It feels right. I wanted to help."

"Well, you should know... I heard some murmurs as I was shaking hands with people as they were leaving. A few of the corporate donors—people who have been with us from the beginning—upped their annual pledges after hearing you speak."

His brow lifted slightly, surprised but amused. "Seriously?"

She nodded, warmth settling in her chest. "Seriously. I think you started something."

He leaned back, flashing a playful grin. "Well, you know… It's not every day you meet a superhero who's also a part-time fundraising catalyst."

She laughed, shaking her head. "A dangerous combination."

Nate leaned slightly forward, fork paused midair. "Wait—how old are you, if you don't mind me asking?"

Amelia smirked, setting down her glass. "Bold move, Mr. Carter."

He grinned, "I'll go first. I'm thirty."

"Okay, fair. I'm thirty-two."

"Older woman," he teased with a wink. "Should I be intimidated?"

"You should be so lucky," she replied, part of her chest flickering at the thought.

She hadn't said it out loud in a while. Thirty-two. It didn't feel old, but it didn't feel young either. Some days, she wondered how one heart could hold two lives—one where Grace lived, and one where she didn't.

Sitting across from each other and separated by only inches of plush space, Amelia pulled her legs beneath her, curling in on herself with unspoken vulnerability.

"You said something earlier… about trust," she said, eyes tracing the outline of the city through the floor-to-ceiling windows. "I don't trust easily. I'm working on it."

"Trust takes time," he replied gently.

"It can, yeah. But that's what's strange. I haven't felt pressure from you. Only… presence."

He didn't interrupt, letting the space breathe.

"I was married once," she said, fingers tightening around the edge of a pillow. "Grant Wells. He's Grace's father."

Nate nodded once, attentive without pushing.

"We met young. Married young. And for a long time, it worked. Especially after Grace was born," her voice dipped. "But when she got sick… things changed. We changed."

She paused, eyes distant now. "We were both grieving before she was even gone. And after... we couldn't find our way back."

Nate leaned forward slightly. "That must've been incredibly lonely."

"It was. Still is, sometimes."

Amelia breathed in deeply, pushing back the tears beginning to surface.

After a moment, Nate spoke. "When my brother Noah died, I was fourteen. I remember watching my parents try to hold it together... and fail more often than not."

Amelia turned slightly toward him, surprised by the soft ache behind his voice.

"They loved each other. Still do. But grief made everything harder. Every little thing became a battle. They didn't know how to laugh anymore—not without him."

He gave a faint smile. "Noah was the one who made everything lighter. He was loud and goofy, always getting into trouble, but somehow he kept the rest of us sane. When we lost him, it was like the entire world lost its color."

Amelia blinked back sudden emotion.

"I'm so sorry," she said gently.

Nate shrugged, the gesture quiet, worn-in. "I just... I get what you're saying. I didn't lose a child, but I lost part of myself when Noah died, and I saw firsthand how it affected my parents."

She nodded, quietly absorbing the truth of that.

"Are they still together?" she asked, softer now.

Nate's mouth lifted into something that wasn't quite a smile, but wasn't sad either.

"Yeah. They are. High school sweethearts. Small town. A little stubborn. But they're still together."

The pride in his voice wasn't loud, just steady—grateful in a way that understood how rare it was to reach the ending most people only hoped for.

"You know," she said, a small fake smile on her face, "aside from a few awkward first dates, Ronnie insisted I try. I haven't really... done this."

Nate looked over at her, curious. "Done what?"

"This," she gestured vaguely between them. "Been with a man like this. At night. In a place like this. It's been a long time."

She hesitated, then added with a dry little laugh, "Fun fact—Ronnie is Grant's sister. That's how I met him."

Nate blinked. "Wow. That's... got to be a little awkward."

"It used to be," she admitted, "but not anymore. Grant moved out of state a year ago." She waved it off gently. "Anyway... we can save that conversation for another day."

He waited, letting her words land before he said anything at all.

"I kept thinking I'd know when I was ready again," she added, her voice unsteady now. "But the truth is... I didn't. I don't. I'm... here."

Her voice cracked slightly on the word "here." She wasn't sure if she meant the penthouse, the city, or this exact moment sitting inches from him. Maybe all of it. Perhaps she just needed to say it out loud.

Nate's brow furrowed slightly, and he leaned forward. "You're not alone in that. I haven't exactly been good at relationships. At least not real ones."

Amelia tilted her head. "You're not exactly short on admirers."

He chuckled, the sound low. "Admiration's easy when they don't know you. But the press—God, they've turned a few casual dates into epic romances. Half of them weren't even people I knew well. But it's easier to believe I'm a headline than a person."

His honesty caught her off guard, and to her surprise, brought a flicker of relief. "That sounds frustrating," she said.

"It is. That's why this—being here, with you—feels entirely different."

"I'm glad," Amelia beamed.

"Honestly, most of the things I read about myself never sound like me," He continued.

"Sometimes I wonder if it's worth it."

They sat in that understanding for a beat. Then, almost shyly, Amelia smiled.

"Can I ask you something kind of... obvious?"

Nate raised an eyebrow. "Always."

She hesitated. "Are you... seeing anyone?"

His answer came without pause. "No. Not even sort of. Haven't in a long time."

Relief washed through her—more than she expected.

"You?" he asked gently.

She shook her head. "No. Just me, my work, and occasionally Ronnie dragging me to terrible brunch dates."

Nate chuckled. "Tragic."

"Honestly," Amelia said, her voice softening, "I think I stopped believing there could be something real. I got used to being the one who stayed behind."

He leaned in closer, his voice soft. "Just so you know, I'm here. And I won't leave unless you want me to."

Her breath hitched, his words resonating deep within her. She was at a loss for words, unsure if she could trust her voice.

Nate kept his eyes on her, unwavering and confident. "You're quite noticeable, you know."

The way he said it made her feel both shy and drawn to him at once. She swallowed and tried to express something similar without stumbling. "Well... you're difficult to forget, too."

His lips curled into a gentler expression. "Nobody has ever said that so cautiously before."

She laughed, grateful for the out. "I'm still deciding if it's a compliment."

And maybe because it felt too raw to sit in that tenderness too long, she reached for something easier. Something a little ridiculous.

"You're playing a superhero," she said, tipping her head, a smirk tugging at her mouth. "Captain Orion."

Nate groaned playfully, "Don't say it like that. It's a serious role."

"Oh, I'm sure. Deep emotional stakes. Laser beams and capes?"

"No laser beams, actually," he grinned. "But yes, a lot of running. A lot of wirework. More stunts than I expected."

She turned to face him more fully now, appreciating the attention being shifted from her. The tension slowly unraveling from her shoulders, she leaned more into the couch.

"Did you do them all yourself?" she asked.

"Most of them. Until I got this." He pointed slightly above his right eyebrow, where a faint line peeked from beneath his hairline.

Her gaze caught on the thin white line above his eyebrow. Strange—she'd never spotted it in any magazine spread or red carpet photo. Even sitting across from him at the hospital, she'd missed it entirely. But here, with only a lamp casting gold across his features and barely two feet between them, she could see everything. The lamplight caught the slight ridge where the skin had healed imperfectly. She leaned closer, drawn by this minor imperfection in his otherwise camera-ready face.

Before she realized what she was doing, her hand had lifted from her lap, fingers suspended in the space between them.

Her hand hovered in the air between them. She hesitated, caught between wanting to touch him and wondering if she should. But the way Nate looked at her—eyes steady, unguarded—gave her the permission she hadn't realized she was seeking.

Her fingertips found the raised edge of his scar, tracing its path. The skin there felt different—a ridge of memory etched into smoothness. Warmth radiated from him, traveled up her arm, and settled somewhere beneath her ribs. Not the sharp knife-twist of anxiety, but something gentler that expanded with each breath.

Nate briefly shut his eyes when her fingers touched him, as though her touch had drawn out something within him he wasn't prepared to acknowledge verbally.

"Is this okay?" she asked softly, her hand hovering near his face, close enough to feel the warmth of his skin.

When he responded, his voice was different—deep and gravelly, imbued with a raw intensity, as though it had emerged from some hidden depth within him, a depth he hadn't allowed her to glimpse until this moment.

"Yeah... this is more than okay."

It wasn't just the words he chose; it was the way they rolled off his tongue, a tone that settled low in her stomach, like the distant rumble of thunder promising a storm. It was a voice she hadn't heard from him before, yet she knew she would never forget it. A voice she longed to hear again, rich with unspoken promises.

Her nerves ignited, a persistent alarm she couldn't entirely silence.

*You don't know where this is going.*

*You don't know if you are ready.*

Yet, despite the warnings, she didn't pull back. Her heart pounded like a drum, resonating through her chest, but her body stayed rooted in place, unwilling to retreat.

And then, when it was too late to second-guess, she realized she didn't want to.

Amelia wasn't sure who moved first, only that the space between them had quietly vanished. Her breath caught, heart thudding against her ribs, begging to be set free. The soft exhale from his nose brushed her lips before anything else did, warm and deliberate, and suddenly the quiet between them wasn't quiet at all — it was humming.

Their mouths met at last—not in haste, not in heat, but with a quiet reverence. Slow and searching, as if they knew one wrong move might make it vanish. His lips were soft but sure, patient in a way that unspooled something heavy and trembling beneath her skin.

He kissed her like a promise. Like he'd waited a long time for this, and he wasn't in a hurry to let it go.

Amelia let herself lean into it, let herself feel the shape of his mouth against hers, the slight scratch of stubble at the corner of her lip, the warmth of his hand curving open-palmed against her cheek. The weight of it steadied her, anchored her somewhere safe and certain. His thumb traced a slow line just beneath her jaw, and her body answered before her mind could catch up — a small sigh slipping free, quiet and involuntary.

She tasted him, too — something sweet lingering from dessert, dark chocolate and berry, softened by something undeniably *him*. It felt decadent. A little dangerous.

When their lips finally touched, it wasn't rushed or desperate. It was careful. Deliberate. Like they were handling something fragile. His mouth pressed against hers with a certainty that made her stomach drop, each subtle shift of pressure uncoiling something that had been wound tight inside her for years.

He kissed her like he meant it. Like this wasn't just a moment, but a beginning. Amelia melted forward, giving herself over to the gentle pressure of his lips, the faint rasp of stubble against her skin. His palm cupped her cheek, thumb resting just below her ear, holding her steady when she might have drifted away.

Her body knew what to do before her mind caught up. A soft sound escaped her throat when his thumb traced the line of her jaw. She tasted chocolate and berries on his tongue, the lingering sweetness of dessert. Something about it felt both innocent and sinful at once—like tasting something she'd denied herself for too long.

He pulled back just enough for them to breathe, their foreheads touching, anchoring them together. The rise and fall of his chest matched her own unsteady rhythm.

Silence wrapped around them like a blanket.

The weight of him against her felt like coming home to a place she'd forgotten existed. His palm remained curved to her cheek, thumb tracing her jawline. At her waist, his fingers splayed possessively, the gentle pressure of his thumb against her hipbone sending liquid warmth cascading through her.

This, she realized. *This is what I've been missing.*

*This is what I want to keep.*

When he finally spoke, his words came as softly as a confession in church, meant only for the space between their bodies.

"Is this okay?" he asked, giving her the same courtesy she'd given him — making sure he wasn't crossing a line she wasn't ready for.

Amelia nodded, her eyes fluttering shut for a moment beneath the weight of it — his care, his patience, his restraint. "Yeah," she breathed. Her voice sounded different too — quieter, gentler. Honest. "This... is okay."

His chest fell with a slow exhale, shoulders dropping slightly as tension left his body—as if her permission had unlocked something guarded inside him.

"Thank God," he murmured, his fingers tightening almost imperceptibly at her waist, as if even the slightest space between them might be too much to bear.

* * *

BEFORE AMELIA EVEN considered opening her eyes, their lips met once more—this time with more length and depth.

Nate's hand rested on her waist while his other hand moved up, fingers gently weaving into her loose hair, his thumb softly brushing the sensitive skin at the back of her neck.

She felt a shiver run through her at his touch. His hand leisurely traced down her arm, his fingertips lightly skimming along, leaving a tender, tingling warmth in their path.

Every part of her was aware of him, of their proximity, and how that space between them disappeared more with each breath.

Amelia allowed herself to melt into the kiss, savoring the way his mouth fit hers with a quiet intensity. His touch wasn't rushed, but it was deliberate. Intent. Appreciative. As if he were committing her to memory.

His hands cradled her—not as if she might shatter, but as if she were something to be cherished. His eyes asked questions his lips didn't form. He waited.

Beneath her, his body remained motionless, an anchor in the still waters. When his eyes found hers again, they held something like wonder—as though he couldn't quite believe the moment was real.

With deliberate care, his palms settled against both of her hips, thumbs tracing slow arcs along the curve where her waist narrowed. Not urging and not demanding, simply steadying.

Her lungs forgot their rhythm when she accepted his wordless invitation. She inched forward until her knees framed his thighs. Her body aligned with his—her weight settling fully into his lap, her face level with his, nothing between them but breath and possibility.

The shift sent a jolt through her core — a slow-spreading heat that bloomed low in her belly and radiated outward until every inch of her skin reverberated with awareness.

Her hands hovered for a beat, uncertain, before settling at last on his shoulders. The warmth of him seeped into her palms, grounding her as surely as his hands at her waist.

Her heart thudded hard beneath her ribs.

She didn't move. Not yet.

Because this — this moment—wasn't about moving.

It was about feeling.

Letting it happen.

Letting him hold her.

And for the first time in so long, Amelia realized she wasn't afraid of being held.

She wasn't sure who breathed first—her or him—but everything in her body felt alert now. His hands remained at her waist, holding her still, thumbs pressing firmly on her hip bones like he thought she might float away if he didn't hold tight. His chest rose to meet hers with every inhale, and where their bodies touched, torso to torso, hip to hip, heat flared in unmistakable waves.

She could feel him beneath her—a steady, pulsing presence that made her breath catch. But it wasn't only that. It was the way his hands didn't demand, the way his body remained still, offering no pressure, no pull—just patience. He let her decide what came next.

She wanted to memorize him. Not only the shape of his body, but the way it felt to be this close—to be wanted without hesitation, to want without fear. Her fingers moved slowly, reverently, tracing the strength in his arms, the curve of his shoulder, the lean muscle of his chest beneath the fabric. Each pass of her hand felt like a quiet act of wonder, like she was learning him one breath at a time. Her touch followed the rise and fall of his chest, steady and warm.

Her fingertips brushed the edge of his shirt, curling into the fabric like testing the shape of a question. When she pulled it slowly upward, he lifted his arms in a silent answer.

As the fabric lifted, her eyes landed on the ink stretched along his left arm, above the inside of his biceps. Two crossed baseball bats, one bearing a faint halo at the top. The lines were clean but worn, as if they had been there for a long time, as if they held meaning.

For a long moment, Amelia couldn't look away from the tattoo, couldn't breathe past the tightness in her chest. Questions formed and dissolved on her tongue, unnecessary.

Her fingers moved of their own accord, brushing over the inked skin with deliberate care. The halo first—that small, telling detail—then along the wooden curve beneath it. Each touch a whisper of understanding.

Nate remained perfectly still under her exploration. When she finally met his eyes, she found them dark with an exposed tenderness that made her throat ache. The memorial wasn't just art; it was Noah, preserved in his brother's flesh.

The shared recognition passed between them without sound—a bridge built of parallel grief that needed no explanation, no translation. It simply existed, as real as the warmth beneath her fingertips.

She moved without hesitation, closing the distance between them with a kiss that belonged only to her.

Nate's response came instantly—a sound caught somewhere between surrender and need as his palms found the curve where her spine met her hips, drawing her against him until nothing separated their bodies. What began as a single point of contact became something hungrier, something that demanded more with each passing second.

The hard planes of his chest met the softness of hers. When she shifted her weight, testing the feel of him beneath her with a deliberate roll of her hips, electricity sparked through her veins, pooling low in her belly, igniting places she'd forgotten could burn.

*Oh. There you are.*

She moved with intention now, her hips finding a rhythm against him that made her breath hitch in her throat and heat bloom across her skin. Not hurried—something more dangerous than that. Something that built like a slow-rolling wave, tightening at her core until she could barely think through the haze of sensation.

This feeling—this hunger—was unlike anything she'd known before. Sharper. Clearer. More consuming.

Nate's head fell back against the cushions, eyes half-closed as though surrendering. His grip tightened at her waist, fingers pressing into soft flesh as he matched her movements with a deliberate upward tilt of his hips. Each breath he took seemed to catch, words forming and dissolving before they could reach his lips.

"Jesus, Amelia…" The roughness in his voice sent a shiver down her spine, settling low and warm. "What you do to me… You have no idea."

A sound escaped her—part sigh, part nervous laughter—as her fingers curled against his shoulders.

"I'm serious," he murmured, his hand sliding beneath the hem of her shirt, fingertips tracing up the bare curve of her back. "You're… all I want. You're wrecking me in the best damn way."

The honesty in his voice—the raw edge of it—sent another shiver rolling through her.

"Tell me if you want me to stop."

God help her, she didn't. Not yet.

Still, she felt it—the tension mounting, the air between them thick with want and restraint. His mouth found hers again, slower this time, but no less hungry, as if he were memorizing her now, too.

Her lips grazed his once more before she pulled back slightly, her breath uneven.

"Nate…" she murmured, her voice unsteady—not unsure, but overwhelmed. Her hips shifted again without thought, grinding softly against him, and his breath came sharper against her throat.

His eyes opened slowly, dark and intent on hers. "Yeah?"

She kissed him again before answering, a soft, open-mouthed touch that elicited another deep sound from his chest. His hands flexed against her waist, holding her there like he couldn't bear the thought of space between them.

"I want to stay… I do." The words slipped out against his lips, soft, almost like a moan. "But I can't. Not tonight."

His breath warmed her skin, slow and controlled. She could feel the tension coiled beneath her, the effort it took not to move. He didn't urge her closer—only held her. Like this moment was enough.

Her hands remained on his shoulders, not pulling away yet. Not quite ready to lose the weight of him beneath her.

He didn't flinch. Didn't loosen his hold. "Okay."

"You're not disappointed?"

"Of course I want you to stay." His thumb stroked along her waist again, slow and sure. "But not at the cost of something that matters."

His mouth found her jaw again, soft and lingering, his lips exploring the shape of her there. She let out a breath—something like a gasp, something like *God, please, don't stop yet.* His teeth scraped gently at the line beneath her ear before he spoke again, quieter but heavier.

"I meant what I said," he murmured against her skin. "I don't take this lightly."

Then, pulling back enough to meet her eyes again, he added, voice low and devastatingly certain, "I want *all* of you. Not just tonight."

Another kiss—this one even slower, deeper, his tongue tracing the seam of her mouth like a question he already knew the answer to. Her fingers curled in his hair, pulling him closer before she could stop herself. Her hips rocked again, and the sound he made—rough, appreciative, *God, Amelia*—went straight through her.

"You're not something I'm trying to get over with," he said, quieter, but no less sure. "You're not a moment. You're... already more than that."

Another kiss. Another slow, aching grind. Her breath stuttered, her thighs tightening around his hips. She couldn't help herself.

"Oh, God..." she breathed, not sure if she meant the words for him or herself.

He smiled against her mouth, something crooked and wrecked and so damn male it made her ache all over again.

"We should stop," she whispered, though her body clearly hadn't gotten the memo—her hips still pressed tight against his, her hands still tangled in his hair. "Really... we should."

Nate huffed a laugh, low and rough. "You say that like I'm the problem." His mouth found her jaw again, dragging one last slow kiss there that made her shiver. "Pretty sure you're the one who can't keep your hands off me."

"That's not fair," she breathed, half-laughing, half-ruined. "You make it hard to remember my reasons."

"Good," he murmured, pressing one last kiss to her throat. "I enjoy having that effect on you."

Her breath caught again, another soft sound slipping free before she eased back enough to meet his eyes. Her lips swollen, her pulse still thudding high.

"I'll call you tomorrow, if you give me your number," he continued, lifting some of the tension.

She gave a small smile, a little skeptical. "Will you?"

"I will." He kissed her again—quick this time, but no less certain—before his hand slid down to lace with hers. "I'll repeat it. I'll call you. Tomorrow."

"I'll call you every day, if you let me." He continued.

Her forehead dropped to his, breathless, her grin widening despite herself.

She laughed softly, thrilled at the thought. "Alright. You've said it three times. That's a legally binding promise."

"Good," he said. "Because I meant it all three times."

Another kiss—gentler now, even slower. As if he wished the moment would linger forever. As if he intended to imprint its significance onto her skin, her lips, her memory.

* * *

IT WAS NEARLY two a.m. by the time they tiptoed back through the hotel lobby with its marble floors that gleamed like black water under the dimmed chandeliers. A different front desk clerk—a middle-aged man with salt-and-pepper stubble and half-moon reading glasses—was now on shift, barely looking up from his dog-eared paperback as the elevator doors opened with a soft chime and the two of them stepped out, their fingers loosely entwined, her pinky occasionally brushing against his wrist.

They walked in quiet steps across the plush burgundy carpet that muffled their footfalls, their laughter soft and conspiratorial, like children sharing secrets. The weight of the night settled around them like a cashmere blanket—warm, comforting, but not pressing in. It was a hush that didn't ask for words, that made the space between heartbeats feel sacred.

The night air kissed their skin as they pushed through the revolving door, cool enough to raise goosebumps along her forearms. Denver's skyline glittered against the ink-black sky, a constellation of office lights and apartment windows. Their steps echoed faintly against concrete, the rhythm in perfect sync, neither of them willing to quicken their pace and break whatever gossamer thread connected them in this moment.

The city slept around them, streetlamps casting pools of amber light at measured intervals, as if the universe itself were holding its breath for this one perfect, fleeting moment between strangers becoming something more.

She paused at her SUV, keys dangling from her fingers. The familiar vehicle seemed somehow different now—not an escape route, but a crossroads.

Nate's fingers wove through hers, his other hand buried deep in his pocket. The streetlight caught the intensity in his eyes.

"I'm not ready for this to end," he said, voice low against the quiet night.

Her grip tightened around his. "So don't end it."

His smile spread slow and warm as he leaned closer. "Then consider this a beginning."

"Semantics," she whispered, but couldn't help smiling.

The kiss he pressed to her lips felt like the first page of a story she'd been waiting to read—gentle yet certain, an ellipsis rather than a period.

He pulled her in entirely, his hands cupping her jaw, the kiss lingering a beat longer than a casual farewell should. When he finally pulled back, his thumbs brushed gently across her cheeks.

"Tomorrow," he said one last time.

She nodded, unlocking the door. "Tomorrow."

Her body trembled slightly as she settled into the driver's seat. Not from fear or nerves. But from the weight of wanting more, wanting him.

She closed the door softly and started the engine.

Before pulling away, she quickly typed an update text to Ronnie:

*Headed home. I'm safe. Also... I might like him. Really like him. Talk
to you later.*

It was a habit, one that neither of them ever skipped.

As she pulled away, she glanced in her rearview mirror. Nate was still standing there, hands in his pockets, watching her go. And something about the way he didn't look away made her believe him.

He would call.

# 9

# the call

NATE CARTER KEPT his promises.

At precisely 7:07 p.m., Amelia's phone lit up with his name, and something inside her chest flickered to life.

During her pre-dawn drive home, she'd prepared herself for disappointment. After all, wasn't it sensible to expect that someone like him—with his movie premieres and magazine covers—would have already forgotten her? That whatever spark had ignited between them would be extinguished by distance and his glamorous reality?

She'd convinced herself that "tomorrow" meant a full twenty-four hours, if he remembered at all. So when his name appeared on her screen—barely fifteen hours since they'd parted—her thumb hovered, suddenly unsure. The notification pulsed once, twice, and something electric raced through her veins, warming places that had been cold for years.

She was sitting barefoot on the couch, hair piled into a loose knot, still in the sleep shirt she'd worn since crawling into bed that morning.

She'd spent most of the day alternating between staring out the window and replaying every second of the night before—his voice, his touch, the way he had looked at her as if she were something worth knowing. The thought of taking a shower had crossed her mind a few times; however, the desire to let his smell linger on her skin overruled her need for cleanliness.

When she answered the phone, her voice cracked a little with surprise.

"You called," was all she could manage.

Nate laughed on the other end, warm and genuine.

"I told you I would. I'm not big on broken promises." He continued, "Honestly, I would have called sooner, but they delayed my flight out of Denver twice, thanks to the weather."

She bit her lip, fighting back the stupid smile creeping in.

"Well, good evening then."

The call flowed easily and naturally. Minutes stretched into an hour without either of them noticing the time.

"So what did you do today?" he asked, his voice warm in her ear.

Amelia curled her toes against the couch cushion. "Nothing worth reporting," she admitted with a soft laugh. "Slept until my body said stop. Tidied up. Answered the work emails that had little red exclamation points."

She hesitated, then added something she hadn't planned to share.

"I did text Ronnie," she said. "When I got home."

"We have this thing," she continued, "where we always text each other when we get home, just to make sure we're alive. It started in college after a couple of weird nights walking home, and it stuck."

"I like that," Nate said. "Makes sense."

"Well, now that she knows I was with you last night, I'm guessing she's going to call or show up at my door any minute. Probably both."

He chuckled. "So, you're going to get grilled by the best friend?"

"Absolutely," Amelia said with a laugh. "If she hasn't already mapped out our entire future step by step, I'll be shocked."

"She sounds like my kind of person," Nate replied. Then his voice softened a little. "You sound... lighter today."

Amelia hesitated. The words were unexpected but welcome. "I guess I am."

There was a pause on the line, not quite silent. She heard the faint rustle of fabric, maybe a zipper.

"What are you up to?" she asked gently.

"Oh, I'm getting a few things unpacked. I landed back in L.A. and waited for what felt like forever for my driver. Then L.A. traffic did its thing." He let out a small exhale.

"You sound tired," she said with a tinge of concern.

"Yeah, I guess I am. Long day, but talking to you has helped."

A smile crept across her face, soft and private. "I'm glad."

After a pause, Amelia spoke, "I should let you get some sleep."

"Only if you let me call you again tomorrow."

"That sounds nice," Amelia said immediately.

"Ok, good, I'll call you tomorrow."

"All right," she said, trying to keep her voice even. "Goodnight, Nate."

"Goodnight, Amelia."

She ended the call and sat there frozen in place. She felt *giddy*. It's the only word she could think of. Not falling in love, not swept off her feet—just... giddy.

Like something had broken loose in her chest and was now fluttering wildly against her ribs.

But the giddiness didn't come alone.

It came with questions. With weight.

Was this happening? Was he really going to call again? And then what? What did he want from her—what *could* he want from her? What would happen when the shine wore off, and he realized she wasn't a headline? She wasn't glamorous. She surely wasn't easy.

What did she expect to happen next? That he'd fly back? Could this become something real? That they could outrun distance, press tours, and paparazzi?

She didn't know. And yet... she wanted to find out.

But as the sun dipped behind the Rocky Mountains, another feeling crept in—quieter, colder.

Reality.

Nate Carter lived in world premieres and private jets. She lived in a suburb outside Boulder with an aging sedan and front porch light that flickered when the wind hit just right.

She filled her days with remote work in yoga pants, juggling donor spreadsheets and driving into Denver for hospital board meetings.

She didn't miss the fact that, no matter how perfect the night had felt, they still orbited entirely different worlds.

And then another truth landed—quiet, but undeniable.

*She didn't really know that much about him.*

Not beyond what he's shared over dessert and their one late-night conversation. Sure, she knew he was a famous movie star; that is why she asked him to attend the gala, but she hadn't even seen any of his movies. She didn't follow celebrity gossip, didn't even have a TV in her bedroom.

The first time she had even seen anything about him was when Ronnie sent a link to a magazine cover. She never even clicked it.

He had a whole public life she'd never explored.

Her phone rested on the cushion beside her, the screen still open to his name.

Maybe she should Google him. Perhaps she should figure out who the world thought he was.

Was there a list of his ex-girlfriends? Were there scandalous stories? Was she the only one feeling this much this soon?

The curiosity itched at her. But just as quickly as it came, she pushed the phone away and shoved it under a throw pillow.

Tonight, she wanted Nate—the one who ate cinnamon bread pudding and kissed like he had all the time in the world.

Tomorrow, she might need to know more.

But tonight, she wanted to hold this version. The version that was hers.

Maybe tomorrow, she'd Google him a little — enough to know what the rest of the world saw when they looked at Nate Carter.

Tonight, she wanted to remember the way he smelled. The sound of his voice. The way he said her name.

* * *

HER PHONE BUZZED again slightly after 9:00 p.m.

*Ronnie.*

Amelia answered with a smile already forming. "Hey."

"Well, well, well," Ronnie's voice sang. "Look who finally emerged from the mystery fog. I expected a recap three hours ago."

Amelia laughed, sinking deeper into the couch. "I have been... processing."

"Oh, I bet you were," Ronnie teased. "Should I cancel your Tinder account now or...?"

"Stop."

"I'm just saying, Lane," Ronnie continued, "you sounded like a middle schooler with a crush when you texted me this morning. I half expected doodles of his name in hearts."

Amelia rolled her eyes, but the smile didn't leave her face. "It was... really nice."

"Nice?" Ronnie scoffed. "That man looks like a Calvin Klein ad and talks like a Nicholas Sparks hero. You're going to have to give me more than nice."

Amelia pulled her knees to her chest. "It was sweet. And easy. And... more than I expected."

Ronnie was quiet for a beat. "Okay, now I'm listening. Keep going."

"He kissed me. I kissed him. We talked. About Grace. About Grant. It felt... grounded."

She continued, "We talked about real-life things. It felt natural. Like I could actually breathe."

Ronnie hummed in approval, "That's a good sign."

"You know, we sure have come a long way from the first gala when you and I got caught in that stupid rainstorm after the dinner," Amelia said suddenly, the memory bubbling up.

"Oh, my God—why in the world did we ditch the cab line and walk five blocks in our stilettos?"

"Exactly. We ended up soaked, starving, and you were furious because your hair frizzed."

Ronnie laughed, sharp and real. "I was not furious."

"You were. You kept muttering about emergency hair products like we were on a survival show."

"Well, yeah. Some of us didn't want to show up to a pizza dive looking like a raccoon. You never know when the love of your life might show up!"

Amelia smiled, warmth settling in her chest. "But we sat there anyway, dripping wet, in our gala dresses, eating greasy pizza with our hands."

"That was a great night." Ronnie snorted.

"It was," Amelia agreed softly. "It was a night that kicked off so much."

"And this one?" Ronnie's voice lowered. "Is this like that?"

"Yeah. I think so... I mean, I hope so."

"And you think it could go somewhere?" Ronnie asked.

"I don't know," Amelia admitted. "He lives in L.A. I'm me. I'm still working to ensure the Foundation stays afloat for another year. We had one night."

"One night," Ronnie said softly, "can change everything."

They stayed on the phone for a while, the way they always did when life felt too big. Ronnie didn't give advice—not really. But she knew how to listen. She also learned how to make Amelia feel at ease. Maybe, just maybe, the impossible wasn't entirely off the table.

After they hung up, Amelia scrolled back through her call log, past Ronnie's name, until she found the one she wanted to see.

**Call Duration: 67 minutes, 18 seconds.**

**Nate Carter.**

She tapped the screen once more to make the name disappear.

But she didn't forget the sound of his voice.

Not that night.

Not ever.

* * *

THE DAYS THAT followed unfolded with a smooth rhythm Amelia hadn't expected.

Sometimes, Nate called in the morning with coffee in hand, pacing the canyon trails behind his apartment, his voice leisurely and unhurried against the backdrop of wind and birdsong. Other times, it was evening, his voice low and slow as he stepped onto his balcony to catch the sunset over Los Angeles. No matter the hour, Nate always seemed to find her—to check in, to ask how her day had gone, to listen.

She didn't know how it had become so natural so quickly. There had been no grand declarations or long-winded promises—just time. Intentional time. For Amelia, that was a kind of romance she hadn't realized she missed.

They talked about everything — and sometimes nothing at all. Conversations stretched long into the night, across mornings and lazy afternoons, until it became second nature to have his voice in her ear.

His favorite kind of food? "Anything I can make without Googling 'how to.'" He admitted this over a laugh, confessing he owned exactly one cookbook and only trusted the pages for pancakes and pasta — both of which, apparently, tasted better after noon.

Amelia laughed, shaking her head. "That's tragic. I'm writing a note to myself right now: never let you make the breakfast reservation."

Another night, they traded childhood stories — hers about summers in Colorado Springs with her grandparents, learning to ride a bike, naming every houseplant on their porch as if they were family pets.

"You *named* your plants?" Nate teased, amused.

"Of course. Gerald, Margot, Dot... You don't?"

"Amelia, I refuse to stay in hotel rooms with the number seven in them. You think I'm judging *you*?"

She'd laughed, her chest aching in that good, necessary way.

One afternoon, he confessed his disproportionate hatred of mushrooms. "It's not rational. I don't care. They're smug little fungi, and I don't trust them."

"You have *very* strong feelings about this."

"Yeah, well, I've made it thirty years without letting one pass my lips. I'm committed."

They shared stupid things, silly things. Things that mattered only because they were theirs.

She told him how she couldn't bring herself to watch scary movies alone, how she always ate the broken chips first so they wouldn't feel like an afterthought.

"That's... oddly kindhearted."

"I have a soft spot for the underdog. Even in snacks."

"You're going to ruin me."

And when he mentioned, almost in passing, the small scar on his hand from a childhood dare gone wrong — a skateboard, a shopping cart, and what he called "the dumbest friends alive" — she'd laughed and asked, "Still friends with them?"

"God, no," he'd said, smiling even though she couldn't see it. "I got smarter."

Across those calls, across days that blurred into weeks, Amelia realized it wasn't *what* they talked about. It was *how* they spoke. How easy it felt. How natural it had become to share even the small, ridiculous parts of themselves.

She told him that while she spent most of her time at her own grandparents' house, the best memories were always made at Ronnie's. Her grandparents— older and uninterested in raising another child—provided a roof, but little else. Her parents were rarely around. So Amelia found comfort in the noisy, bustling kitchen at Ronnie's, where people laughed, argued, and always made room for one more at the table. She'd never really been a TV kid—never even had one.

"It's funny," she said one night, "I used to feel left out when everyone talked about their favorite shows. I just... didn't have one."

Nate's voice warmed on the line, "I'll fix that."

"Oh, you're taking on the whole backlog?" she teased.

"I am now," he said. "We'll start with the essentials: baseball movies, a few childhood classics, maybe a little guilty pleasure reality TV. Don't worry, I will make a plan."

Amelia grinned, curling up on the couch. "I trust your judgment... but not your reality TV taste."

"Ouch, you wound me, Mils."

"You'll survive."

It was easy. And it was steady.

Some nights, she fell asleep with his voice still in her head — laughing, teasing, talking about nothing at all. On other days, he'd text her pictures of the view from his apartment or some ridiculous meme she didn't quite understand, but she saved it anyway because it came from him. She liked how it grew between them: unhurried, certain, with the ease of something meant to last. Like a good habit worth keeping.

But still... curiosity lingered.

One quiet afternoon, while sipping iced coffee in her favorite oversized sweater and ignoring a spreadsheet she was supposed to be updating, she finally did it. She Googled him.

It started simple: "Nate Carter." Her fingers hesitated over the keys as if she were confessing something.

The search results exploded. Film credits, red carpet photos, dating rumors, etc. There were even several articles on Nate's suspected workout regimen—an entire internet of speculation, headlines, and clickbait.

She scrolled through all of it with a strange sort of detachment, her brain catching on the glossy images of a man who felt both familiar and far away. It was odd, seeing him through everyone else's eyes when she'd already begun seeing him through her own.

She skimmed more than she read. A few things made her smile—he'd once donated a large sum of his first big check to a children's hospice in Santa Barbara. He'd proudly brought his mom to an award ceremony last year. There was even an interview clip where he admitted to crying during *The Notebook.*

Then there were other stories. The women. The speculation. The anonymous quotes. Paparazzi photos taken from too far away, published without context. Some felt silly. Others were a little harder to ignore.

She shut her laptop after thirty minutes, feeling a strange sensation. Not disappointed exactly. Just... reminded.

*He lives in a different world.*

But she'd always known that. Even so, here they were—still talking, still laughing, still discovering the pieces that made each other whole.

But as she looked back at her blinking email inbox, a different weight settled in—the growing buzz around the gala. There were follow-ups to send and potential donors to thank.

The foundation landed in two local press articles, and her phone buzzed with fresh inquiries. She knew the reason—and she was grateful.

*Nate.*

The attention was beneficial and necessary—but she also knew how quickly it could slip away. The whole thing was precarious, as if one wrong step would make the momentum vanish. It was the moment she'd worked for—the moment to grow the foundations' reach.

But now she had to keep it going. She had to make sure the gala wasn't a one-time splash. She had to protect what she'd built.

That evening, Nate called her from the passenger seat of a car. She could hear the city moving around him—horns, voices, the hum of traffic.

"You sound busy," she teased.

"I'm trying not to get carsick," he replied. "We're crawling down Sunset, and my driver's listening to smooth jazz like it's a hostage situation."

She laughed. He doesn't like smooth jazz, noted.

"How was your day?" he asked.

She told him about a meeting with a potential donor who inquired about contributing substantially. About the chicken sandwich, she regretted ordering from a local sandwich shop for lunch. She shared she loves working from home most days, as it allows her to get more work done, plus she gets to wear comfortable clothes.

He listened to every word like it mattered.

Then, without meaning to, she asked, "Do you ever Google yourself?"

Nate let out a quiet laugh. "No. God, no."

"I did," she confessed, biting the inside of her cheek.

"I figured you would eventually."

"I didn't go too deep," she said, curling her toes into the rug below her. "But... It's a lot. You're a big deal."

"I'm not," he said. "That's just noise. PR. Most of it's not even accurate."

"I know," she replied, and she did.

"Did you see anything that scared you off?"

She thought for a moment. "No. But I saw things I'd like to ask you about one day."

There was a pause.

"Then ask me," he said gently. "Anytime."

She nodded, even though he couldn't see her. "Okay."

Nate, possibly realizing she wasn't prepared to ask those questions, shifted the topic.

"Okay, I have a serious question for you," Nate said. "If you could only eat one kind of ice cream for the rest of your life, what would it be?"

Amelia grinned. "Are we talking classic flavors or anything goes?"

"Dealer's choice."

"Then it's a tie. Coffee toffee, and mango sorbet."

Nate laughed. "Mango sorbet? That's such a health-conscious answer."

"Excuse me, it's refreshing and delicious. What about you?"

"Rocky Road. No hesitation."

"Wow," she said, mock-serious. "I don't know if I can trust someone who eats marshmallows on purpose."

"Low blow, Mils."

There was a pause, then she added, "Okay, now your turn — most embarrassing childhood favorite movie?"

Without missing a beat, he said, "*The Mighty Ducks.*"

"No shame in that."

"Oh, I had the jersey—the hat. I went by Charlie for a solid year. It was... a phase."

She laughed, clutching the phone a little tighter. "I love that."

"I even carried around a hockey stick my mom found at a rummage sale," he added, deadpan. "Didn't play hockey. Didn't even own skates. And there wasn't a rink within a hundred miles."

That made her giggle — a warm, easy sound. "That's some serious commitment."

"Oh, definitely. I carried it everywhere, as if I were training for the Olympics. I'm still waiting for someone to recognize my dedication."

She laughed again, the sound soft but genuine. "Consider me impressed."

"Okay, but follow-up question," she said quickly. "What's your guilty pleasure TV show?"

There was silence. Then, begrudgingly, "The Great British Bake Off."

Amelia beamed, delighted. "You're kidding."

"I am not. It's calming. Also, the bread rounds are serious business."

"Oh, I can't wait to roast you for this."

"I can live with that."

"Actually," Amelia added, "I love that. Something sweet and cozy. That's very Captain Orion of you."

His laugh was low and unguarded. "You make me soft and cozy. That's the problem."

The line between them wasn't merely a call anymore. It was something steadier now. Something real, piece by piece, in the hours they kept choosing each other.

Then his voice shifted—warmer now. "I miss you."

It caught her off guard, the way those words landed and settled in her chest.

"You saw me eight days ago," she teased, trying to soften her reaction.

"I know. That's the problem," he said. "It wasn't enough."

She didn't respond right away, her heart fluttering against her ribs.

"I want to see you again," he added, voice deeper now. "If you want to see me again, too, of course."

Amelia exhaled slowly. "I'd like that."

"Yeah?" he said, almost sounding surprised.

"Yeah."

"I have been talking to my manager, Mike—and Cassidy too—trying to carve out some time," he said. "Maybe a long weekend in Denver?"

"That would be exciting, Nate," she said, nearly squealing.

"I was thinking the same thing."

They spent the rest of the call imagining what they might do if he came to visit. Try new foods. Watch old movies. Take walks in her neighborhood. Laugh a lot.

Amelia pictured it—him standing in her kitchen, walking down her street, sitting with her on those well-worn porch seats.

It came easily. Too easily.

And just as quickly, she tried to pull herself back.

*Don't get ahead of yourself. Don't build stories that haven't happened yet.*

But the images stayed. Persistent. Clear.

Nate in her world. Nate in her life. Nate... staying.

And when they finally hung up, Amelia looked down at her phone and smiled. She hadn't meant to fall so fast.

But maybe—just maybe—she wasn't falling.

Maybe she was being caught.

# 10

## close enough

THE MORNING OF Nate's arrival stretched and dragged in the way only waiting can. Amelia's house was already spotless—she'd wiped the counters twice, restacked the magazines on her coffee table, and made an extra grocery run even though her kitchen was fully stocked.

Even her car hadn't escaped her restless energy. She'd gotten up early, taken a trash bag outside, and methodically cleared every granola bar wrapper and stray coffee cup from the floorboards and console. She vacuumed the mats, too, because somehow it felt important—like she couldn't offer Nate a seat in her world if there were crumbs underfoot.

Still, she felt anxious, circling her living room, hoping it might soothe her.

By the time the black town car turned into her driveway, the mid-May sun had already warmed the sidewalks, but the breeze still carried a faint trace of Colorado's lingering spring chill. The trees lining her neighborhood had leafed out, delicate green against the bright sky. It was a spring morning that hinted at summer but hadn't fully let go of winter.

The car came to a slow stop in front of her house. The engine idled briefly, then the passenger door opened.

Her pulse thudded a little harder. She rubbed her palms against her pants, willing the nerves to stop.

She stepped outside, pretending her hands weren't shaking.

When Nate stepped out of the car, he looked impossibly casual in a grey Henley shirt, jeans, and sunglasses pushed onto his head. He moved like someone who didn't quite belong on a magazine cover but had ended up there, anyway. His dark hair fell slightly mussed from the flight, but he greeted her with an immediate smile.

When he saw her standing in the driveway, he stopped for a second, as if his brain needed to catch up to his eyes.

"You're real," he said, grinning.

Amelia let out a short breath and walked toward him. "You made it."

"I told you I would," he replied, and without hesitation, he leaned in for a brief, warm hug.

"I was thinking I imagined you," he murmured against her hair.

"You imagined a woman in yoga pants and a messy bun?"

"All the time."

When they pulled back, she noticed his shoulders drop a fraction, something he'd been carrying before finally letting go.

The front driver's door opened next, and a tall, solidly built man stepped out, with warm brown skin, striking green eyes, and a steady presence.

"This is Luke Walker," Nate said, gesturing toward him. "He's my head of security. He'll be around."

Amelia smiled and extended her hand. "It's nice to meet you."

Luke offered a polite handshake back. "Pleasure to meet you, Ms. Lane. I'll be around, but you won't even notice me. I've got a room at the Terry House B&B down the road, and I'll stay close."

Nate grimaced slightly. "Mike insisted. I rarely love the extra security, but... It's important."

Amelia smiled gently, instantly sensing the discomfort in Nate's tone. She took note to ask him about that later.

"I appreciate you making sure he's safe," she told Luke, meaning it.

Luke nodded once and gave her a slight wink. "Only doing my job. I'll put the luggage at the front door and check in later."

With that, Luke gave them space, heading to the trunk of the car.

Nate turned back to Amelia, eyes lighter now. "Hi."

"Hi," she echoed, her nerves loosening a little.

He stepped a little closer, not quite touching but close enough that she felt it — that warmth, that gravity he carried without trying. His eyes traced over her face, reacquainting himself with something he'd missed.

"You smell the same," he said quietly, almost to himself. "God, I missed that."

Her breath caught, but she didn't answer. Not with words.

Because he smelled the same too, that mix of something clean and warm, faint cologne tangled with whatever soap he used and a little of the city still clinging to his shirt. She hadn't realized until right now how much she loved that about him. How much she'd missed it, too.

Nate glanced around, then a softer smile tugged at his mouth. "So this is Longmont."

"This is Longmont," she confirmed, gesturing to the house behind her. "And this is home."

"It's so nice here," he whispered as he took in the trees, homes, and the warm presence of Amelia.

"It's a pretty great place to be, that's for sure," Amelia replied, with a bit of pride in her voice. "Shall we go inside?"

As they neared the house and spotted Luke setting his bags by the entrance, Nate spoke more quietly. "Mike was adamant about having security. I'm not too happy about it, but... it's for safety. I don't want you to stress over it."

"It's fine," she replied sincerely. "If anything, it gives me a bit of a fancy feeling."

Nate managed a slight grin in response.

* * *

AMELIA'S HOUSE WAS a small three-bedroom 1940s bungalow, lovingly worn but well cared for. The white clapboard exterior and welcoming front porch were perfectly Longmont—modest, sunlit, and warm.

Inside, original hardwood floors stretched from the front door through an open living space that Amelia had filled with a blend of soft neutrals, local art, and woven blankets folded over the back of her couch.

Photos lined the hallway—shots of her and Ronnie in their teens and twenties, along with more than a few snapshots of Grace. Nate lingered, letting his hand trail along the edge of a small frame.

The dining room opened into a bright galley kitchen, where Amelia had already set out fresh flowers in a mason jar.

Amelia led him through the entryway and straight into the living room.

"So, this is my home," she said, suddenly aware of how modest it must seem compared to his world.

"This place feels like you," Nate said, setting his bag near the couch.

"I hope that's a good thing," she replied.

"It's wonderful," he remarked without hesitation. "Lovely. Peaceful. Warm and inviting." He slowly spun around, absorbing the sight of the wooden floors, the eclectic throw pillows, and the subtle fragrance of vanilla and flowers.

Amelia exhaled softly, unsure why that hit so deep.

"I love it here," Nate continued, his eyes landing on the small potted plant struggling for life in the corner.

"You have been here five minutes," she laughed.

"And I already know I like it."

"I'm glad."

A breeze drifted in through the cracked kitchen window, pulling the soft clinking of wind chimes into the space, along with the clean, earthy scent of freshly cut grass.

Something about the stillness in the space—Nate here, in her home—made her want to share the best parts of it with him.

"My favorite part of the house is the back deck," she said, motioning toward the sliding glass doors off the living room.

They stepped outside together. Amelia tucked her hands into the sleeves of her sweater.

The deck spanned the rear of the house, adorned with string lights and sheltered by a maple tree that extended its branches protectively above. Flower boxes overflowed with newly blossomed white and pink tulips. Along the fence, lilac bushes stood tall and lush, their initial blooms unfurling in gentle hues of lavender and violet.  The breeze carried their sweet, unmistakable aroma across the deck, infusing the air with a subtle promise of the coming summer.  The sun warmed the planks beneath their feet, transforming the deck from a mere backyard feature into a living memory—a space where people had gathered, leaned, and shed tears.  It was not just beautiful, but a place that had been lived in and cherished.

"I spend a lot of time out here," Amelia said, wrapping her arms around herself. "I guess... it reminds me of a different house I used to have. The one I lived in with Grace and—well, Grant."

Nate's head tilted slightly, listening.

"When we lost Grace, the marriage couldn't survive it." She traced a finger along the deck railing, her nail catching on a splinter. "Grant wanted to sell the house—said we needed a clean slate. I fought for it, but in the end..." She swallowed, her gaze drifting toward the maple tree. "I found this place two blocks from our old home. Close enough that I can still walk past her bedroom window some mornings."

Nate's expression softened, the lines around his eyes deepening with understanding.

"Some days I take the long way to work," she whispered, "just to drive by."

She looked at the worn wood under her feet. "It's not exactly the same, but it's pretty close." The silence lingered between them. "She would have loved this deck," Amelia murmured, almost as if speaking to herself.

"Thank you for sharing that with me," Nate said finally, his voice soft.

They lingered on the deck a little longer before heading inside.

* * *

BACK IN THE LIVING room, Nate's gaze lingered on the photos tucked along the mantle and the small pink blanket draped carefully over the arm of the couch.

"She's everywhere, isn't she?" he said gently.

Amelia smiled, sadness soft but present. "Yeah, I like it that way."

It had taken her a long time to let those things stay. At first, she thought they would break her. Now they helped her breathe.

"How about I show you around before we eat something?" she said, blinking rapidly. "You've got to be hungry after that flight."

"Starving," Nate admitted with a warm smile. "Lead the way."

The stairs creaked slightly under their weight as they climbed to the second floor. Amelia gestured down the narrow hallway, where afternoon light spilled through an open door.

"Guest room," she said, pausing at the threshold where he could see a simple iron bed dressed with a patchwork quilt in faded blues and creams. "Nothing fancy, but the mattress is decent."

Next came a small room she'd converted into a workspace—just enough room for a desk beneath the window where golden hour light streamed across stacks of manila folders.

"My sanctuary when I'm not at the hospital," she said, straightening a framed certificate on the wall. "Though sometimes the fundraising paperwork follows me home, anyway."

When they arrived at her bedroom, she paused for a moment. Her fingers lightly touched the doorframe, staying there briefly as she considered whether to enter. Not that the room hid any secrets — it was simply hers. No man had ever set foot in this space.

Nate observed her hesitation. "You don't have to show me everything."

"It's fine," she murmured, mostly to reassure herself, as she slowly opened the door.

The room was inviting and filled with sunlight even in the late afternoon, featuring soft blush-colored walls that added warmth without being overwhelming. The bed was adorned with a pale pink quilt over white linens, giving the space a gentle, well-worn comfort. Against the far wall stood a lovely antique armoire, its intricately carved doors slightly open, hinting at floral fabrics within.

In the corner, a wooden quilt rack displayed a few folded throws, all delightfully worn—soft cottons, hand-stitched squares, with colors gently faded over the years. Beneath it, a wicker basket held more blankets in muted shades.

Graceful lamps with glass bases provided a soft, golden glow on each side of the bed. Her nightstands, different yet charming, were stacked with beloved books, a ceramic dish for jewelry, and on the far one, a framed photo of Grace—smiling, with sunlight dancing through her hair.

In the corner, near the window that overlooked the small backyard, a worn chair sat with a folded throw draped over the arm, inviting in its simplicity.

Through a slightly open door, the ensuite bathroom was in view–featuring white tiles, a vintage vanity, and a skylight that captured the waning light above the shower. It wasn't anything extravagant, but it belonged to her.

She watched as Nate's eyes moved slowly over the space, taking in every detail without rushing. Something about his presence here didn't feel invasive — it felt oddly safe.

*Unexpectedly right.*

"It's not much," she said, suddenly aware of how intimate this felt. "But it's comfortable."

Nate stepped inside, his hands tucked into his pockets, turning once in a slow, quiet circle.

"It's beautiful. Like you," he said. Nothing added, nothing hidden—the truth, plain and clear.

Her pulse fluttered, quick and unsteady. She didn't know what she had expected him to say, but not that.

She swallowed, tucking a loose strand of hair behind her ear. "Thank you."

"Well, that's the tour," she said, nudging her shoulder toward the hallway as she led him out of the room.

The weight in her chest eased as they stepped into the hallway.

Nate followed easily as they went back downstairs, his steps matching hers.

* * *

AMELIA SERVED A simple meal—comfort food that required little fanfare but filled the kitchen with warmth: golden-skinned roasted chicken, potatoes that yielded easily beneath the fork, and green beans from the farmer's market that still held the brightness of morning harvest.

Nate made himself at home in her small kitchen, leaning against the counter as he stole warm slices of bread, teasing her relentlessly about her "serious vegetable roasting techniques."

The nerves Amelia had carried all morning dissolved. The kitchen filled with easy laughter and soft conversation—the kind that made her remember what comfort could feel like.

He inquired about her day, her work, and the books she was currently reading.

Nate shared how uneventful his flight to Denver was, and how surprised he was that the airport was built so far away from the city.

They made light of Luke's disappearing act, speculating that he might be close by, either engrossed in a crossword puzzle or discreetly observing the neighborhood from his car as though he were starring in a low-budget spy film.

After dinner, they sank into the living room couch, feet tucked beneath them, trading stories about childhood. Nate described his hometown in Idaho—small, flat, a place where everyone knew everyone. His parents had grown up there too, making the Carters a familiar name around town.

As he spoke, Amelia noticed something shift in him — the way his posture eased, how his shoulders dropped in a way they didn't when he talked about work or press or Hollywood. This was the part of his life he carried with quiet pride. It softened him. Grounded him.

Amelia listened carefully, letting his words build a picture in her mind — a younger, less guarded Nathan Carter. A house with grease under fingernails and casserole nights, and people who said 'I love you' as if it were ordinary.

"I envy that," she admitted after a pause. "The warmth. The family dinners. The steady support."

He didn't push, didn't ask. Just waited, easy and patient.

"My childhood was... different," she said finally. "Not terrible. Just... fractured." She traced the rim of her glass with one finger. "Pieces that never quite fit together the way they should have. I never really felt like I had a solid or safe place."

Nate leaned back slightly, studying her—not with pity, but with something quieter.

"You built your own safe place," he said, his voice warm with quiet admiration. The corner of his mouth lifted in that way that made his eyes crinkle. "That takes a kind of strength most people don't understand."

She looked at him, her voice soft but steady. "I just didn't want to feel invisible anymore."

Nate held her gaze for a beat, then tilted his head in playful solemnity. "Well, mission accomplished. I can confirm you're very visible. Possibly even glowing."

That earned the smallest smile from her, one she didn't hide.

The evening drifted easily toward nightfall. Their dessert plates still sat on the coffee table, their drinks half-full, the air between them soft and steady in the way things were when neither person wanted the night to end.

When Nate stretched out on the couch, Amelia threw a pillow at him.

He caught it effortlessly and grinned. "Hey, what was that for?"

"You looked too comfortable," she shrugged, though the playful warmth in her cheeks made her wonder how much she actually meant it.

He tossed the pillow back, and their laughter layered itself into the house as if it had always belonged there.

She realized she hadn't felt this at home with someone in years.

Their conversation drifted in that comfortable, weightless way until, at some point, Amelia stifled a yawn behind her hand.

Nate caught it, a small, knowing smile pulling at his mouth. "That's my cue to be a gentleman and get you to bed."

She laughed softly, shaking her head. "I don't know why I'm tired. You're the one who traveled."

"Yeah, but I've got jet lag adrenaline working for me. You look like you're about to drift off mid-sentence." His knee bumped gently against hers. "Let me be the responsible one tonight, Mils. Just this once."

There was no argument to be made. Not really.

She led him upstairs to the guest bedroom, sliding open the dresser's top drawer to reveal neatly folded towels. Her foot deliberately pressed against a spot on the floor near the bathroom. "Fair warning—this board has a voice of its own after dark," she said, the corner of her mouth lifting. "One step at midnight and you'll have the whole house as your audience."

"I appreciate the hospitality," he said from the threshold.

Her smile deepened, eyes warming. "Having you here feels right."

Something unspoken passed between them as he stood there—tonight's quiet comfort carrying whispers of something lasting.

When he bent to kiss her cheek, his fingers brushed against her arm, leaving a trail of warmth that spread through her like watercolor on paper.

"Goodnight, Amelia."

"Goodnight, Nate."

As she padded toward her room, her heartbeat echoed in every part of her body. Life thrummed in her veins — and for the first time in a long time, it seemed to pulse through the walls of her home, too.

The stillness had lifted. It no longer felt like it belonged to her alone. Tonight, the space felt different—like it had quietly opened its arms to something new. Maybe even to him.

# 11

## the pull of you

AMELIA LAY AWAKE, flat on her back, the ceiling fan turning slowly above her. She stared into the darkness of her bedroom, her heartbeat loud in her ears, a restless thrum in her chest.

Nate was down the hall.

Nate. In her house. In her guest room.

The same man who had made her laugh over dinner, who had leaned close while they shared dessert, who had looked at her as if she might vanish if he blinked.

She had gone through all the proper motions—goodnight, door closed, lights off—but there was nothing restful about this moment.

She rolled onto her side.

Then her back.

Then her side again.

She pulled the blanket higher over her bare legs, knowing it wouldn't help. Every nerve in her body hummed with electrical energy. Her thoughts kept circling the same question, looping endlessly like a skipping record: *What was he wearing right now?*

Grey sweatpants? Boxers? Nothing?

God, she hoped it wasn't nothing.

The idea made her breath catch and her legs shift restlessly beneath the sheets.

*Get it together.*

She'd wanted to kiss him all night. She wanted to lean across the couch and taste the curve of his smile. But she hadn't trusted herself. Not with him here. Not in her house. Not when she knew how quickly she would fall if she let herself even slightly lean.

A soft groan escaped her lips. She buried her face in the pillow, but it also didn't help.

She glanced at the clock: **11:32 p.m.**

An hour since she'd said goodnight. An hour of watching the minutes crawl.

Giving up, Amelia slipped out of bed, tied her silk robe tight around her matching pajama set—a soft pink tank with delicate straps and shorts that clung enough to feel dangerous—and tiptoed toward the door.

*Just water*, she told herself—*just the kitchen.*

The moment her bare feet pressed into the old wood floors, they betrayed her with a loud groan that seemed to echo off the walls. She froze, wide-eyed. Another step. Another groan. It was as if the house had conspired against her, each board beneath her feet broadcasting her every move. She tried the safe path she'd memorized, but somehow, tonight, her feet found every disloyal plank. Each creak and moan screeched into the quiet, as if announcing: She's awake! She's awake!

By the time she crossed the hallway, she was practically stomping on a symphony of betrayal. She might as well have rolled out a red carpet and invited him downstairs.

*Subtle, Amelia. Very subtle.*

When she finally reached the kitchen, she exhaled in relief, grateful for the silence. Her house was small enough to make discretion nearly impossible, but maybe Nate hadn't heard her. Perhaps she could get her drink and return to her room unnoticed.

Then she saw it—his backpack still sitting near the couch, the faint indentation of the throw pillow where he'd leaned on his elbow during dessert. The space still held his smell and warmth. And it made her pulse quicken all over again.

*Maybe this was a mistake*, she thought, turning back toward the stairs.

"Going back up so soon?"

She spun around. Nate was there, leaning casually in the doorway, wearing black joggers and no shirt. *Holy hell.*

His bed-tousled hair and sleep-rough voice—low, raspy, far too casual—clashed with the way his eyes devoured her.

Her mouth opened, but no words formed. She blinked, caught, cornered, and completely unable to think straight.

He crossed his arms, his forearm muscles flexing as his gaze slid slowly, deliberately, from her bare legs to the knot of her robe. His mouth ticked into a lazy, lopsided smile.

"Do you usually wander your house looking like that, or am I just lucky tonight?"

She blinked, her throat suddenly dry. "I-uh-I was just... water."

"Sure, Mils," he murmured, the nickname sliding from his tongue like honey. "Just water."

When he called her Mils, her legs wobbled, and her body jolted with surprise.

"You heard me walking around?" she asked, mortified.

"Hard not to. You hit every creaky board in the place. Sounded like you were bringing in a marching band."

His grin deepened. "Not that I minded. I love your house talking back."

Her pulse skipped. "It rarely sounds that loud. I—I know the safe path."

"Safe path, huh?" His eyes sparkled, amused. "Pretty sure you abandoned it tonight."

She bit her lip, unsure whether to laugh or apologize. "It's not usually like this. It's as if the house knew I was up to something."

He took a slow step closer. "Were you?"

Her breath caught. *Yes*, she thought. "I was just thirsty."

"Me too." He wasn't talking about water. She knew that. She knew exactly what he meant. But his voice held no pressure, only quiet honesty. And something about that dismissed her more than any line could.

His eyes dropped to the curve of her bare thighs, his smile growing hungrier.

"I don't think I'll ever be the same after tonight."

She covered her face with her hand, her laugh muffled and breathless.

"I couldn't sleep either," he said, sauntering into the kitchen as if this was the most natural thing in the world. His eyes flicked briefly to her robe again, his jaw tightening almost imperceptibly. "I've been lying there for an hour thinking about how close you are."

The silence thickened, heavy but not uncomfortable.

He quickly looked through the cabinets until he found the right one. He reached for two small glasses, his movements calm but confident. He filled them both with water, handed one to her, then leaned back against the counter, mirroring her stance.

"Not sure I'll ever sleep again, honestly," he said, taking a sip.

"Why's that?"

"Because now I know you look like this when you can't sleep." His eyes dragged over her again, slow and hungry, making her skin burn in the best way.

"Silk pajamas, messy hair, and legs like *that*?" He dragged a hand down his face. "You're dangerous, you know that?"

Her hand trembled slightly around the glass. The weight of his gaze on her silk robe, the way it tied tightly around her waist, the way her shorts peeked out from underneath—it all made her feel suddenly wildly *aware* of her skin.

"It's just a tank and shorts," she whispered, suddenly unsure of her footing.

There was heat everywhere—in her cheeks, in her chest, in the growing ache low in her stomach. It was a pulse, an insistent rhythm she could no longer ignore.

"It's you." His voice darkened, low and intimate now. "It's always you."

The words landed in her chest with a force she hadn't expected. Part of her wanted to deflect, to lighten the moment, but another part—a part she barely trusted yet—wanted to believe him. To let herself believe him.

And maybe she already did.

Maybe that's why her walls were crumbling so easily.

She'd been so sure that opening herself to someone again would feel like falling from a cliff. But this didn't feel like falling. This felt like stepping into sunlight after too many cold winters.

He set his glass on the counter, took hers from her trembling hands, and placed it next to his. Then he slipped his hands around her waist and pulled her into him.

His lips were on hers before she could think. Slow at first, savoring, then deeper, his hands firm on her hips, fingers curling into the silk fabric.

She melted instantly, her body pressing into his as the kiss unraveled her defenses. Her hands threaded into his hair, pulling him closer, needing him closer.

The soft *thud* of her body meeting the counter barely registered before his hands gripped her hips, lifting her effortlessly and setting her down on the edge. The cold bite of the granite met the curve of her thighs, a sharp contrast to the hard, unmistakable warmth of him pressing in close.

Her breath caught—half gasp, half want—as his body settled fully between her legs, his heat grounding her, claiming the space.

The warmth of him there — the solid press of his need — made her gasp into his mouth.

He groaned in response, low and rough, the sound vibrating against her lips.

"You're making me crazy, Mils," he whispered, his breath ragged as his hands slid under the hem of her tank, his fingers brushing the bare skin at her waist. His lips grazed the curve of her jaw, his breath hot and uneven.

Her legs tightened around him, pulling him closer, and her hands flattened instinctively against his bare chest. Warm. Solid. Hard muscle beneath hot skin, his heartbeat drumming against her palm—a quiet dare wrapped in silence. He felt too good — too real — heat radiating from him in waves that curled low in her belly.

"You're not exactly helping me stay sane either," she breathed, her fingers curling against his skin, knowing she couldn't quite convince herself to let go.

"Good," he growled softly, his mouth dragging along her neck, tasting the skin there with slow, deliberate pressure. "I don't want either of us thinking straight right now."

His fingers reached for the small of her back, drawing her even closer, and she moved with him, slowly rocking against him in a rhythm that made the air between them practically sizzle.

His groan deepened, desperate and low. "Tell me what you want, Mils."

Her mind scrambled for words as his hands roamed, his mouth pressing reverent kisses along her collarbone.

"Is this real?" she whispered, breath catching against his skin. Her voice was barely audible, but heavy with wonder, disbelief, and longing.

Nate stilled for a second, then lifted his head, his eyes dark and full of everything he hadn't said yet.

"Yeah," he murmured, voice low and sure. "It's real. You're real. God, you're real."

Then he kissed her harder, deeper, as if answering her in the only language he trusted. His body pressed into hers, leaving no room for doubt.

And just like that, she had her answer.

This man was real.

His voice was a plea and a promise. "Anything you want. We can stop. We can go slow. I'm not in a hurry. I just want you. Only you."

Her heartbeat thundered, but her mind didn't run like it used to. It didn't talk her out of this. Instead, it filled with memories of him—his laugh, his tenderness when he told her about his brother, the way he'd let her set the pace all along. She felt weightless, floating somewhere between instinct and surrender.

He wasn't asking to break her open. He was asking to be allowed in.

And maybe that was the difference. Perhaps that's why this didn't feel reckless.

Despite that, the slightest flicker of hesitation pressed at her ribs—the ache of memory, the echo of Grant's name, and the life they had.

Could she permit herself to move forward?

Her chest tightened—and then Nate's hands skimmed her waist again, his mouth pressing another patient kiss to her neck, his breath steady and real and here.

She didn't have to forget the past to say yes to the present.

She could carry both.

Maybe she was already doing it.

She laced her fingers behind his neck, her voice breathless and sure. "I want you to take me upstairs."

His eyes locked onto hers, fierce and tender. "Yeah?"

"Yeah."

A slow grin spread across his face—it promised trouble and safety all at once. "Good. Because I'm not sure I could've let you go."

Without another word, he pressed another long kiss to her mouth, then gathered her robe from the floor and draped it over his arm.

He laced his fingers through hers, guiding her through the quiet house and up the stairs.

When they reached her bedroom door, she turned to face him, her heart pounding as she let him inside her space once more—but this time, for more than a tour of her bedroom.

The door clicked shut behind them, and she realized—she wasn't scared anymore.

Not of this.

Not of him.

Not of what came next.

# 12

# hello, beautiful

AMELIA AWOKE just as the first light seeped into her room, the steady purr of the ceiling fan soothing her semi-conscious mind. She lay still for a moment, eyes closed and covers undisturbed, fearing that any movement might dispel the enchantment of the previous night.

But it hadn't.

She turned her head slowly on the pillow and found him curled on his side beside her, his bare chest rising and falling in slow, steady breaths.

He was here. In her bed. In her life. And the quiet thud inside her chest told her she didn't want this to be a one-weekend thing.

Last night. *God, last night.*

Her skin still tingled where his hands had mapped their way over her body—gentle and attentive when she needed it, confidently firm when he knew she could take more. He was deliberate. Measured. He hadn't only touched her; he'd studied her, as if learning her was the point, maybe memorizing her was something *he* needed.

And she'd let him. She'd wanted him. Every piece of him. The weight of his body against hers, the strength in his arms when he took control, the soft things he'd whispered into her neck when their breaths turned ragged.

"Tell me this is where you want me... because I won't stop otherwise."

Her response was a mere whisper, her lips struggling to form the words against his skin.

"Here... yes... please."

His mouth traced the line of her jaw, his words reaching places his hands never could.

"Say it. Tell me I'm where you want me."

"You... are.  Oh, you are..." Her fingers gripped him tightly, her body responding before her lips could articulate. "Don't stop... please."

Her chest warmed, her stomach fluttering as the memories replayed in a slow, golden loop.

Careful not to wake him, she let her eyes wander. His hair was still sleep-tousled, his jaw peppered with the faintest shadow of stubble.  His face, smooth in sleep, was breathtakingly handsome but unguarded now—boyish, even.

Her eyes followed the delicate scar above his eyebrow. In the soft morning light, it appeared more pronounced, almost intimate.  She had touched it instinctively in the Crawford penthouse, but now—with the quiet of the morning enveloping them—she allowed herself to examine it. To appreciate it. To trace it once more.

Her fingers lightly caressed the mark, as softly as a whisper. But before she could linger, her attention shifted.

His arm. His left arm.

He slept on his right side, giving her a full view of the tattoo on his left arm—two baseball bats crossed like an X, with one of them crowned by a delicate halo.

She'd seen glimpses of it before, but now, she saw all of it. Every detail. Every line.

It was quiet, meaningful. Not flashy. And somehow, that made it feel even more sacred.

She extended her hand and gently traced it, her thumb caressing the halo, committing the lines to memory as if it were a secret known only to her.

Nate stirred at her touch, his brow creasing faintly before relaxing again. Then his lips curved into a slow, sleepy smile.

"Hello, beautiful," he rasped, his voice thick with sleep.

A grin tugged at her mouth. "Morning."

He reached for her immediately, curling his arm around her waist and tugging her closer until their legs tangled, her head resting easily on his chest. His skin was warm, his heartbeat steady beneath her cheek.

He let out a low, sleepy groan when she settled against him — unintentional, wrecked, and so full of wanting it made her feel flushed all over again. That sound. That sound alone could undo her, could get her to agree to anything, at any time. He didn't even know what it did to her.

Neither of them rushed to speak. There was no hurry in the morning light—no need to race toward the day.

"Sleep okay?" she murmured.

"Best I've had in... years," he said, pressing a soft kiss into her hair.

They stayed like that for a while—snuggling, trading lazy kisses, fingers tracing idle patterns across bare skin, whispering soft nothings as if they had all the time in the world.

"I was thinking," Nate eventually said, his voice still low, "what if we walk down Main Street this morning? Grab some coffee, maybe breakfast? Can you show me around your town?"

"That sounds perfect," Amelia breathed, her chest tightening in that too-happy way that made her feel light and terrified at once.

"And then tonight," he added, "we stay in. Order takeout, start that movie marathon I promised you."

"Sounds perfect."

He grinned, eyes fluttering shut again briefly. "I like your neighborhood. I like your house."

"You like my creaky floors."

"Yes, I do," he chuckled, "and I like the way you walk on them."

Amelia sighed contentedly, her palm resting flat on his chest. She didn't know how she'd landed here, but part of her believed maybe she didn't have to question it.

Nate eventually shifted, stretching his arms overhead. "I should check in with Luke," he said through a yawn. "He was pretty chill about me disappearing last night, but I should at least tell him I survived."

"You can text him," Amelia murmured, her fingers splaying lazily across his ribs.

"Yeah," he exhaled. "And I should probably... call Cassidy. She's called a few times."

Amelia's heart stuttered a little. She lifted her head to meet his gaze. "Oh?"

"Yeah," he said, sitting up slightly and running a hand through his hair. "I don't know what she wants yet. I'll call her later."

Not now. Later.

Sitting up and swinging his legs over, he paused at the edge of the bed, looking down at his left arm. "I got this tattoo a year after Noah died," he said softly. "Had to be sixteen before they'd let me. It did not thrill my parents, but they understood."

Amelia sat up, her gaze fixed on the ink. "It's beautiful."

"It's him," Nate said simply. "Everything he was."

And something about that knowing—mutual and unspoken—anchored the space between them. It didn't need words. It carried its own weight.

His phone buzzed from the nightstand, but he didn't reach for it. Instead, he sauntered toward the en suite bathroom, utterly comfortable in his own skin, the light catching the lines of his back and the curve of his shoulders.

*Holy hell, this man!*

Amelia watched him go, her chest tightening differently now.

She wasn't sure what Cassidy wanted. The uncertainty hovered—faint as an echo, but impossible to ignore.

Did Cassidy approve of where Nate was? Was she calling to tell him he was wrong? To ask him to get back to LA?

Amelia didn't know. And she wasn't sure Nate knew either.

But he'd left his phone on the nightstand.

And right now, that was enough.

She sank back against the pillows, the memory of his smile still warm on her skin.

She breathed in deeply, savoring the lingering scent of him—of them—wrapped in the sheets, soft and clean, touched with her shampoo and something warmer, something distinctly his.

She closed her eyes and let herself stay there, breathing them in.

* * *

LATER THAT MORNING, Amelia's front door announced their departure with a gentle creak. The late spring air greeted them—crisp and bright with possibility. She'd pulled on her favorite jeans and that moss-green sweater that always made her eyes look more aquamarine than blue, her hair twisted into a loose braid that draped across her collarbone. Beside her, Nate moved with the casual confidence of a man who'd never questioned his right to take up space, his Boise State hoodie hanging just loose enough at the shoulders to suggest it had been loved for years.

As they reached the end of her driveway, Luke emerged from his car parked on the street.

"Morning, boss," Luke greeted with a casual salute as he walked over.

Nate chuckled, "Don't call me that."

Luke shrugged with a smile. "Old habits die hard. Thanks for texting me your plans for today. I'll trail behind, and you won't even notice I'm there."

Nate nodded appreciatively, and Amelia felt reassured by Luke's quiet efficiency. His presence didn't seem intrusive; instead, it was a comforting layer of security she hadn't realized she needed.

They strolled through her quiet neighborhood, framed with tall, mature trees and tidy lawns. Amelia's steps slowed slightly as she pointed out a few local landmarks.

"I moved to Longmont after I graduated from college and married Grant," she explained, her voice soft. "We both found jobs in Boulder, and Longmont felt... perfect. Quieter. Close to the mountains. Close to our jobs."

Nate glanced over, absorbing her words carefully. "Is the old house nearby?"

"Just a couple of blocks from here," she said, almost whispering and nodding to her left.

She'd thought about showing him the house. It had been on her mind ever since she knew he was coming to visit. There was a part of her that wanted to walk him past it, to let him see where Grace used to play, where the porch light used to flicker, where a whole different version of her had once existed.

However, now that he was present, and they were walking side by side through the neighborhood, their hands gently grazing each other, she doubted whether it was the appropriate moment. Certain feelings remained too fresh, too burdensome to share with someone else. Especially someone she was still eager to impress rather than burden.

Maybe next time, she thought. Maybe when she was sure she could take him there without unraveling.

She didn't say any of this out loud. And maybe that said enough.

Nate's hand brushed against hers briefly as they walked, a silent acknowledgment of the weight in her words.

Their fingers laced together naturally as they crossed the final block toward Main Street, the pace of the town gently picking up around them.

The scent of sizzling bacon and buttery omelets drifted from open café doors, mixing with the crisp air and the sweetness of blooming spring blossoms. Engines idled in a polite procession as early morning business deposits backed up the small, one-lane bank drive-thru. Shop owners unlocked their front doors with familiar waves to each other, flipping signs from *"Closed" to "Open"* as they prepared for the steady rhythm of the day. The town was stretching awake, the hum of it soft but sure—the day officially starting.

When they entered the intimate, bustling corner coffee shop, it did not surprise Amelia when heads immediately turned. One barista—wide-eyed and openly staring—fumbled a tray of coffee mugs, the crash making half the café spin around.

"It's Nate Carter," someone whispered near the pastry case.

Nate's easy, familiar smile curved as if he'd heard it a thousand times before—because he had. He didn't posture or play it cool; he simply offered a small wave, his presence somehow making the moment feel casual instead of chaotic.

Amelia watched as a young couple hesitated by the register, whispering to each other before one finally worked up the courage to ask for a picture. Nate said yes, of course he did. His kindness wasn't for show—he crouched down a little so their kid could fit in the frame, made them laugh, and complimented someone's band t-shirt on the way back to her side.

After autographing two barista aprons and taking a few more selfies, Amelia noticed how effortlessly he navigated this aspect of his life, entirely at ease.

Not strange at all.

Meanwhile, she wasn't entirely sure how to exist in the spotlight. Should she stand closer? Should she smile at the cameras? Ignore them?

This wasn't LA. This was her town. And part of her wanted to protect it.

But the other part—the bigger part—felt proud of him.

After they finally decided on their drinks—he went for a black coffee, while she chose a vanilla oat latte—Amelia also recommended her preferred breakfast dish: a honey-drizzled croissant sandwich filled with eggs, avocado, and sharp cheddar.

"Try it," she said, eyes brightening. "It's the best thing here, hands down."

"Then I'll have the same," Nate said without hesitation, flashing her a quick wink.

The cashier, who had been doing a respectable job of keeping her composure until now, let out an audible gasp, her hand fluttering to her chest as she processed the full force of Nate Carter's attention.

Amelia fought the urge to laugh as Nate casually stepped aside to wait, utterly unfazed.

When their order was ready, they tucked themselves into a corner table by the window where the late morning sun warmed the worn wooden table between them. The scent of fresh espresso, toasted bread, and something sweet filled the air.

"This place is charming," Nate said, wrapping his hands around his cup.

"It's one of my favorites," Amelia said. "It's where I go when I need to think."

He sipped his coffee, watching her over the rim. "Thank you for bringing me here."

They both took their first bite of the croissant sandwich at the same time.

Nate's eyebrows shot up immediately in appreciative surprise.

"Oh, wow," he said, covering his mouth slightly. "You weren't kidding. This is incredible."

"Told you," she said with a slight, triumphant grin, taking another bite.

He nudged her foot under the table. "Good taste, Mils. I'm impressed."

He paused for a moment, then glanced up at her with a soft, curious grin. "By the way... I've been calling you that—Mils. I don't know where it came from. It just sort of... stuck. Do you mind it?"

Her heart did a little flip. "Mind it? I love it."

She blurted it out too fast, too eagerly, and immediately felt her face warm.

"I mean—I like it. I like you calling me that. No one's ever... It's just you."

Nate's grin deepened, clearly enjoying her flustered honesty.

"Good," he said, tapping her foot again under the table. "I was hoping you'd say that. Feels like a habit already... one I'm not sure I could break. Kind of like you."

Her stomach churned intensely, and she was genuinely relieved to have eaten a few bites of food. Without those, she wasn't sure she could keep herself from feeling nauseous.

*How was one supposed to respond to such a thing?*

"Thank you, Nate," she managed, his name feeling strange and warm on her tongue all at once.

She let out a breath of laughter, soft and a little shaky, and nudged her cup with her fingertips.

"Tell me about home," she said, grateful for the change of subject.

"Idaho," he started, leaning back in his chair. "Little farm town, about an hour outside Boise. Parma. Home of the Parma Panthers."

She shook her head, but her smile was encouraging.

"We grew up a little outside of town. My mom works as a school secretary at Parma Middle School, and my dad was a wildland firefighter. He still works our small piece of farmland now."

His gaze softened as he spoke. "Noah and I were pretty much inseparable. We spent summers building tree forts, riding ATVs, and roping each other into ridiculous dares. We both played baseball for the Panthers. Noah was incredible. Captain of the team. He could hit anything. Me? Not so much. But I wanted to do whatever he was doing."

Amelia's chest ached gently, but she loved hearing him speak about his brother.

"After Noah… after the accident, I couldn't leave. I graduated from high school and attended Boise State, where I studied communications. I figured it would keep me close to my parents. They needed me. I needed them, too." He smiled faintly.

"I still go back as much as I can. I love being out in the country. It's home. I sometimes bring my mom to LA. She loves it—getting her hair done, dressing up a little. She's adorable in the city."

He shrugged lightly, his thumb tracing a circle along his coffee cup. "I never thought about acting back then. It just sort of… found me."

Amelia rested her chin on her hand, completely absorbed. "Thank you for telling me."

He reached across the table and brushed his thumb over her knuckles. "You make it easy."

Nate's thumb paused in her hand. "So, no siblings at all?"

"No," Amelia said, shaking her head. "I'm an only child. Honestly, it's probably for the best. My parents were barely there for me—I can't imagine what it would have been like if there were more of us."

Nate's brows furrowed slightly. "That must've been lonely."

"It was," she admitted. "But I had Ronnie. And her family. They filled in a lot of the gaps."

He squeezed her hand gently. "I'm glad you had her."

The soft buzz of his phone interrupted their moment. Cassidy's name flashed across the screen. Nate glanced at it briefly, his jaw tightening, and then, without hesitation, he silenced the call and flipped the phone face down.

"She can wait," he said, his attention fully returning to Amelia.

Amelia nodded, but something unspoken lingered in her chest.

They lingered over the last sips of coffee, reluctant to end their conversation, then stepped out into the fresh morning air of Main Street. The sun had climbed higher now, casting their shadows behind them as they strolled past storefronts. Nate admired a vibrant mural of the Rocky Mountains spanning an entire brick wall, while Amelia pointed out her favorite details. When they reached the corner with the faded "Bookworm's Haven" sign hanging above a blue door, she tugged his hand gently toward the entrance.

They drifted between tall wooden shelves that smelled of vanilla and dust, their fingers brushing over worn spines and dog-eared pages that whispered stories of previous readers. Sunlight filtered through the shop's cloudy front window, catching dust motes that danced around them like silent companions. Nate found her in the fiction aisle, as she cradled an old copy of *Wild* by Cheryl Strayed. Its cover faded. His lips curved into a soft smile when their eyes met.

"This is the one," she said, tucking it under her arm, her fingertips lingering on the book's textured edge.

At the counter, where a brass bell sat next to a stack of bookmarks painted with local wildflowers, Nate plucked the book from her hands before she could reach for the worn leather wallet peeking from her purse.

"I'm getting this," he said, pulling out his card. "I want every excuse for you to think about me later."

Her stomach turned over once more. The words settled deep within her chest, but she merely smiled, suppressing the impulse to say she didn't require a book for that. She already would, for many other reasons.

The elderly woman at the checkout counter offered them a cheerful yet absent-minded smile, oblivious to Nate's identity as she processed the book purchase. She turned to Amelia and said, "You've found a good one, dear," affectionately patting Nate's hand as though he were her grandson. "Keep him close." Nate grinned, obviously enjoying the remark. "That's the idea, ma'am," he replied.

Amelia couldn't help but laugh, warmth blooming under her skin as they stepped back out of the storefront, the little bell above the door jingling behind them.

They continued their leisurely wandering, hand in hand, down the heart of Main Street, taking their time to pause and peer into the windows of sleepy shops just beginning to awaken for the day. The gentle morning light cast a soft glow on a quaint print shop, its window adorned with a small collection of hand-painted signs. The signs were charmingly crafted, displaying welcome plaques and nursery prints in soothing pastels that seemed to whisper promises of warmth and comfort. Next door, the quintessential small-town insurance office stood with a quiet dignity, the name painted in precise, blue lettering on the glass above an aging wooden door that creaked with character. Nate's eyes lit up with delight when he spotted a cheerful kitchen supply store. Its display was a feast for the eyes, with rows of gleaming copper pots and vivid enamel bakeware stacked artistically, each piece reflecting the warm sun and inviting passersby to imagine the culinary delights they could create.

"This town's got good taste," he teased, nudging her shoulder gently as they walked.

They reached the next storefront, its display window crowded with mismatched treasures and dusty curiosities. Nate slowed, staring through the glass like he'd found something he hadn't realized he'd been missing.

"An antique store?" His grin widened. "Okay, I haven't been in one of these in years. Can we go in?"

Amelia smiled, already reaching for the door. "I was hoping you'd say that."

Inside, the air carried a subtle blend of the earthy aroma of aged wood and the crisp, clean scent of lemon polish, mingling together in a nostalgic embrace. A soft bell chimed gently above them as they entered, announcing their arrival into the serene labyrinth of densely packed shelves. Nate's excitement visibly spiked, his eyes lighting up at the sight of a carefully arranged display of vintage farm tools near the entrance. The tools, each with their own story etched in rust and wear, stood like sentinels of history, drawing him in with their rustic charm.

"Okay, this is wild," he said, holding up an old branding iron. "My uncle used one just like this. I haven't seen one in years."

Amelia studied the way his eyes crinkled at the corners when he examined the branding iron, the tension in his shoulders melting away with each new discovery. This version of Nate—fingers tracing worn metal, voice dropping to a reverent whisper when he recognized something from his childhood—existed in a world where red carpets and paparazzi flashes seemed like distant fiction.

They wandered slowly through the rest of the collection, pausing to share quiet stories and half-forgotten memories. Somewhere between an old feed bucket and a pair of cracked leather gloves, their hands found each other—intertwining without thought or ceremony. Neither of them pulled away. It didn't feel new. It felt right.

For a moment, the only sound was the soft creak of the wooden floor beneath their steps, as if the space itself respected their silence.

Then Nate's phone buzzed again. Amelia glimpsed the screen.

Cassidy. Again.

This time, Nate didn't even look. He just kept walking, his hand firm in hers.

And somehow, she didn't question it. His hand in hers, the silence between them—it all felt right.

# 13

# more time

THE AFTERNOON SUN dipped lower as Amelia and Nate strolled back to her house, their easy rhythm unbroken even by the occasional glance or phone camera they passed along their route. They walked close without thinking, shoulders brushing, hips bumping now and then, as if their bodies had quietly agreed not to stray too far apart. Amelia felt lighter than she had in years while the quiet pulse of the day was settling gently around them.

After the antique store, they'd wandered with no real destination, letting the slow pulse of the town guide them. They'd stopped for lunch at a small corner bistro with crooked tables on the sidewalk and paper menus clipped to weathered boards. Nate had ordered a burger the size of his face; Amelia had stuck to soup and salad, still laughing at the way he'd teased her for "eating like a bird."

They'd bought a hand-thrown ceramic mug from a local artist—Nate had insisted it looked like something she'd reach for every morning—and a worn baseball cap from a cluttered thrift shop because he wanted the faded patch on the front. They peeked into a tiny record store, browsed old vinyl with no need to talk, and left with a scratched-up Springsteen album Nate promised would sound better with a bit of static, anyway.

At one point, they found themselves seated on a weathered wooden bench, steaming coffees nestled in hand, as they indulged in the quiet pleasure of people-watching. In front of them, across the bustling street, a lively group of teenagers was engaged in a humorous and chaotic endeavor—attempting to stack themselves atop a single, wobbling longboard. Their laughter echoed through the air as the board teetered precariously, ultimately yielding to gravity's pull.

The hours slipped by seamlessly, one into the next, like pages of a well-read book, as the day unfolded with a languid grace. It stretched long and leisurely, the way truly good days do when the clock's ticking fades into the background, leaving only the savor of the moment.

They reached her front porch with dragging feet, as if some invisible thread had snagged on the sidewalk behind them, trying to hold this perfect day in place just a little longer.

Nate halted at the stairs, surveying his surroundings as if committing the scene to memory. "Thank you for showing me around your town, Mils." His voice was soft, but there was a weight behind it. "I mean it. I get why you love it here. Feels like... I don't know. I could actually see myself living in a place like this."

Amelia's breath caught. The words felt casual coming from him, almost offhand—but they landed in her chest with a thud. She wasn't sure what surprised her more—that he'd said it, or how much she wanted to believe it.

She smiled, unable to hide the way her heart leapt. "Careful, Carter. You keep saying things like that, I might start believing you."

His grin widened as he opened the front door. "Good. You should."

Inside, Nate shrugged out of his hoodie and placed their small collection of treasures on the coffee table. He flopped down onto the cushions with a sigh, stretching his long frame across half the couch and patting the space next to him.

"So, movie marathon? I believe that was the plan."

Amelia grinned, curling up on the couch beside him. "It was," she nudged his knee playfully. "I'm guessing you brought a list?"

"Even better," he said, leaning forward and unzipping the backpack he had left last night. "I brought actual DVDs."

She laughed. "Wait—DVDs? I think I still have a player, but I've never used it. I'm not even sure I hooked it up."

Nate's expression turned comically horrified. "This is a tragedy. We're fixing this."

He pulled out a small stack of DVDs, splaying them across the coffee table proudly. Among them was *Captain Orion*. He tapped the case with a smirk. "You still haven't seen this one."

Amelia wrinkled her nose in playful protest. "I know. I was supposed to watch it before the gala. Cassidy was very insistent."

"Well, now you get the deluxe edition—with director's commentary from the lead actor." He leaned in conspiratorially. "Trust me, the commentary's worth it. I'll tell you which stunts I actually did and which ones nearly broke me."

She laughed, resting her chin on her hand. "Sold."

"Okay, but first—we need food."

"Takeout?" she suggested.

"Yes, definitely takeout."

They both stood, drifting into the kitchen where Amelia pulled open the small side drawer near the fridge. Nate peered over her, placing his chin on her shoulder, eyebrows lifting at the sheer volume of crumpled paper menus stuffed inside.

"Is this... all takeout?" he asked, sounding both amused and impressed.

"Sadly, yes. It's an unhealthy amount. I'm aware."

She rifled through the stack, her eyes lighting up the second she found the menu she'd been hoping for. "Ah—here we go. There's this amazing Thai place a couple of blocks over. Their drunken noodles are to die for. And they make the best crispy spring rolls."

"I'm in," Nate said immediately, flashing her that easy, boyish grin. "Same order as you. I trust your taste after that croissant sandwich."

With that, he sauntered back to the couch, sprawling across the cushions, already claiming the space for the night.

Amelia watched him settle in, her heart tugging at how effortlessly he seemed to belong here. Shaking it off, she picked up her phone and dialed in their order.

Nate leaned back on the couch, his arms lifting in a long, lazy stretch, his voice drifting out with a soft, satisfied sigh. "I could get used to this."

The words landed squarely in her chest.

Thank God she was still rattling off her address to the kid on the other end of the phone—because if she hadn't been mid-sentence, she might have choked on air.

*He could get used to this?*

*Me too*, she thought, clutching the phone a little tighter.

* * *

AS THEY WAITED for the food to arrive, they busied themselves with tidying up the living room. They folded the blanket, fluffed the pillows, and collected the small pile of trinkets Nate had left on the coffee table. After a while, they both confessed a desire to change into more comfortable clothes.

Upstairs, Nate followed her to the bedroom, his overnight bag slung over his shoulder. He set it down by the dresser and casually brought his bathroom items into her en suite like it was the most natural thing in the world—his toothbrush, toothpaste, two travel-sized colognes, and a small black bag of whatever else men seemed to need.

They got cleaned up together in the tiny bathroom, bumping elbows at the sink, trading kisses and teasing glances in the mirror, stealing space and laughing through it. It was nothing dramatic—brushing teeth and washing faces—but Amelia couldn't remember the last time something so mundane had felt this close to belonging.

She slipped into a soft, cotton three-piece pajama set—dusty blue, with a camisole, cardigan, and drawstring pants. Cute. Comfortable. Absolutely not sexy.

Nate, meanwhile, emerged in a fitted white t-shirt and another damning pair of sweatpants—the kind that should be illegal on a man with his frame. Amelia nearly tripped over her own feet.

She would not survive him in sweatpants. There was simply no way.

The air in the bedroom seemed to flee all at once, and for a second, Amelia forgot how to breathe. Her pulse thudded in places it had no business thudding, and every rational thought scattered like dust in the light. If they didn't get out of this room, she was going to surprise even herself and make them both forget dinner entirely.

"We should, um—we should go downstairs," she said quickly, brushing past him with a nervous laugh that didn't quite reach steady. "Food's probably almost here."

Nate followed behind, grinning as if he knew exactly what kind of fire he was playing with.

"So now you know how I feel," he called lightly, "every time you wear one of these dangerously cute pajama sets and pretend it's not a weapon."

She shot him a look over her shoulder, half scandalized, half amused—and fully affected.

They were halfway down the stairs when the doorbell rang—rescuing Amelia from having to respond and sparing a whole bag of Thai food from spending the night on her porch.

By the time she returned from the door, Nate had already pulled out the coffee table for a bit more room and turned on the lamp beside the couch. She set the takeout bag down between them, and together they unpacked the steaming containers, chopsticks, napkins, and two chilled glasses of water. It enveloped the room in the warm and inviting aroma of spicy basil and peanut sauce.

"Okay," Nate said, grabbing the *Captain Orion* DVD. "Moment of truth. Let's see if this DVD player still works."

They fumbled briefly with the dusty remote and ancient cables, but miraculously, the machine powered on. The movie's loading screen filled the small TV, and Nate pumped his fist in victory.

"Still got it."

Amelia laughed, settling back onto the couch and picking up a spring roll. "You know, it's weird. I've never watched one of your movies."

"Why's that?" he asked, unwrapping his chopsticks.

"Honestly? I didn't want to get caught up in the version of you that everyone else thinks they know. I wanted to meet you first." She hesitated, then added quietly, "And… I don't watch movies much. They remind me of dates. And I don't date."

Nate looked over at her, his expression softening in that way it always did when she said something that mattered.

"Well," he said, nudging her knee with his, "I'm changing that. This is most certainly a date."

She raised an eyebrow. "Is it now?"

"Oh yeah," he said, grinning. "Takeout, pajamas, me in these devastating sweatpants… classic date night."

She laughed, shaking her head, and he leaned a little closer.

"Also," he added under his breath, "it's probably because I haven't been in that many movies."

"Modest," she said with a smirk.

"Honest," he countered.

She nudged his leg again. "Guess I'll make an exception—for you."

They were about to hit play when Amelia's phone buzzed on the coffee table.

*Cassidy.*

Amelia raised an eyebrow and picked it up. "Hello, this is the Nate Carter hotline. How can I direct your call?"

There was a beat of silence on the other end before Cassidy's sharp voice cut through. "Hi, Amelia."

Amelia sat up straighter. "Hi, Cassidy—"

"Is Nate with you?" Cassidy's tone softened suddenly, laced with concern. "Is he okay? I've been trying to reach him all day."

Amelia's playful edge evaporated. "He's here. He's fine. He's… happy."

"Glad to hear it," Cassidy continued. "Would you mind putting him on the phone?"

She handed the phone to Nate without saying a word.

Nate sighed, pressing the phone to his ear. "Cassidy, I know. I'm sorry. I should've called you back."

His jaw was tight at first, his tone apologetic but clipped. But then, as he listened, his expression shifted—first to curiosity, then to something brighter.

"You're kidding. Seriously?"

There was a pause as Cassidy rattled off whatever news had her so persistent.

A slow grin spread across Nate's face. "No, no, this is great. Yeah—I'd love to. Thanks for pushing it. I owe you."

He glanced at Amelia, his excitement impossible to hide.

"Okay, I'll call you tomorrow. And sorry again. I won't go dark on you next time."

He ended the call and turned to Amelia, grin still in place. "So, apparently, they rescheduled my LA press tour. Which means..." He leaned in, voice warm. "I get to stay longer. If you'll have me."

Amelia's heart soared, her breath catching in the best way. "Yeah. I'd like that."

"I was hoping you'd say that."

She folded her legs beneath her and gave him a quiet smile, content to stay like this a little longer. "I have to go to work one day next week, though. Staff meeting. But maybe you can come with me—if you want to see what I *actually* do."

"Would love to," he said without hesitation.

Without thinking, Amelia leaned forward and kissed him—soft and sure. Nate's hand found her knee, his thumb brushing slow, lazy circles as he deepened the kiss enough to make her toes curl.

When she finally pulled back, still smiling against his mouth, she whispered, "I'm happy you're staying."

His forehead rested against hers. "Me too."

They stayed there for another moment, content in the quiet, until a soft knock sounded at the front door.

They looked at each other with curiosity before Nate got up to answer the door.

It was Luke.

"Hey, boss," Luke greeted casually. "Got the update from Cassidy. It sounds like we're sticking around a little longer."

"That's the plan," Nate said, stepping aside to let him in.

Luke's gaze flicked briefly to Amelia. "Is that cool with you?"

Amelia smiled warmly. "Yeah. Very cool."

Luke relaxed slightly. "I'll plan and extend my stay at the B&B."

Amelia hesitated, then offered, "You should come to dinner tomorrow. I'll cook. It'll be nice."

Luke looked surprised, but pleased. "I'd like that."

Nate chimed in, "Invite Ronnie, too. She needs to meet Luke."

Amelia grinned. "You're right. She'll love that."

Luke excused himself, promising to check in the next day. As soon as the door closed, Nate plopped back onto the couch with a satisfied sigh.

"Now. Finally." He picked up the remote. "You ready to see me in all my spandex glory?"

"Born ready," Amelia teased, nudging his shoulder.

They dug into their takeout, the food a perfect balance of heat and sweetness, and pressed play.

The movie flickered to life, but Amelia watched Nate as much as she watched the screen. The way he relaxed beside her, the easy curve of his smile, the small notes he whispered about each scene.

Somewhere between the spring rolls and the final act of *Captain Orion*, she realized she hadn't just let him in.

She wanted him to stay.

And maybe—possibly maybe—he would.

They didn't rush to turn the movie off when it ended. They let the credits roll, the soft hum of the soundtrack filling the quiet. When Nate's arm slid around her, it wasn't a question. She leaned in, their heads resting together as the screen faded to black.

The weight of the day, the buzz of connection—it all settled into something steady. Something that didn't need to be defined.

When they finally stood to clean up the coffee table, neither of them said a word about where they would sleep. There was no hesitation, no awkward shuffle toward separate rooms. They moved together, step by step, as if they'd already made a choice.

Nate paused in the hallway, a slow, quiet smile tugging at his lips. "I'm gonna follow you, Mils."

And she loved the way it carried the quiet weight of home in every syllable.

# 14

# dinner for four

AMELIA WOKE SLOWLY, drawn up from sleep by the warmth of sunlight and the even warmer gaze resting on her.

Nate was already awake, propped on one elbow beside her, gently brushing his fingers through her hair.

She blinked at him, groggy but smiling.

"You watching me?" she murmured.

"Couldn't help it," he said softly, tucking a strand behind her ear. "You look peaceful. Which is new."

She stretched beneath the sheet, her tank top twisted around her waist, legs tangled with his. "I feel peaceful," she said honestly, surprised by it.

They stayed like that for a while—quiet and lazy, fingers tracing invisible patterns across bare skin, exchanging sleepy kisses and softer thoughts. A morning that made everything else blur around the edges.

Eventually, Nate slipped out of bed and disappeared into the bathroom. Amelia heard water coming to life, the hiss and pulse of the shower.

A moment later, his voice floated through the room. "Come here for a second."

She padded over, still in her tank top and soft cotton shorts, and stopped outside the open walk-in shower.

She lingered in the doorway, face half-hidden in the billowing steam. "You called?"

Nate leaned his head out from behind the glass door, water streaming down the planes of his chest. "I just need a kiss."

She approached the shower's edge, steam curling around her ankles. "One kiss?"

"Mm-hmm."

The moment her lips met his, he hooked his arm around her waist and pulled her straight into the shower.

She gasped as the warm water hit her back. "Nate!"

He grinned, eyes dark and playful. "Oops."

Her clothes clung to her instantly, soaked through and molding to every curve. Nate stepped back ever so slightly, his gaze trailing over her slowly, appreciatively. The tension changed—deepened—settled into something molten and deliberate.

He reached for the straps of her tank top, easing them down her shoulders with devastating slowness. His fingers ghosted over her skin as he peeled the wet fabric away, exposing her inch by inch.

She shivered—not from cold, but from anticipation.

He lowered his mouth to her chest, praising each peak with soft kisses that turned sharper, more possessive. His mouth was worshipful, his teeth teasing. She arched into him without thinking, her hands tangled in his hair, silently begging him not to stop.

Then he knelt slightly, working her shorts and underwear down at the same slow, agonizing pace. His fingers skimmed her thighs, his mouth following until she was bare and breathless.

By the time he stood again, her body was humming with need.

Without a word, Nate took both her hands in his and gently pressed her back against the tiled wall. The sharp chill contrasted with the heat of the water and the fire in her blood.

He leaned into her, his hips finding the space between her thighs, his arousal undeniable.

She moaned softly at the contact—his closeness, the heavy press of him, already threatened to undo her.

He kissed her neck, her collarbone, her lips—slow and deep — until it drenched them in more than just water.

His mouth brushed her ear. "You know I haven't been able to stop thinking about that shower bench since the first time I saw it."

She exhaled a shaky laugh. "You're ridiculous."

But she didn't say no.

When he released her hands, she followed his lead. He stepped back to the bench, sitting with his legs spread, his eyes never leaving hers.

"Come here," he said, his voice low, rough with restraint.

She crossed the space between them, slow and trembling.

He reached for her hips and gently turned her, guiding her to face away. With the slightest pressure, he coaxed her to lower—carefully, deliberately—until she was seated on him, taking him in one aching inch at a time.

Her breath caught.

"That's it," he whispered, his hands strong at her waist. "Take all of me."

She did.

The stretch, the weight, the fullness—it overwhelmed her. He held her there for a moment, signalling that he couldn't bear to move yet.

Then, slowly, she moved. Hips rocking. Breath catching. Matching his rhythm. Faster. Then slower. Then just right.

They found their pace together—bodies in sync, hearts barely keeping up.

She came undone with his name on her lips.

And he wasn't far behind.

Afterward, they stayed tangled together under the water, hands exploring gently now, mouths brushing in quiet awe.

"I've never felt anything like that," she whispered, her forehead resting against his.

Nate's smile was soft, his voice quieter still. "Me neither." He brushed his nose lightly against hers. "You make everything feel... different. Better."

Her breath caught, a smile tugging at her lips. "I don't even know what to say to that."

"You don't have to," he murmured. "You're here. That's enough."

They stayed like that for a while; the water cascading over them, neither one ready to move.

Eventually, Nate gave a soft laugh, his lips grazing her temple. "Pretty sure we're about three minutes away from the water heater giving up on us."

Amelia smiled, reluctant but amused. "Guess we should quit while we're ahead."

They finished the shower slowly, washing each other with lazy, lingering touches and quiet laughter, like neither of them wanted to let the moment slip away.

By the time they made it downstairs, Amelia's skin still tingled.

The morning slipped by as she and Nate lingered on her back porch, their bare feet propped on the weathered railing, steaming mugs in their hands. The soft breeze carried the distant hum of a neighbor's lawn mower, the comforting clink of a wind chime from the house next door.

They swapped stories about work—Nate confessing how surreal it sometimes felt to act in front of green screens, making dramatic faces at tennis balls suspended from wires. Amelia laughed, imagining him in his Captain Orion suit, pretending to battle invisible monsters.

"It's not as glamorous as people think," he said, shaking his head. "Half the time, I'm running in circles in front of a fan while someone shouts stage directions at me."

Amelia's laughter bubbled up, light and easy. "Hey, I spend half my day chasing down spreadsheets and emails no one ever reads. I think we're both pretending in some ways."

They drifted from stories about work to the music that had shaped them— Nate's love for classic Springsteen, Amelia's weakness for acoustic covers— and the books they each kept reaching for on quiet days.

Nate admitted he had once dreamed of being a baseball coach. "Long before Hollywood found me," he added, brushing his thumb over the handle of his coffee mug. "I thought I'd spend my life in a dugout, not on a soundstage."

She loved that. She loved learning the pieces of him that had nothing to do with the spotlight.

*The versions of him that belonged to no one else.*

After lunch, they sprawled on the living room floor, sorting through an old box of Amelia's photos and mementos—yellowed ticket stubs, faded

Polaroids, and clippings from old school projects.

Nate picked up a snapshot of Amelia as a teenager, braces flashing, standing in front of a rickety carnival ride.

"Is this… is this a mullet?" he asked, raising an eyebrow.

Amelia gasped, grabbing for the photo, but Nate held it out of reach. "It wasn't a mullet. It was the early 2000s! That was cool back then."

Nate laughed, eyes sparkling. "I don't know, Mils. That looks dangerously close to business in the front, party in the back."

She shoved his arm playfully. "You're lucky I like you."

"Yes, I am," he replied instantly.

His smile softened, his gaze dropping to the next photo—a younger Amelia holding Grace in her arms. Her throat tightened, but she let him study it.

"She's got your eyes," he said quietly.

Amelia swallowed around the lump rising in her throat. "Yeah. She had a stubborn streak to match."

Nate's hand found hers on the floor, his fingers curling around hers without hesitation, easy and instinctive.

Eventually, Nate leaned back against the couch, stretching with a satisfied sigh—right as his stomach gave a loud, unmistakable growl.

Amelia raised an eyebrow, grinning. "Was that a threat or a cry for help?"

"I think it was a formal request for dinner," he said, rubbing his stomach. "Also, a sign that I deserve something substantial after facing the attic box of teenage Amelia."

She laughed, shaking her head. "All right, then. But you're coming to the store with me. And you're carrying the bags."

"Deal."

Amelia glanced at the clock and stood, brushing invisible crumbs from her yoga pants. "We should probably get moving, then. If we wait too long, I'll lose motivation and we'll be stuck with cereal."

They both slipped on sneakers and headed for the door together, the sunlight stretching long and warm across the sidewalk as they planned their grocery list aloud.

They drove to the grocery store, teasing each other about shopping cart driving skills and arguing over the best pasta shape. Amelia insisted on cooking her signature lemon butter chicken with roasted garlic potatoes and a simple arugula salad tossed in homemade vinaigrette.

Nate happily volunteered to be on salad duty, although he warned his lettuce-chopping skills left much to be desired.

At the wine aisle, Amelia reached for a familiar bottle—a crisp white she trusted.

Nate eyed the shelf, then glanced at her with a teasing smile. "Is this your 'I've had a long week' wine or your 'we're eating pasta and pretending we have our lives together' wine?"

She laughed. "Both. It's versatile."

He scanned the labels and grabbed a second bottle—a rich red with a label that looked far too dramatic for their night in. "Let's live a little."

She shot him a mock-suspicious look. "If that one tastes like disappointment, I'm blaming you."

"Fair," he said, dropping both bottles into the cart with a grin. "But hey, at least we'll be hydrated."

At the front of the store, the cashier paused halfway through scanning their items; her gaze flicking between the screen and Nate as if she was trying to convince herself she wasn't hallucinating. She rang up a bag of baby potatoes, then stopped entirely, just... staring.

When she got to the wine, her hand hesitated over the bottle.

"Oh, here," Nate said smoothly, reaching into his wallet. "You can check my ID."

He handed her his driver's license with a casual smile, but the poor girl's hands were shaking so badly she could barely hold it steady, much less read the birthdate. She stared at the card, waiting for it to blink or disappear.

Amelia did her best not to laugh. Nate didn't even try.

They were still chuckling by the time they stepped out into the parking lot; the door sliding closed behind them.

"That poor girl," Amelia said, grinning.

"She's probably in the back room right now texting five people," Nate replied. "I feel like I should've signed a napkin or something."

Back at the house, they set to work in the kitchen, the mellow drift of music filling the space between them. Nate chopped clumsily, occasionally stealing sips of wine while Amelia marinated the chicken and prepped the potatoes.

Luke arrived first, stepping through the front door with his usual calm presence.

"Hey," he greeted. "Figured I'd swing by early. I got word that with our extended stay, they're sending another guard out to rotate patrol with me in the evenings."

"More company?" Nate asked.

Luke shrugged. "So that you know. Nothing to worry about, but the extra set of eyes won't hurt."

"Sounds good to me," Amelia said, handing Luke a glass of water. "Dinner's almost ready. Sit, relax."

Luke leaned casually against the counter, chatting easily with both of them as Nate tossed the salad greens into a bowl with entirely too much enthusiasm.

A few minutes later, there was a brisk knock at the door.

"That'll be Ronnie," Amelia smiled as she wiped her hands on a towel and crossed the room.

When she opened the door, Ronnie burst inside with her signature energy, balancing a box in one hand and a bottle of wine in the other.

"I brought dessert from La Belle Bakery in Denver," Ronnie announced. "You're welcome."

"You're the best," Amelia said, pulling her into a hug.

As Ronnie stepped further inside, her eyes flicked quickly to Luke, taking him in. "Oh—hi. I'm Ronnie." She extended her hand, warm and curious. "You must be…?"

"Luke," he said with a polite nod, shaking her hand firmly. "I'm Nate's security."

Ronnie's brow lifted slightly, a flicker of intrigue passing through her. "Security, huh? Well, you're doing a great job. He's still in one piece."

Luke gave a slight, amused shrug. "I try."

She flashed him a grin, her curiosity clearly piqued, but not in a pushy way.

"Glad you're here."

There was something in the way their eyes met—a flicker of interest, maybe something more—but the moment passed quickly as Nate came over to greet Ronnie with a warm hug.

The four of them settled into a natural rhythm, Ronnie diving into conversation like she'd known Luke forever. She had that way about her— effortlessly pulling people in.

Amelia watched the flow of it, the way Luke genuinely laughed at Ronnie's quips, the way Nate seemed to enjoy being part of this little circle that already felt familial.

Dinner was ready soon enough. They gathered around Amelia's small but cozy dining table, plates piled high with lemon butter chicken, roasted potatoes, fresh salad, and a little basket of warm bread Nate had insisted on grabbing from the store.

"This looks amazing," Ronnie said, already reaching for the potatoes.

"I hope it tastes as good as it smells," Amelia said, sliding into her seat beside Nate.

As they began eating, the conversation drifted easily—favorite foods, embarrassing moments from school, Ronnie's wild stories about college parties, and Luke's deadpan one-liners that somehow made everyone laugh harder.

Nate kept sneaking appreciative glances at Amelia, and she caught him every time.

When the conversation turned to travel stories, Luke shared some of his work experiences over the years. Nate seemed genuinely curious, leaning in as Luke talked about the logistics of traveling with high-profile clients, the importance of staying in the background, and the weirdest things he'd had to handle on the job.

"Ever had to rescue someone from an actual tabloid stakeout?" Ronnie asked, wide-eyed.

Luke smirked. "Once. In Prague."

"Oh, tell me everything," Ronnie leaned in, hanging on every word.

Amelia couldn't help but notice how comfortable they all seemed—how quickly this dinner, which she had worried about over-planning, felt so natural.

As the evening went on, Nate refilled Amelia's glass and brushed his hand lightly against hers every chance he got.

Ronnie caught the gesture, her gaze softening as she looked between them.

"I like this," she said suddenly, her voice warm. "This... feels good."

"It does," Amelia agreed, her chest full of something she wasn't quite ready to name.

Luke nodded once, a quiet but clear agreement.

When they finally cleared the plates and brought out Ronnie's bakery dessert—a perfectly flaky lemon tart—they all lingered at the table, sipping wine, sharing stories, letting the night stretch long.

Amelia memorized the sound of their laughter, the way Nate's voice dipped low when he leaned close to her, the ease in Luke's posture, the sparkle of mischief in Ronnie's eyes.

This wasn't just a good night.

It was a beginning.

* * *

AFTER DESSERT, THE group drifted out to Amelia's back porch, the night air crisp and cool. Nate ducked inside briefly, returning with a couple of throw blankets draped over his arm.

"Here," he said, handing one to Amelia and tossing the other across Ronnie's lap. "I'm not having you two freeze out here."

Ronnie laughed, wrapping the blanket around her shoulders. Luke, quietly observant, slipped off his jacket and draped it around Ronnie's back with a casual ease that surprised them all.

"Thanks," she murmured, adjusting the surrounding jacket.

They settled into their seats; the air was chilled but bearable, the porch light casting a soft glow.

Ronnie shifted, curiosity bubbling up again. "Okay, Nate—I've got to ask. How did you get discovered? Being from Idaho, you don't exactly seem the type to stumble into Hollywood."

Amelia straightened slightly. She hadn't even thought to ask. The question snapped her attention fully toward Nate.

"Yeah," Amelia added, intrigued. "I don't know how that happened. I mean, how does someone go from Idaho to a superhero?"

Nate chuckled, his breath visible in the cold. "Well, believe it or not, I didn't plan any of this. I attended Boise State University to earn a degree in communications. Figured I'd work behind the scenes forever. I got a job out of school writing news broadcasts for a local station in Boise. Spent a couple of years doing writing and video editing, mostly in the background."

"Seriously?" Ronnie asked, pulling her blanket tighter.

"Yeah. And then one day, one of the weekend special anchors retired. They wanted to create a new weekend segment to spotlight local attractions and stories across Idaho. I applied for it—not because I thought I'd get it, but because I wanted to try something new."

He smiled, the memory warming him even as the night air cooled his skin. "They gave me the job. And that's when I created *You Are Here.* It was this little travel segment. I'd go all over Idaho—small towns, festivals, hiking trails, and local food joints. It was the best gig."

Ronnie's eyes widened. "Wait. That's why your face looked so familiar when Amelia first mentioned you coming to the gala. I think I saw something about that years ago. My uncle used to watch local Idaho stations sometimes."

Nate laughed. "Yeah, I was the *You Are Here* guy. At the end of each segment, I'd always sign off the same way. 'This is Nathan Carter, and You Are Here.'"

Amelia's chest tightened in the best way—something about that phrase, the way it tied to everything they'd shared, to everything he seemed to stand for.

"That's adorable," she said softly. "Do you still have clips of it?"

Nate rubbed the back of his neck. "Somewhere. But I'm sure it's all still floating around the internet."

Ronnie was already pulling out her phone, her fingers flying across the screen. "Hang on—don't move. I'm finding it."

Within seconds, she had loaded a video. The porch filled with the sound of a much younger Nate, his voice a little higher, his smile equally smooth as he confidently introduced a segment about a cherry festival in northern Idaho.

He wore a neon green Nike polo tucked into khaki shorts, his hair a little too gelled, standing in front of a giant cherry pie. Ronnie nearly dropped the phone, laughing.

"Oh, my God. That shirt," she said, pointing. "Lane, tell me you're seeing this. This is peak youth group energy."

"Ronnie, no," Amelia immediately chided.

"It's giving major Eli Whitmer vibes."

Amelia groaned, placing her head in her hands. "Please don't bring up Eli."

Nate looked amused. "Do I want to know who Eli is?"

Amelia sighed. "High school boyfriend. Very... wholesome."

"He was president of the FCA," Ronnie added helpfully. "That's Fellowship of Christian Athletes for those not fluent in southern suburbia. He carried his Bible in a zippered case with highlighters."

Amelia buried her face in her blanket. "Stop."

"And!" Ronnie held up a finger triumphantly. "He once ate an entire peanut—shelled and all—on our junior year field trip."

Luke blinked, unable to resist the urge to join in the fun. "I'm sorry... the whole thing?"

"The whole damn thing," Ronnie laughed. "He said he'd never seen peanuts in shells before. Thought that was just how they were served. Kept crunching them like it was normal until Mr. Langston started yelling."

"I think I blocked that out," Amelia muttered.

Luke tilted his head. "Wait. How had he never seen shelled peanuts?"

"Eli was... sheltered," Amelia offered diplomatically. "Homeschooled till eighth grade. Really into youth group mixers and object lessons."

She hesitated, then sighed. "Also allergic to dairy. But he always forgot. Took me to Pizza Hut on our second date. Cheese pizza and the salad bar, naturally. I spent the end of the night cleaning up his vomit in the bathroom while he prayed over a paper towel. I don't even know why I let it go on after that."

Nate looked horrified and delighted. "And this boy dated you?"

"Briefly, " Amelia muttered. "And with much prayer."

Everyone laughed. Nate gave her an exaggerated bow. "You've clearly upgraded."

She rolled her eyes, but the blush in her cheeks gave her away.

Nate chuckled. "So, besides Eli and Grant, who else should I know about?"

Amelia shook her head, then hesitated. "Not really anyone. I mean, not seriously. A few first dates here and there. But it's mostly just been them."

"Hey, no judgment," Nate said warmly. "My first girlfriend was Misty in ninth grade. She was a Wiccan."

Luke sat up a little straighter. "A what now?"

"Misty the Wiccan," Ronnie repeated with delight. "Do tell."

"She was a Wiccan," Nate said casually. "Think, full moon rituals, crystals, the whole deal. She once told me she could summon my grandma."

"That's sweet," Amelia said, raising an eyebrow. "Was your grandma...?"

"Dead? No, she was very much alive," Nate deadpanned. "Still is actually. I just didn't have the heart to tell Misty she was summoning someone who played bridge every Tuesday."

He grinned, shaking his head at the memory. "She used to drag me to this metaphysical crystal store at the mall. They wedged it between the Orange Julius and the arcade. Every time, I'd spend over an hour elbow-deep in a box of loose quartz and tiger's eye while she lit incense in the corner and spoke to someone's dearly—or not-so-dearly—departed aunt."

He paused, his expression suddenly serious. "Also... until about three years ago, I thought the word incense was incest."

He made a point to enunciate the last word.

"Incest," he said again, in case they didn't hear him right.

The table practically seized with laughter. Ronnie had to put her wineglass down to prevent it from spilling. It doubled Luke over, wheezing, and Amelia clutched her blanket to her chest, willing it to keep her from falling apart.

Nate held up a hand, trying to finish his thought through the chaos. "No, seriously—listen."

They all made varying efforts to compose themselves—Ronnie wiping tears from her eyes, Luke fanning his face, Amelia biting her lip—but it wasn't working.

Nate nodded solemnly. "Yeah. For years, I'd ask people if they liked incest. Or worse—I'd walk into a room, take a deep breath, and say, 'Mmm, smells like incest in here.'"

He shook his head, fake regret on his face. "I couldn't figure out why everyone kept giving me side-eye. The day I learned the truth, I wanted to dig a hole and live in it."

That set them off again. Ronnie practically slid off her chair, Luke wheezed out something unintelligible, and Amelia buried her face in Nate's shoulder, giggling uncontrollably.

When he finally had his breathing back under control, Luke looked genuinely puzzled. "Wait. What's a Wiccan?"

Ronnie whipped her head toward him. "You're kidding."

He shook his head. "Is that a type of candle? Or a bike? Sounds like a yoga brand."

Nate burst out laughing. "No, man. It's like... modern witchcraft."

Luke raised his glass in the air with a smirk. "Must be some midwestern shit."

The table erupted. Nate nearly spilled his wine. Ronnie howled. Amelia leaned into Nate, giggling until her sides hurt.

"She was a witch, Luke," Ronnie clarified between giggles. "Like, moon rituals and spirit candles and the whole broomstick starter pack."

Luke nodded slowly. "Still weird."

They all leaned back in their chairs again, still chuckling, the laughter giving way to comfortable silence.

Ronnie wiped a tear from the corner of her eye, still catching her breath. "God, my cheeks hurt."

Amelia laughed, the sound bubbling up before she could stop it. Her smile stretched wide—genuine and unguarded—as something light unfurled in her chest.

Beside her, Nate looked around the table, his eyes crinkling with quiet wonder. "Can we stay in this moment forever?" he said, half-teasing, but full of truth.

The moment lingered, wrapped in shared warmth and mutual understanding.

Eventually, they all stood, the hour growing late. They made their way to the front door, gathering jackets and offering sleepy goodnight wishes.

Luke glanced at Ronnie. "Want me to walk you to your car?"

"Yeah, that'd be nice," she said, her voice a little softer than usual.

As Ronnie pulled Amelia into a hug, she whispered quickly, "Pray for me."

Amelia smiled against her shoulder, whispering back, "Pray for us both."

When they pulled apart, their shared grin said everything.

Luke opened the door with quiet ease, holding it for Ronnie as if it were second nature.

Nate and Amelia exchanged a glance but said nothing, letting the quiet speak for itself.

When the door closed behind them, Amelia leaned briefly against it, her chest full in the best way.

She turned off the porch light and stood for a moment in the quiet. Laughter still echoed faintly in her ears, but it was the quiet that stayed with her now—the kind that felt complete.

Maybe ordinary nights were the ones that stayed with you the longest.

# 15

# the matchmakers

AMELIA HAD EXPERIENCED countless mornings in her life—but none quite like this one. Nate's presence lingered on her skin like a whispered secret.

From her perch on a kitchen stool, coffee warming her palms, she watched him navigate her cabinets with sleepy determination, his smile already forming before his eyes were fully open.

Last night's intimacy still resonated through her body like the afterglow of a perfect sunset.

It hadn't just been good—it had been transformative.

She'd discovered something beyond physical pleasure.

Not the tentative exploration of new lovers, but the profound recognition of possibility.

Like stumbling upon a door she never knew existed, one that opened to everything she'd been missing.

Because no one—not even Grant—had ever done that before. No one had ever savored her slowly, with intention and dedication. The warmth of Nate's tongue between her thighs completely overwhelmed her, making her legs shake, her breath hitch, and her eyes shut tight against the intensity of the sensation. And he didn't stop. Not when she writhed. Not when she called out his name. Not when she was pleading, trembling, and on the verge of losing control, barely able to hold herself together.

Then, right when she thought she couldn't take a second more, he'd started kissing his way back up her body—slowly, almost reverently—before grabbing her hips and flipping her gently onto her stomach.

That alone had taken her breath.

No one had ever done that either.

And then he'd moved over her, his chest against her back, his hand steadying her waist as he slid inside—deeper, fuller, thicker from that angle. She'd gasped so sharply she forgot to exhale.

All she could say—*the only thing she could say*—was, "Oh my God...Please, don't stop."

And he hadn't.

Daylight poured through the windows as she sipped her coffee, watching him move barefoot across her kitchen like he'd misplaced something there years ago and had finally come home to find it.

He bent low to peer into one of the lower cabinets, then suddenly straightened with a triumphant grin.

"Bingo," he said, holding up a box of Captain Crunch as if he'd won the lottery.

She lifted her mug to hide the smile that threatened to take over her face. God help her, she was in trouble.

"You're sure you want to come with me today?" she asked, her voice still rough from sleep—though she wasn't sure if it was from the morning or from all the things she'd whispered into his neck hours earlier.

Nate turned toward her without answering right away. He set the cereal on the counter, crossed the space between them, and slid in behind her stool—wrapping his arms around her waist, his chest warm against her back.

"I'm sure," he said softly, brushing his lips against the curve of her neck. "You think I'd let you go without me after last night?"

She leaned back into him without thinking, her body already remembering the shape of his.

"Didn't figure you for the clingy type," she teased.

"Only with you."

The way his hands tightened slightly against her hips sent a shiver straight through her, her pulse kicking to life, similar to last night.

She closed her eyes briefly, letting herself lean back further into his chest. The memory of his touch, his mouth, the weight of his body above hers—it was all right there, still simmering beneath her skin.

"Besides," he added, his lips brushing the shell of her ear now, "I think I promised Janice I'd see her again."

Amelia swallowed the lump forming in her throat, trying to keep her voice even. "She'll be happy to see you."

"So will I," he whispered, dropping one last kiss on her shoulder before finally stepping back.

She turned to face him, her heart thudding hard against her ribs.

"Coffee and cereal first," she managed.

"Obviously," he grinned, already reaching for two bowls.

He poured generous servings of Captain Crunch into each, added milk, and gave both bowls a dramatic stir—clearly taking the task way too seriously. Then he handed hers over with both hands like he'd plated a five-star meal and wanted full credit.

"Your gourmet breakfast, madam," he said, straight-faced but barely holding back a smile.

She rolled her eyes and took it, trying not to grin too hard.

They grabbed their mugs and bowls and made their way out to the back porch, the morning sun warm across the wooden planks.

They had merely sat down at the table, cereal bowls in hand, when Nate's phone buzzed. He glanced at the screen and picked up immediately.

"Hey, Luke."

Amelia leaned in, catching the low rumble of Luke's voice, though she couldn't make out the words.

"Yeah, yeah. That's fine," Nate said, a slight grin tugging at his lips. "No, we'll keep it low-key. Thanks, man. I'll let her know."

When he hung up, he slid his phone back into his pocket and turned toward her, clearly amused.

"So... change of plans," he said. "Luke's taking the day off—he said he'll see us tonight instead."

Amelia blinked. "Really? That's… unlike him."

"Right?" Nate nodded. "Apparently, he's arranged for a local guy to cover for him today. Someone named Tyler. He's going to trail us while we're in Denver. Nothing serious."

She tilted her head, trying not to laugh. "Is that necessary? It's a hospital workday, not the Oscars."

"Maybe not, but word's gotten out that I flew into Denver and didn't fly back out. Luke just wants to stay ahead of things. Plus, Tyler's going to be with us the rest of the time I'm here, anyway."

Amelia took a bite of cereal, her smile curling as she looked out at the backyard. "Hmm. Isn't it funny how Ronnie just *happens* to have the day off, too?"

Nate's eyebrows lifted, catching on immediately. "Huh. Imagine that. Pure coincidence, I'm sure."

"Total," Amelia said, giggling. "We might've accidentally played matchmaker last night."

"They kept finding reasons to talk," Nate said, rising and offering his hand to help her up. "I liked it, though. It was a good night."

Amelia slipped her hand into his, savoring the easy weight of his grip. "Well then, let's enjoy our day while our friends enjoy theirs."

* * *

THEY RODE INTO Denver together, Nate in the passenger seat with his arm slung casually over the window like he'd been riding beside her for years. Amelia couldn't stop smiling at how natural it felt—the way he settled into her car, the way his laughter filled the space as they replayed stories from the night before.

"Okay, but I still can't get over Luke casually mentioning he went through a cowboy hat phase," Nate said, grinning as he looked out at the road ahead. "Like it was nothing."

"I still can't believe he wore it to prom," Amelia said, grinning. "That's not just a phase—that's a lifestyle."

"And the belt buckle," Nate added. "Did you see Ronnie's face when he said it was engraved?"

"She nearly choked on her wine," Amelia said, grinning.

Nate smirked. "Although, let's be honest—she might've been choking more on the mental image of Luke in tight cowboy pants."

Amelia burst out laughing, shaking her head. "Yeah, that probably did it."

Their laughter rolled through the car, the sound bright and easy, carried forward by the sunlight streaming through the windshield.

Eventually, they both fell quiet, catching their breath. Amelia leaned her head back against the seat, pressing her palm lightly to her stomach.

"Ow," she said with a groan and a grin. "My face and abs officially hurt."

"Worth it," Nate said, still smiling as he looked out the window.

They rode in comfortable silence for a minute or two, the kind that didn't need to be filled.

Halfway there, Nate caught her sneaking a glance at him.

"What's going on in that head of yours, Mils?"

She loved the way he said her name like that—it was his, something personal and earned.

"I guess I'm wondering how you're going to handle a day with spreadsheets and donor calls," she teased.

"Sounds riveting. I'm ready to be wildly impressed."

She shook her head, biting back a smile as she changed lanes. "You might regret this."

"Nope," he said, certainty threaded through his tone. "I don't think I could regret anything that gets me more time with you."

It wasn't a line. She knew it. And that made it more difficult to breathe normally.

When they arrived at the hospital, Nate adjusted his hat and sunglasses, clearly hoping to keep a low profile. Amelia had her doubts—it wasn't often a man like Nate Carter wandered through the children's wing without notice—but she appreciated the attempt.

They moved through the familiar halls, Amelia leading the way with confident ease. This was her space. She belonged here.

Their first stop was her office, a small but cozy space lined with sticky notes, project binders, and a few framed photos—a young Grace in pigtails, a shot of Amelia and Ronnie on a hiking trail, the Grace Wells Foundation logo in a simple silver frame. Nate paused by her desk, trailing his fingers along the edge.

"She's beautiful," he said softly, gesturing to the photo of Grace.

"She was," Amelia replied, her voice steady but soft. "And this... this is where I get to keep her story alive."

Nate's hand settled gently on her back, a silent affirmation.

Before Amelia could let the weight of that linger too long, a light knock sounded on the door.

A young man—probably late-twenties—stepped inside, standing tall with the posture that suggested military training and a no-nonsense approach. He wore dark jeans, a clean black polo, and an earpiece clipped behind one ear.

"Mr. Carter. Ms. Lane," he said with a polite nod. "Tyler Morgan. I'll be trailing you both today. Luke sends his regards."

Amelia stepped forward and offered a small smile. "Nice to meet you, Tyler. And please—call me Amelia."

He gave a brief nod, eyes scanning the space once before settling comfortably by the door.

They spent the morning weaving through Amelia's work routine—emails, phone calls, prepping sponsorship packets. Nate lingered nearby, genuinely curious, occasionally asking questions that made her realize how deeply he was paying attention.

By late morning, they made their way to the PICU wing. A group of nurses waved excitedly when they saw Nate, their professionalism briefly cracking as their starstruck smiles broke through. He took the attention in stride, pausing for photos, signing a few badge clips, and making each person feel significant.

Janice appeared around the corner, her arms wide as she called out, "Mr. Carter! I was hoping I'd see you again."

"Janice, you're the reason I came back," Nate said, his charm effortless.

"You say that now, but wait until you hear my dance requests," she quipped.

Amelia watched the two of them with a quiet sort of gratitude. Nate wasn't pretending. He wasn't performing. He was *here.*

Nate leaned in and hugged Janice, and unless Amelia was imagining things, a slight squeal escaped before Janice's face turned a very telling shade of red. With a grateful wave goodbye, Janice headed back toward the reception desk while Amelia and Nate continued down the hall.

As they walked, Nate visited a few of the families staying long-term. He crouched to talk with one boy about superhero movies, took photos with another who was celebrating a treatment milestone, and sat for nearly half an hour with a teenager who wanted to ask him about film editing.

Amelia stayed close, watching Nate settle into each moment without rushing, without distancing himself. He asked real questions. He listened.

"You're good at this," she said quietly as they stepped into the hallway.

He looked over, brow raised. "Good at what?"

"This. People. You don't just... show up for the photo op."

His smile was soft. "Neither do you."

They lingered in the hospital cafeteria for lunch, tucked into a quiet corner where Amelia could eat her favorite soup without interruption. She told Nate stories about Grace—the way she insisted on extra sprinkles on everything, her love for the hospital's red wagons, the way she once declared she wanted to be a 'ballerina astronaut.'

Nate listened as if each story were a rare treasure.

"I would've liked her," he said finally, stirring his iced tea.

"She would've loved you," Amelia replied, her throat tightening.

They took the long way back to her office, visiting a few more staff members who had grown fond of Nate in two days. Tyler shadowed them quietly, always nearby but never intrusive.

By mid-afternoon, they settled back in her office, scrolling through donor spreadsheets and laughing at how boring Nate found the process.

"How do you do this all day without losing your mind?" he groaned dramatically.

Amelia smirked. "Coffee. Lots of coffee. And stubbornness."

"Should've guessed."

She continued, "I also work from home most of the time, so I take a break whenever it gets to be too much."

Nate settled into the chair, arms behind his head, his legs stretching out under the table—casual, confident, and entirely too distracting.

"You know," he said, "I've done a lot of interviews. I've been on many sets and attended more premieres than I can count. But this—sitting in your office while you curse at spreadsheets—might be my favorite thing I've done in a long time."

Amelia laughed, rolling her eyes. "You're such a liar."

"Dead serious," he said, his gaze steady.

She looked at him, the weight of the moment settling between them. The way he showed up in her world, the way he folded so easily into her routine— it felt real. Tangible.

"Thank you," she said softly.

"For what?"

"For not treating this like a celebrity side quest. For making space for this to be something more."

He stood, rounding her desk, and leaned against it, close enough that she could smell his cologne, warm and familiar now.

"I'm not going anywhere," he said. "If you'll let me stay."

The air thickened, her pulse quickening in the best way.

Before she could reply, there was a knock at the door—one of her team members reminding her about the weekly staff meeting.

"I've got to run to this meeting," she said. "It won't be long."

Nate stood upright and stretched. "No worries. I think I'll wander a bit—go check in on some kids again. Maybe stop by the third and fourth floors."

"You sure?"

He nodded, already grabbing his hat. "Yeah. I've got a few friends up there now."

They parted at the office door, Amelia making her way down the hall toward the conference room while Nate disappeared in the opposite direction.

The staff meeting was straightforward—featuring event updates, donor reports from the gala, and upcoming outreach events—but Amelia couldn't focus. Her eyes drifted toward the hallway every time someone walked by the door. She could picture him out there, laughing with nurses, crouched beside kids in wheelchairs, getting pulled into conversations he had no intention of escaping.

When the meeting finally ended, she was one of the first out the door. She smiled and waved off questions and conversations, her mind already elsewhere. Everyone seemed more interested in confirming if Nate was still somewhere in the building than in the next fundraiser deadline. If she were being honest, she was as well.

Amelia made her way up to the fourth floor, her steps quick and purposeful. As she turned the corner, she immediately saw him—seated once again in room 404.

The sight stopped her.

Even from the doorway, she recognized the familiar curve of the well-worn baseball glove propped on the windowsill, the cracked leather softened from use. Caleb's bat leaned in the corner, and the faded Atlanta Braves cap hung from a hook on the IV pole. The exact details had been there the first time Nate visited—when he ended up staying nearly an hour, swapping baseball stories and movie lines with a kid who had every reason not to smile, but did anyway.

And now Nate was back in the same chair, hunched forward, fully locked into the moment.

He and Caleb were deep in conversation, voices low but animated, like old friends picking up right where they left off.

Amelia hovered for a moment at the door, taking it in—the easy way Caleb's face lit up when Nate laughed, the way Nate leaned in, elbows on his knees, giving Caleb every ounce of his attention. He wasn't there as a celebrity or a guest. He was there as a friend.

She finally stepped into the room, her voice soft. "Hey."

Caleb turned, grinning. "Hi, Ms. Lane."

"We were arguing," Nate said, glancing up at her with a smirk, "about whether Captain Orion's new helmet should have night vision or X-ray."

"Both," Caleb said without hesitation. "Obviously."

Amelia chuckled and crossed her arms. "You're not making it easy on the design team."

Caleb shrugged, all mischief. "I'm just giving the people what they want."

Nate gave Caleb a playful glare. "We're going to need a whole new effects budget."

Caleb leaned back against his pillow, satisfied. "That's not my problem."

They all laughed, and for a moment, the weight of everything lifted. Amelia's heart tugged as she watched them—this joy wasn't for show. It was grounded, real, passing between them like a quiet thread.

She glanced at the clock on the wall. "Alright, I'm officially calling it. My workday is over."

Nate stood, slow and thoughtful, his expression a little more subdued now. He ruffled Caleb's hair gently and held out a fist. "Thanks for the advice, Coach."

Caleb bumped it with a grin. "Don't screw it up."

"Doing my best."

Amelia leaned down and kissed Caleb's forehead. "Tell your mom I'll stop by next week."

"Will do. Thanks for coming, both of you."

When they stepped into the hallway, the door clicking softly behind them, Nate was quiet for a long moment.

They walked side by side toward the elevators, the late afternoon light slanting through the windows and casting long shadows across the hall.

"He reminds me of Noah," Nate said finally, his voice rougher than before.

Amelia turned to look at him, but he kept his eyes ahead.

"I don't mean they're the same, just..." He exhaled. "Sometimes I wonder what Noah would've been like if he'd made it through. Caleb's got that same stubborn spark. Same way of laughing when things aren't funny. He makes *you* feel better—like somehow, you showed up to help him, but he's the one carrying *you*."

Amelia's heart clenched gently. "I see that."

She reached for his hand and held it as they walked. He didn't stop her.

"I think Caleb makes me want to be better," Nate said. "Not just for him, or for Noah—but for myself… maybe there's more I'm supposed to be doing."

Amelia said nothing while squeezing his hand and letting him finish his thoughts.

"I'm going to call Mike," Nate continued. "And Cassidy. Start putting something together. I don't know what it is yet, but it has a purpose. Something real."

They paused at the elevator, the metal doors gleaming softly in the golden light.

"I think Caleb already knows you're doing more," Amelia said, looking up at him. "You showed up. You cared. That's more than most."

Nate met her eyes, the weight of everything they weren't saying hanging quietly between them.

"I just don't want to waste it," he said softly.

"You're not," she whispered.

When the elevator doors slid open, they stepped inside, still hand in hand.

By the time they reached the parking garage, the sun had mellowed into a quiet haze, bathing the concrete in amber and dusted gold.

"You hungry?" Nate asked as they reached her car.

"Starving."

"Then dinner's on me."

She grinned, unlocking the doors. "I can't say no to that."

As they pulled out of the garage, Nate adjusted his seat with a satisfied sigh. "Feels like I've got my spot back," he said, glancing her way.

Amelia laughed, easing into traffic. "Don't get too comfortable."

"Too late." He reached for the glovebox and peeked inside. "Though I am a little disappointed, there aren't granola bars in here. Honestly, I expected better."

She groaned. "You're never letting that go, are you?"

"Not a chance. I was emotionally unprepared that day."

She shook her head with a smile. "You're a real comedian, funny guy."

"Don't encourage me."

They drove back to Longmont in a quiet that didn't need filling. The vibration of the road, the rhythm of tires against pavement, the occasional glance shared between them—it all settled into something tender and unrushed. When they got home, Amelia ordered pasta takeout from a local favorite that delivered fast.

They ate barefoot in the kitchen, leaning against the counters, their shoulders brushing, their laughter easy.

The rest of the night unfolded simply. No grand gestures or need to plan tomorrow. Two people who couldn't seem to stop reaching for each other, while sharing the same couch, the same movie, the same space.

And when they finally went to bed, there was no question that they would go together. That's just where he belonged now.

# 16

# hug shop

T HE STREET LOOKED just as it always had. The sidewalk still had its cracks, and the mailbox on the corner still leaned to one side. Amelia knew the route so well she could have navigated it blindfolded, but today, she observed everything keenly.

She hadn't suggested driving. There was no need. Grace's house was near enough to feel tangible, near enough to hurt.

They strolled, hand in hand, as the morning sun softened the edges of everything except memory.

Amelia led the way, steady but slow, as if each step toward the house carried its own measured weight.

Nate didn't rush her. He matched her stride, never asking how close they were or what to expect when they got there.

When they turned the corner, Amelia's feet faltered slightly. The sight of the house always did that. It looked the same as it always had—blue shutters, white trim, the slight sag in the front porch railing—but seeing it with Nate beside her shifted something inside her. It made the memories sharper. Closer.

"There it is," she said, her voice almost a whisper. "That's the house."

Nate stopped with her, his eyes traveling over the weathered siding and the small porch that leaned just enough to suggest years of good living and a bit of neglect. "It's beautiful."

"It was our first home," she said, her thumb finding the silver 'G' pendant that hung from her neck. "Grant and I scraped together the down payment right after our wedding—just enough space for what we thought would be our little family of three. I can still see myself carrying Grace through that doorway, wrapped in her yellow blanket. Eleven months later, she wobbled across those porch boards, arms outstretched, laughing the whole way."

Nate's gaze softened. He said nothing, allowing the story to settle.

"Those porch boards," Amelia continued, her voice drifting as her fingers traced the silver 'G' pendant, "they creaked just enough to soothe her on sleepless nights. I'd rock her until dawn sometimes, her tiny fist wrapped around this necklace." Her lips curved into a smile that didn't quite reach her eyes. "Every time she touched it, she'd whisper, 'Mama's treasure,' like she understood exactly what she was to me."

Nate's hand found hers, his thumb gently pressing into her palm. "She sounds like she had you wrapped around her finger."

"She did." Amelia's lips twitched in the ghost of a smile. "Every morning, those little feet would slap against the hardwood floors, racing toward whatever adventure she'd dreamed up overnight. That backyard became everything—a royal court where she'd serve invisible tea, a stadium where she'd score impossible goals, a wilderness where her flashlight cut through sheet-tent darkness. Her kingdom, every inch of it."

They stepped closer, peering through the slats in the side gate. The backyard, though a little overgrown now, still held the bones of those memories. The magnolia trees stretched wide and tall, their waxy leaves catching the sunlight as the first soft pink blooms unfurled.

"She loved those trees the most," Amelia said, her throat tightening. "She'd collect the petals when they fell, stuff them into her pockets, or make little piles in the corners of her room. She called them her 'dream petals.' She believed if she kept them close, her dreams would be safe."

Nate tightened his grip on her hand. "I love that."

"She used to say," Amelia continued, her voice softer now, "that when the petals landed on you, it meant they were giving you a hug."

Amelia's breath caught for a second, but she smiled through it. "I told her that was the most beautiful thing I'd ever heard, and she just giggled and said, 'Well, that's what they do.' Like it was the most obvious thing in the world."

Nate lifted her hand and pressed a soft kiss to her knuckles. "That's perfect," he said softly. "I hope they find me someday."

Amelia's chest tightened, but this time it wasn't from sadness—it was from how much she wanted to be right there with him, in all of this, for as long as he'd let her.

Nate brushed a loose strand of hair behind Amelia's ear. "She sounds like a person who made the universe brighter."

"She did." Amelia blinked quickly, steadying herself. "It wasn't just the house. She *was* the home."

They lingered there for a long time, as if the memories alone could draw Grace's laughter back through the walls, through the breeze rustling the magnolia leaves.

Amelia wanted to show Nate every detail—to walk him through the house, to tell him where the kitchen table sat, where the toy bins overflowed, where the nightlight had glowed in Grace's room. But the house wasn't hers anymore.

One day, maybe.

One day, if the universe were kind, there would be a For Sale sign out front.

But not today.

She pressed her fingertips briefly to the gate, almost repeating a goodbye, before turning toward the sidewalk.

"There's one more place I want to show you," she said, her voice low but certain.

Nate didn't ask where. He simply fell into step beside her.

"Whenever you're ready," he said.

They walked for several quiet blocks; the houses giving way to open fields and a small, peaceful cemetery edged with old oak trees. The wrought-iron gate creaked faintly as they passed through.

It didn't take long to find Grace's spot. Amelia knew the path by heart.

The headstone was simple but beautiful, carved from soft gray stone with delicate magnolia blooms etched around the edges.

***Grace Veronica Wells***
*Our Treasured Daughter*
*Your Light Remains*
*Forever Blooming*

Amelia knelt, her fingers trembling slightly as she traced the magnolia carvings, pausing on the letters that formed her daughter's name.

"She loved that her middle name was Veronica," Amelia whispered. "She always said it made her extra brave, like Ronnie."

Nate crouched beside her, offering her the closeness without invading her personal space. "She sounds like she was all kinds of brave."

"Most kids want to open a lemonade stand in the summer, but Grace had a different business prospect," Amelia said, her voice trembling with the weight of memory. "One of her favorite ideas—the one she clung to for the longest—was that she wanted to open a hug shop."

Nate's brow lifted, curiosity lighting his expression. "A hug shop?"

Amelia nodded, a soft, tearful laugh escaping her. "Yeah. She came up with it when she was about five years old. She told me one early morning in the hospital that some kids in the world were too sad, and that the problem was no one was giving enough hugs."

She paused, her thumb brushing over the edge of the cool stone. "So she said she was going to fix it. She was going to open a hug shop where anyone could come in and get a hug whenever they needed one."

Nate's lips curled into a small, tender smile, but he didn't interrupt.

"She had it all worked out," Amelia went on, her voice warming through the ache. "She said it would have a big pink sign that said 'Hugs.' No appointments. No money. You walk in, and she'd be there with her arms wide open, waiting for you."

Amelia could almost see her—Grace's little arms stretched wide, her serious, determined face.

"She told me that if someone were extra sad, she would give them two hugs.

And if someone came in angry, she would let them sit in the 'cool-down chair' first, then hug them when they were ready."

Nate's throat bobbed, his own emotion building quietly as he pictured it.

"She even wanted to have a little bell on the door," Amelia added, her fingers tracing the delicate magnolia carvings. "So she'd always know when someone was coming in to see her."

Amelia swallowed the lump in her throat and let the smallest smile crack through. "She said the world would feel better if more places guaranteed a hug the second you walked through the door."

Nate's voice was soft, reverent. "She wasn't wrong."

"No," Amelia whispered. "She wasn't."

"She could have changed everything."

"She already did." Amelia's breath hitched, her hand pressing flat to the stone.

"She changed me."

"It's been four years," she said, her voice almost weightless. "And some days, I still wake up thinking I'm going to hear her feet running through the house. I still catch myself buying the yogurt she loved. Sometimes I wish I could just turn around fast enough and she'd be right there."

"I wanted to keep the house," she whispered. "I fought for it. But Grant… he couldn't do it. He couldn't stay in that house without her. I think in his mind, leaving was the only way to survive."

"Maybe that's what he needed," Nate said carefully. "But it wasn't what you needed."

"No," Amelia said, tears slipping down her cheeks. "It wasn't."

The wind stirred again, and a few leaves from the trees above drifted down, landing softly near the base of the headstone.

"She would've said that's a sign," Amelia whispered.

"Then maybe it is," Nate replied.

They sat still for a long time, letting the moment settle deep into their bones.

Amelia leaned forward, pressing a kiss to her first two fingers before gently placing them on the carved **G** on the headstone. She stayed there for a moment, her touch lingering, then stood slowly, brushing the dust from her jeans.

Nate rose with her, his hand finding the small of her back as they turned to walk the quiet path back through the trees.

When they reached the sidewalk, Nate stopped, turning to her fully. "Thank you for showing me."

She looked up at him, her eyes tired but steady. "Thank you for coming."

Nate's hand slid gently from her back to her hand, linking their fingers as they fell into step together. Neither of them spoke as they walked.

Amelia let herself sink into the silence.

For so long, this place—this neighborhood, this walk—had been sacred. Untouchable.

The house she had loved. The backyard where Grace had laughed. The grave where her daughter now rested. These had always been places she visited alone, corners of her life that felt too delicate to share.

She marveled quietly at the way he fit. The way he carried the weight of these memories with her, without trying to fix them, without crowding her grief. He didn't pull or push—he simply stayed.

It wasn't only that he made her laugh, or that his hands fit so perfectly around her waist, or that he kissed her with fervor. It was the way he made space for her. The way he seemed to settle right into the hollowed-out places she'd long since stopped expecting anyone to reach.

Maybe she hadn't only let him in.

Maybe he'd found his way here all along.

Her chest tightened at the thought, but it wasn't fear this time—it was something warmer. Something that might even be hope.

She squeezed his hand a little tighter.

They walked in easy sync the rest of the way home, their footsteps quiet against the familiar streets. And for the first time in a very long time, the ache of what was no longer there didn't feel so sharp.

She could still miss Grace. She could still love her with every shattered piece of her heart.

And maybe—just maybe—she could let herself love something new, too.

*Maybe she already had.*

* * *

WHEN THEY REACHED Amelia's house, they found Luke perched on the front steps, phone clutched in one hand. The familiar furrow between his brows had deepened into something unfamiliar—not his professional vigilance, but genuine alarm. His eyes met Amelia's, and the silent message there made her feet rooted to the sidewalk. Her stomach lurched sideways as if she'd missed a step on a staircase. Nate's palm, warm against her lower back, became her anchor as the world tilted beneath her.

"There's something we need to talk about," Luke said as they approached, rising to his feet.

His tone was calm, but the undercurrent was unmistakable. Something had shifted.

Amelia slowed, eyes narrowing. "What's going on?"

Luke slipped his phone into his pocket and exhaled through his nose. "There were a few people here earlier. Cameras. They were trying to look through the windows. Taking pictures."

Amelia's breath caught. "At my house?"

He nodded, his jaw clenched like a vise. "We intercepted them before anyone breached the perimeter. But the damage is done." He pulled out his phone, swiped twice, then turned the screen toward them. "Coffee shop. Hospital entrance. Even loading groceries into your car." His eyes darkened. "Twitter's already calling you Nate Carter's new flame."

Nate muttered a low oath, dragging his palm over the stubble on his jaw. His shoulders hunched forward as if bracing against an invisible weight. "This is exactly what I was afraid of. My world bleeding into yours."

Luke shook his head. "It was always going to catch up, eventually."

Amelia blinked, still catching up. "Wait... Why would anyone care about us at the grocery store?"

Luke hesitated, then glanced at Nate. "Because you're the mystery girl."

She blinked again. "What?"

Nate shifted uncomfortably, his voice low. "It's... kind of what the media does. If I'm seen with someone—especially more than once—they speculate. And if they don't know who it is... they label you."

"That doesn't even make sense. I'm not—" She cut herself off, her pulse kicking. "This is my home. My life. How can they be so intrusive?"

"I know," Nate said quickly. "I know, I'm so sorry. And I hate that it's happening now."

Luke stepped in, his voice firmer now. "You're safe. That's the priority. Tyler and I are on it—we'll reinforce the perimeter, add extra drive-bys for the next couple of days. Nobody's getting through without going through us first."

"But you can't take down what's already online," Amelia said, the realization sinking in.

Luke's expression softened, but he didn't sugarcoat it. "No. I can't. But I'll track it. I'll make sure it doesn't escalate."

She nervously combed her fingers through her hair, realizing just how vulnerable she felt, even standing in her own driveway. "How did they discover my address?"

"They followed someone," Luke said simply. "Maybe one of us. Maybe a store clerk. All it takes is one post with the right tag."

Nate moved in closer, his voice now softer, yet still laced with guilt. "I should have expected this. I should have warned you."

Amelia gazed at him intently, and the frustration that had been boiling within her subsided just a bit. Because he wasn't panicking or pulling away. He was right there. With her. Facing the situation together.

She grasped his hand firmly. "I'm okay," she said, more to reassure herself than anyone else. "As long as you're here."

Nate's shoulders relaxed. "I'm not going anywhere."

Luke clapped Nate on the shoulder, the gesture carrying weight. "We'll keep it under control," he said. Then to Amelia, "You just focus on what matters. We'll handle the rest."

Amelia nodded slowly, her pulse still skipping, but her footing steadier than it had been a moment before.

They stepped inside; the door clicked shut behind them, sealing them into their shared quiet.  The house still smelled faintly of coffee and the lavender-scented candle she'd lit that morning.

The outside world could clamor and press in all it wanted.

But here, within these walls, they still had space to breathe.

And for now, that was enough.

# 17

# my girl

THE REST OF the day passed in quiet comfort. After the tension of the morning and the weight of visiting Grace's house and grave, the only thing Amelia wanted to do was to be still. And Nate seemed perfectly content to let her.

They watched a movie on the couch that evening, something lighthearted and silly that neither of them paid attention to. Amelia dozed off halfway through, her head resting on Nate's chest, lulled by the soft rise and fall of his breathing.

Nate didn't move. Not once. He shifted his arm only to pull her in closer, brushing his thumb along her shoulder in slow, steady lines. It wasn't about the movie. It wasn't about filling the quiet. It was simply about being near her.

When she finally stirred, blinking herself awake and realizing she'd been asleep for almost an hour, she sat up quickly. "Oh my God, I fell asleep on you."

Nate's mouth curved into a lazy, satisfied smile. "I liked it."

"I'm sorry, I just—" she rubbed her face, suddenly self-conscious. "I didn't mean to pass out on you."

"I loved every second of taking care of you, Mils," he said, his voice low, steady, and so sure that it made her chest ache in the best way. "You don't have to apologize for needing rest. Not with me."

Her throat tightened. She wanted to tell him how good that felt. How safe she felt with him. But the words caught somewhere in her ribs, so instead she leaned into him and pressed a soft kiss to his shoulder.

When she pulled back slightly, she caught his gaze—steady, kind, unflinching.

"You really don't mind?" she asked, her voice softer now, vulnerable in a way she wasn't used to letting herself be. "I mean… this isn't exactly the glamorous life you're used to."

Nate's brow furrowed, confusion in his eyes. "What? Lying on a couch with the most incredible woman I've ever met, watching movies and taking naps? Sounds pretty perfect to me."

She gave a small laugh, shaking her head. "You know what I mean."

He tilted his head, using his free hand to gently lift her chin, so she met his gaze. "Yes, I mean it. I want this. Not the fame or the chaos. Just this. Just you." His words enveloped her heart with undeniable certainty, resonating deeply within her.

"You make it impossibly hard not to fall for you," she admitted, her cheeks warming.

"Good," he murmured, his grin slow and sure. "Because I'm already gone for you."

Her breath hitched, her heart stumbling over itself.

"And just so we're clear," he added, his tone light but his eyes serious, "if you keep falling asleep on me, I fully intend to make that a habit."

"You do?" she whispered, smiling into the flutter of nerves rising in her chest.

"Absolutely. My new favorite thing," he teased, pressing a soft kiss to her temple. "Taking care of you is not a chore, Mils. It's a privilege."

Her chest ached in the best way as she tucked herself briefly against him one more time, her hand curling lightly into his shirt. She felt his arm tighten around her waist, his palm warm against the small of her back. And beneath the softness of the moment, there was a quiet tension rising—charged and intimate, but unhurried.

She shifted slightly, only to realize the way his breath hitched—the subtle way his body responded to hers. He wanted her. She wanted him, too.

The closeness, the quiet, the weight of the day had only drawn her nearer to him, not worn her down. If anything, it had stripped her defenses.

Amelia tilted her chin up, her lips brushing just below his jaw. "Is this real?" she whispered again, the words trembling in the space between them. "Tell me I'm not dreaming."

Nate's hands slid up her back, slow and sure, and his mouth found hers with a depth that unraveled her. "It's real," he murmured into her kiss. "We're real."

His voice wrapped around her, tender and firm, and it hit that place inside her he always seemed to find—an ache that wasn't new, but felt deeper every time. She melted into him, letting his touch and his presence draw her closer to something she no longer wanted to resist.

His hand curled into her hair, the other gripping her hip as she pressed closer, both of them leaning into the heat rising fast between them.

He let out a soft groan against her lips, momentarily pulling away to murmur in a low, husky voice, "If we don't stop soon, I'll have you right here on this couch." Amelia's breath hitched, her body warming and her pulse racing beneath her skin.

She gazed at him with heavy-lidded eyes, her voice a mere whisper, "Then have me."

And with that, he did.

Somewhere in the fleeting moments between her back colliding with the plush embrace of the cushions and his hands gliding with a gentle urgency beneath her shirt, time seemed to suspend its relentless march. His lips pressed against hers with an insatiable hunger that swept away every coherent thought like leaves in a storm. As she shifted her position, straddling him completely, a sound emerged from deep within his throat—a raw, guttural expression that was the most unguarded, primal thing she had ever heard from another human being. It resonated through her entire being, like a profound truth never spoken aloud, intended for no other ears but hers.

"Jesus, Mils..." he groaned, his voice wrecked against her neck. "You're gonna kill me."

She gasped as his hands tightened on her hips, steadying her as she moved. "Take me, Nate," she whispered, desperate and breathless. "All of me."

* * *

AS SHE STEPPED toward the kitchen, Amelia caught sight of her bra, half-tucked under the coffee table. She paused, a smile tugging at her lips despite the heat rising to her cheeks. Her body still carried the imprint of their connection—muscles pleasantly sore, skin pulsing with remembered touch. Each step reminded her of what they'd shared, a physical memory her body wasn't ready to release.

The cool tile against her bare feet anchored her as she pulled open the refrigerator door. Light spilled across her face as she surveyed the contents: yesterday's pasta, those roasted vegetables he'd complimented. Simple food for this delicate moment. She wanted something that wouldn't require thought or conversation—just nourishment to extend this perfect, fragile peace between them.

A few minutes later, Nate joined her, and they rummaged through the fridge side by side, moving in a wordless but harmonious rhythm. The cool air from the fridge mingled with the warmth of the kitchen, creating a subtle blend of sensations. Before they sat down, Amelia slipped out of the room, only to return moments later, wearing the soft gray robe from their first night together—the fabric draped over her skin, whispering like a half-remembered dream against her senses. When Nate caught sight of her, his eyes lingered for a heartbeat—soft, reverent, and almost awestruck. A quiet, knowing smile played on his lips, and she felt its gentle tug resonate all the way to her spine.

She carefully plated the food and carried it out to the back patio, where the air had cooled just enough to justify a light jacket. Nate slipped into his hoodie, the fabric rustling softly, and followed her with two glasses of water in hand. The patio lights above them twinkled like distant stars, casting a gentle glow that wrapped around them. For a moment, it seemed as if the world had paused in its perfection.

They ate in a comfortable silence, the kind that spoke volumes without needing words. Occasionally, they nudged each other's elbows playfully or stole bites from each other's plates, their laughter mingling with the night air. Amelia's shoulders finally eased from their tense hold. After such an emotionally charged day, this simple, quiet dinner beneath the canopy of stars was precisely what they both needed to find solace and peace.

Nate twirled his fork in the last of his noodles and leaned back with a contented sigh. "Alright, random question."

Amelia raised an eyebrow. "Those are usually your best ones."

He grinned. "When's your birthday?"

"February sixth," she said, reaching for her glass. "You?"

"November eighteenth," he replied. "Which means I was always that kid who brought cupcakes to school when everyone else was gearing up for Thanksgiving break."

Amelia laughed. "Let me guess—your mom always made the cupcakes?"

"Absolutely, she did. They were the best," he confirmed. "I used to pretend I didn't care, but if someone forgot to say happy birthday, I'd sulk for hours."

She smiled at the image. "I used to *want* heart-shaped pancakes. Saw them in a book once and couldn't let it go."

Her fingers brushed the rim of her glass. "But... that wasn't a thing in my house."

Nate watched her for a beat, quiet. "If anyone deserved heart-shaped pancakes, it was you."

She let out a gentle, somewhat wistful laugh. "You say that now, but just wait until you're with someone who's thirty-two and still secretly dreams of them."

Nate leaned in, a smile playing at the corner of his lips. "It's a good thing I like thirty-two. And heart-shaped pancakes. And most importantly, you."

Her breath hitched, the playful atmosphere between them suddenly infused with a tender warmth.

He tapped his glass with a finger, thoughtful yet confident. "Got it. On your next birthday, we're going all out—pancakes, your favorite flowers, the whole nine yards. You won't have to ask for a thing."

Amelia was at a loss for words, so she stayed silent. She couldn't decide if she were more thrilled about the prospect of a special birthday or the fact that Nate implied he'd still be around.

He leaned back, legs extending beneath the table until his ankle brushed hers. "Mom went all out for birthdays. Streamers hanging from every doorway, cakes shaped like baseball diamonds or rocket ships." His voice softened. "But Noah—he brought the magic. Once, he wrapped twenty different boxes inside each other for my present."

Amelia slowly reached across the table and let her fingers brush his. "Sounds like he was a great brother."

"He was."

They sat in silence for a beat, the warmth between them stretching comfortably across the table.

Then she asked, "When was the last time you had a birthday you really enjoyed?"

He tilted his head, considering. "The last one before Noah died." His voice was quiet now, its tone softened. "He went all out—decorated my school locker, filled it with balloons, and made me wear a crown to school. It was ridiculous."

He smiled faintly. "But it was perfect. I didn't know it would be the last one we had together like that."

Amelia's expression softened, her hand still resting near his. "He showed up for you."

"Always," Nate said, eyes distant for a beat. "I'd give anything to go back to that day. Even for a few hours."

A silence settled between them—not heavy, but reverent.

"Well," she said gently, "you've got another one coming up."

Nate looked at her, something steady flickering in his eyes.

"I haven't looked forward to my birthday in years... but now?"

He paused, eyes still on her.

"I think I might."

She didn't look away; she knew what he meant. "I hope so."

They fell quiet for a moment, the air around them easy but thick with meaning. Then Nate glanced sideways and added, "You know, my parents still call me Nathan."

Amelia blinked, surprised by the shift. "Really?"

He nodded. "Hollywood made Nate. But Nathan's the name that followed me through scraped knees and peewee sports and detention for climbing the gym roof."

She smiled, tilting her head. "Nathan, what?"

"Nathan Dean Carter," he said, dragging the back of his knuckles across the table toward her plate. "Dean was my grandfather. He was quiet, but solid. Never missed a single baseball game."

Amelia's lips curved softly. "That suits you. Nathan Dean."

"Yeah?"

"Yeah," she said, then added, "Amelia Ann Lane."

"Ann," he repeated slowly, as if savoring it. "That fits too."

She raised an eyebrow. "Why? Because it's simple?"

"No," he said, voice lower. "Because it's the kind of name you'd whisper when you want something you're afraid to ask for."

Her breath caught.

She looked down for a moment, her fingers curling around the edge of her glass—not to hide, but to steady herself. The way he said her name... it did something to her. Stirred something soft and dangerous and real.

She wasn't ready to reply to that—not out loud—so she let the silence stretch, let the air carry it between them.

A subtle noise in the yard caught her attention. Initially, she assumed it was Luke or Tyler on their usual patrol. Having them nearby had become routine. Perhaps Tyler had taken a shortcut through the backyard instead of going around the front.

However, when she turned toward the noise, her heart sank. A shadowy figure stood in the distance, indistinct, yet clearly not Tyler. And definitely not Luke.

"Nate," she murmured, her heart racing. "There's someone out there."

"Hey, sweetheart, you gonna make me work for my photo?" a voice slithered out from the shadows. The taunt, casual, and cutting pierced the night air.

Nate's chair scraped loudly against the patio as he shot to his feet. His eyes darted to where the voice came from, his body lines instantly sharp and alert. "Who is that?"

She pointed, her hand trembling. "By the trees—slightly past the fence line."

Another voice joined the first, nastier. "Come on, smile at us, Miss Lane. You're famous now, right?"

"Hey!" Nate's voice rang out, loud and firm, cutting through the evening air. "Who's there?"

The figure shifted but didn't back away.

"I said, who's there?" Nate barked again, his body stepping slightly in front of Amelia's, his hand dropping to her shoulder in a firm, steady grip.

The first man laughed, a sound that made Amelia's stomach twist. "Relax, Captain Orion, we're just fans."

Amelia's chest squeezed tight. "Do you think it's—?"

"I need you to go inside. Now, Mils." His voice was calm but urgent. "Lock the door behind you."

Her feet stayed planted. "But what about—?"

His eyes cut back to hers, firm but not panicked. "Go. Please. I'll be right behind you."

Before she could move, the second man lunged from the shadows, his camera thrust forward like a weapon. "Say cheese, Amelia!" The night shattered with white light, leaving her vision swimming with purple afterimages.

"Amelia." Nate's voice dropped lower, urgent. "We don't know who that is or what they want. I need you inside where it's safe. Now."

His words, coupled with the unspoken fear beneath them, eventually broke through her haze.

"Okay," she breathed, backing up quickly. "Okay."

She snatched her plate without thinking, bolting for the sliding glass door as her heartbeat pounded in her throat.

"Lock it," Nate called after her as he advanced toward the yard.

The moment she clicked the lock into place, another voice hissed from the dark. "How's it feel, Nate? Having your little charity girlfriend trapped inside?"

From inside, she could still see Nate—a dark outline now—moving quickly across the yard, his voice sharp as he shouted again into the dark, "Hey! This is private property! You need to leave!"

But the men didn't leave. One broke into a jog, weaving through the yard's shadows, angling toward the side of the house. The other moved in on Nate—too fast, too deliberate.

Nate shouted again. "You're trespassing!"

The man lunged, camera raised like a weapon. Nate met him head-on, grabbing his arm, twisting him sideways.

"Get the hell out of here!" Nate's voice thundered.

The man stumbled, his camera swinging erratically, the strap pulling taut as he struggled to regain his footing. With renewed determination, he sprinted toward the back fence, effortlessly vaulting over it and vanishing from sight.

Nate, however, was not as fortunate. His balance wavered as his foot snagged on a protruding garden stake just as he launched himself forward. He crashed to the ground with a heavy thud, one arm scraping painfully against the jagged pile of wood that lay scattered nearby, the sharp edges biting into his skin as he broke his fall.

Amelia's breath hitched in her throat as she witnessed the scene unfold. Her eyes widened as she saw Nate press his hand quickly over the wound, a fleeting gesture of pain and resolve, before he moved with a determined urgency toward the side gate. In a heartbeat, he slipped out of her line of sight, leaving only the rustling of leaves in his wake.

She slid down against the door until her knees hit the floor, fingers splayed across the cold glass.

"Nate?" The word broke in half as it left her lips, drowned beneath the thundering of her own heartbeat. She leaned forward, straining to see into the darkness where he'd disappeared. Her lungs seized. "Nate!"

Nothing.

She fumbled to grab her phone, her fingers slipping as she suddenly realized she did not know whom to contact. Nate's phone remained on the table outside, visible from her vantage point.

Each heartbeat dragged on as if it lasted a minute, and every second brimmed with anxiety. She frantically paced in front of the door, her chest tight and her mind racing through worst-case scenarios.

What if they injured Nate? Should she venture outside? Should she contact the police?

As she continued to pace, she began dialing 911 when the front door suddenly rattled with three sharp, urgent knocks, followed by three more. Amelia's heart pounded against her ribs as though it wanted to break free. Her feet felt glued to the floor, even as the knocking persisted.

Her breath came in quick, tight gasps as she tiptoed to the front of the house.

"Amelia! It's Tyler! It's me, open the door!" His voice cut through the door, firm but urgent.

She flung the door open, relief crashing through her so quickly her knees nearly buckled.

Tyler stepped inside, quickly scanning the house. "Are you okay? Are you hurt?"

She shook her head, her voice still caught somewhere in her throat. "I'm okay. Where's Nate?"

"We're still getting the full picture," Tyler said, his words clipped but steady. "Some paparazzi snuck into the backyard. Luke and I think they've been watching the house since this afternoon. I need you to stay right here."

"Are they gone?" Amelia's pulse rattled hard in her chest.

Tyler's radio crackled. He responded quickly; his hand pressed to his earpiece.

"Copy. Yeah, I've got her. She's safe."

A beat of silence as Tyler listened.

"Luke's handling the perimeter," Tyler told her. "Nate's okay, but he took a hit to his arm. EMS is en route."

Amelia's knees buckled. "What? EMS?"

Tyler's voice softened slightly. "It's precautionary. We want to make sure he is OK."

A new wave of dread tightened around her body. She sank onto the couch without realizing it, her legs folding beneath her. Tyler stepped into the kitchen and returned a moment later with a glass of water. She took it, her fingers trembling enough to make the surface ripple.

"Try to sip," he said gently. "You're safe now. We've got eyes on everything."

Amelia nodded, but didn't drink. She held the glass with both hands, steadying herself, and stared at the front door as if she could will it to open.

Tyler stood near the window, one hand on his radio, the other resting casually near the holster at his hip. His voice was low and measured each time he responded to a call sign, but she caught fragments of it.

"Suspect detained."

"Confirming ID now."

"Copy that. Holding position."

She got up and paced the living room—slowly at first, then in tight loops between the kitchen island and the coffee table. The water went untouched. Her robe felt too warm, then not warm enough. She folded her arms. Unfolded them. Sat down again. Stood back up.

Red and blue lights flashed through the windows now, washing the walls in shifting colors. Shadows of paramedics and officers flitted past the glass, making it feel like the house was surrounded.

"I need to see him, Tyler. Please—"

"I know. But right now, he needs to be treated first. You'll see him in a minute."

"I just..." Her throat felt too tight. "I need to see him."

More time passed. Twenty minutes? Thirty? She couldn't tell.

Tyler checked in with someone else. "Front clear. Nothing else flagged on surveillance." Then, to her, "They're wrapping up now. Luke's escorting him back."

She couldn't concentrate. Her heart was racing, and she continued to pace back and forth, trying to push away the worst-case scenarios she knew were unfounded.

Suddenly, the lock turned. The door swung open, and Luke stepped inside.

"He's alright, but the medics want to tend to him in their vehicle before we take him inside," Luke spoke with a professional demeanor, but his eyes briefly softened as he looked at Amelia. "Come out with me and see for yourself."

He extended his hand, calloused palm upturned in the half-light of the entryway.

Amelia's legs moved on autopilot, her bare feet numb against the cool hardwood as she followed Luke through the living room, past the abandoned water glass still beaded with condensation.

The front yard was chaos—red and blue lights slicing through the night air, uniformed officers with flashlights cutting harsh beams across the lawn, neighbors in bathrobes and slippers huddled in twos and threes behind half-drawn curtains, their faces pale ovals of concern.

And there was Nate, sitting on the back of an ambulance, his bloodstained BSU hoodie crumpled in his lap like a wounded animal, his right arm wrapped in pristine white gauze that gleamed under the harsh overhead lights as a paramedic with latex-gloved hands worked quickly, methodically.

But he was upright. Awake. His skin was ashen beneath his five o'clock shadow, but his eyes were clear.

When his eyes found hers across the twenty feet of suburban battlefield between them, his posture straightened like a soldier coming to attention, shoulders squaring despite the visible wince of pain that tightened the corners of his mouth.

"Hey, Mils," he called out softly, his smile small but defiant. "You okay?"

She didn't answer—she just moved, weaving through the chaos until she was beside him.

"I'm fine," she said, her breath hitching. "But you're not."

"I will be." His eyes softened as he reached out to squeeze her hand. "The moment we're back inside."

Luke nodded to the paramedic, then gently touched Amelia's shoulder, his fingers barely grazing the thin cotton of her robe. "Let's get you two out of the circus." The neighbors' whispers floated across the lawn like dandelion seeds, landing everywhere, impossible to gather back up.

Amelia's fingers trembled as she grabbed Nate's left hand, feeling the warmth of his palm against her ice-cold skin. She helped him up, wincing when he swayed slightly against her. Together, they navigated the uneven flagstones of the path, her bare feet flinching at the cold stone. Luke walked ahead, his broad shoulders blocking the prying eyes of onlookers as they made their way up the three wooden porch steps that creaked under their weight.

Luke and Tyler followed them inside, hanging back in the entryway, their professional stance softening as the door clicked shut, sealing out the chaos of flashing lights and murmured speculation.

Amelia lunged forward before the door had fully closed. Her arms encircled Nate's waist, fingers clutching fistfuls of his shirt as she pressed her cheek against his chest. His heartbeat drummed against her skin—steady, alive—while her own body betrayed her with tremors she couldn't control. She clung to him, terrified that loosening her grip might somehow make him vanish.

"I was so scared," she whispered, tears spilling over. "I didn't know where you were. I didn't know—"

"I'm so sorry, Mils. I'm so sorry you had to go through that." His arms wrapped around her, hands cradling the back of her head like he could shield her from the world. "I should've been more careful. I brought this to your doorstep."

"You didn't do this to me," she whispered. "They did."

She pulled back, pressing her palms against his chest. "Where are you hurt? Tell me."

Nate glanced down at his arm and shook his head. "It's just a scratch."

But Amelia was already inspecting him, her fingers hovering over his ribs, shoulders, then freezing when they reached the white gauze wrapped around his forearm. "There's blood seeping through the bandage, Nate." Her voice cracked. "When I couldn't see you out there, I thought—I couldn't even let myself think it."

She clutched his BSU sweatshirt against her chest, staring at the crimson stain that had spread through the torn fabric, marking where the gash had sliced from his elbow nearly to his wrist.

The weight of everything settled between them—fear, adrenaline, the fragile relief that he was still standing. Words slipped away, lost in the hum of distant sirens and the heaviness of what could have been. Her breath slowed, but her grip didn't ease. Nate's hand rested over hers, grounding them both.

And then—silence.

"I've got more security coming," Luke leaned into the room to speak. "There'll be someone at the front and back of the house at all times now. We're locking this down."

Luke shifted his stance, his expression softening slightly as he turned to Amelia. "You'll both need to give a statement to the Longmont PD. They're handling the local side of things. I told them you've had enough for tonight, so they agreed to meet you tomorrow."

Amelia's insides twisted into a cold knot.

*The police want a statement from me?*

Nate immediately caught the hesitation in her eyes. He stepped closer, his hand settling warmly on her back. "We'll figure it out together. I'll be with you."

Luke nodded. "It's pretty routine. Just confirming what you saw and heard. But I didn't want you to be surprised."

"Okay," Amelia said softly, her voice steadier than she expected. "Thank you for handling it."

Luke's gaze briefly flicked to Nate, his respect clear. "You two get some rest. We've got this."

Nate clapped his friend's shoulder, his voice lower now, barely loud enough for Amelia to hear. "Thanks for protecting my girl."

Luke gave him a look that said it wasn't up for debate and then excused himself to coordinate the extra team with Tyler.

Amelia's pulse fluttered at Nate's words—*my girl.*

That's exactly what she wanted to be.

His girl.

It slammed into her all at once. Not that she cared for him, not that she wanted him.

She *loved* him. God, she loved him.

And the second she thought she might lose him—really lose him—every wall she had ever built... shattered.

There was no protecting her heart anymore. It was his. She wasn't even sure when she'd handed it over, but she knew he'd been holding it before tonight.

When the door clicked shut behind Luke and Tyler, Nate cupped her face, his eyes searching hers with so much tenderness it unraveled her completely.

"I never want you to feel unsafe again. Not with me. Never with me."

Her hands slid up to his shoulders, her thumbs brushing his neck, grounding them both. "I don't feel unsafe with you. I never have."

Tears pressed hard behind her eyes, not from fear but from the relief that he was here, that he was okay, that she could finally feel the full weight of what she'd been trying not to admit.

"I love you," she whispered, the words trembling on her lips.

His chest hitched, the weight of her words hitting him squarely. "You do?"

She nodded, her fingers tightening on his shirt. "Yes, I do."

The look that passed over his face—shock, relief, adoration—sent her reeling.

"I love you, too, Mils. God, I love you."

His mouth found hers, their kiss building until it was no longer possible to pretend they would stop. Nate pressed his forehead to hers, his voice a desperate whisper. "Let me take you upstairs."

"Yes," she breathed, her hands clutching at him.

They didn't make it far—each step was a pull, a surrender, a promise.

What unfolded was nothing short of every aching, breathless thing they had been building toward.

Tonight, there was no more fear.

No more distance.

Only them.

Only love.

# 18

## making a statement

THE BUZZING OF Nate's phone started before the sun fully rose, persistent and sharp, clawing its way into their quiet.

Amelia stirred first, her body tangled in warm sheets and the steady weight of Nate's arm draped across her waist. She blinked up at the ceiling, the events of the night before flooding back with sharp clarity. The backyard. The shouts. The knock at the door. The way her pulse had clawed its way up her throat in fear.

And then—Nate's arms. His safety. His steady hands. His love.

She turned slightly to watch him, his breathing slow and even, his features relaxed in the morning light. How had someone like him wandered into her world—and stayed?

She settled back against him, allowing herself the smallest luxury of time. To hold this. To hold him.

But time, as always, was a slippery thing.

Nate's phone buzzed on the nightstand, the sharp vibration cutting through the quiet. He didn't stir.

Another buzz. Another text.

She could feel the slight tension in his arm, the subconscious pull of awareness as his body woke.

The phone buzzed again, more persistent now.

"Someone's popular," Amelia mumbled, her voice still thick with sleep.

Nate's groan vibrated against her back. "Ignore it. I'm not moving."

She smiled softly, closing her eyes for one more breath. "It might be Luke."

Nate exhaled, pressing his face into her shoulder. "Or Mike. Or Cassidy. Or the paparazzi wanting to know what I eat for breakfast."

"Do you want to check it?"

"Not even a little." He kissed her shoulder lazily. "You're the only thing I want to check on this morning."

Her heart skipped. The memory of last night's terror now softened by this—this realness, this warmth.

But the phone buzzed again.

Reluctantly, Nate reached for it, his thumb skimming the screen.

A soft sigh escaped him. "Mike's losing his mind. Cassidy's called six times. Luke's already sent me two updates."

"Anything urgent?"

He continued to skim. "Cassidy's trying to get a pulse on things. Mike's trying to get me to agree to a press statement. Luke's locking down the perimeter even tighter. He says to expect Detective Mallory this morning to take our statements."

"Great," Amelia muttered, already feeling the weight of that. "Can't wait."

Nate kissed her temple. "You're not doing this alone. We'll face it together."

"Promise?"

"Promise."

But before she could get out of bed, Nate's grin deepened. He gently pressed her back against the pillows, his body shifting above hers as he whispered, "But first…"

His mouth found hers, soft but insistent, his hands bracketing her hips as if being apart from her for even one more breath would break him. Amelia's pulse leapt, her fingers sliding into his hair as his weight settled over her.

"We've got time," he murmured between kisses, his voice rough and warm against her skin. "We've always got time for this."

She laughed softly, her chest tightening with the overwhelming rightness of him. "You're impossible."

"Yeah, but you love me," he teased, his lips trailing to her collarbone.

"Yes, I do." She arched into him, her body already aching for the closeness they'd built, the safety he'd offered her again and again. Every wall she'd ever built gave way beneath his touch, never meant to last in the presence of something this honest.

Their morning stretched in lazy, breathless waves—slow, tender, and deeply connected—as if their bodies were finally catching up to what their hearts had already decided.

When they finally settled, their breathing evening out as they lay tangled in the soft morning light, Amelia traced lazy circles on Nate's bare shoulder.

"Best distraction I've ever had," she murmured.

Nate chuckled, tightening his arm around her. "Happy to help."

* * *

THE KNOCK ON the door came less than an hour later.

Detective Ray Mallory—a sturdy, kind-faced man from the Longmont Police Department—introduced himself with a firm handshake and a quiet, respectful tone.

"Ms. Lane?" he said, offering his hand. "Detective Ray Mallory, Longmont PD. Thank you for making time."

Amelia nodded, her grip steady despite the nerves in her stomach. "Of course. Please, come in."

Mallory turned to Nate, extending his hand again. "And you must be Mr. Carter. Appreciate you being here too."

"Happy to help however we can," Nate replied, his voice calm but watchful.

Mallory nodded, giving Nate a quick once-over—his height, his posture, the way his body subtly angled toward Amelia. "You alright? I heard you took the brunt of it."

"Just a slight cut," Nate said, flexing his bandaged arm slightly. "I've had worse on set. But thank you for checking."

The detective gave a faint smile. "I imagine your job prepares you for more than just line memorization."

"Some days more than others," Nate replied dryly, earning a small smile from Amelia despite the tension.

The detective gave a narrow nod, his eyes scanning the room as if he'd done it a thousand times. He was middle-aged, with light gray hair beginning to thin and a slight limp in his left leg that Amelia couldn't help but notice as he crossed the threshold. His uniform was crisp but well-worn, as if he'd spent years showing up for people on their worst days. There was something calm about him. Steady. And Amelia was grateful for that.

"It will not take too long," he promised as he pulled out a small spiral notebook and sat at the dining table. "But I want to walk through everything carefully. Tell me what you remember. Even the small stuff matters."

Amelia sat across from him, her hands clasped tightly in her lap until Nate joined her, his hand resting gently on her knee, his thumb brushing steady circles that reminded her she wasn't alone.

Mallory set his notebook on the dining table and began walking Amelia through the statement process, carefully guiding her through each memory, each detail.

"What time did you first notice someone in the backyard?"

"It was already dark," she said, her voice steady but distant. "We'd almost finished dinner. It was maybe... eight-thirty? Maybe a little later."

"And before that, did you see or hear anything unusual earlier in the day?"

She shook her head. "No. Just normal things—neighbors walking their dogs, people driving by." She paused, then added, "But I guess that was the problem. I noticed nothing unusual, but they must have been watching us already."

He asked about what the figure looked like, what Nate had said, and how quickly things escalated.

"Did you ever see the individual's face?"

"No. Only a shadow at the fence line. They never came into the light enough to make out any details."

"Did they say anything to you or Mr. Carter?"

Amelia swallowed. "Yes."

Mallory looked up. "Go ahead."

"The first man said..." she hesitated, the words scraping her throat, "Hey sweetheart, you gonna make me work for my photo?"

Nate's jaw tightened, but his hand stayed steady on her knee.

"Then the second one said, 'Smile at us, Miss Lane. You're famous now, right?"

Mallory's pen paused briefly, then resumed. "Taunting you."

Amelia nodded. "They wanted us to feel... exposed. Cornered."

Mallory glanced at Nate. "And you confronted them?"

"Told her to go inside first," Nate said. "Tried to de-escalate. But when one of them rushed forward with the camera, I stepped between them. That's when the physical part started."

Mallory nodded. "And the injury?"

"Fell. Caught my arm on a pile of wooden stakes or edging. Sharp enough to slice deep."

Mallory nodded slowly, his pen gliding across the page. He asked her to recount the sequence—what she did when Nate told her to go inside, what she could hear from the other side of the glass door.

"Did you see what happened in the backyard after you went inside?"

"No," she whispered, her chest tightening. "I couldn't see him anymore. I—I didn't know where Nate went. I didn't know what was happening. It was... it was the worst part. Not knowing."

Her voice cracked then, and Nate's hand tightened on her leg, his thumb still moving, still steady.

"You did everything right," Detective Mallory said, his voice softening enough to settle her frayed edges. "We've already started reviewing footage from nearby homes and traffic cameras. And one suspect is already in custody."

Amelia blinked. "Seriously?"

Mallory gave a slight nod. "Picked up near here—ditched the camera equipment and tried to blend in on foot. Your security team responded promptly. That helped a lot."

Nate nodded. "Luke and Tyler handled things fast."

He continued with a few more questions about the front door, Tyler's arrival, and whether Amelia had seen the camera gear, which the paparazzi had dropped when they fled.

"It all happened so fast," she admitted. "One minute we were eating dinner... the next, it felt like the walls weren't safe anymore."

Mallory gave another slight nod, his understanding quiet but solid. "That's how it goes sometimes," he said. "The world shifts, and it takes a little while to feel your feet under you again."

When the questions got harder, Nate's hand stayed steady, grounding her. He didn't speak unless she needed him. Unmoving. Unwavering. Her anchor.

"I should've seen it coming," Nate muttered as the interview wound down, eyes darkening. "This isn't the first time someone's crossed a line."

Mallory gave him a long look. "They went beyond a line tonight. Trespass. Assault. And if we find the other man, there may be a conspiracy. This isn't on you."

Mallory left his business card on the fridge before he departed, promising to follow up soon.

"If you remember anything else, or if you need to talk through something, call," he said, tapping his card once for emphasis. "You're not alone in this."

When the door closed, Amelia let out a long breath she didn't know she'd been holding.

The silence that followed felt strangely heavy. Her body hadn't caught up to the fact that the threat was gone, but her heart was still sprinting. She pressed her palm lightly to her chest, trying to coax her pulse to settle.

Nate rose from the table first, pulling her into his arms, pressing a soft kiss to her hair. "You did amazing, Mils."

"That's done," he said softly, wrapping his arms around her tightly.

"Yeah," she said, leaning into him. "That's done."

There was a long beat of stillness between them. Then she added, "I'm so glad one of them is in custody. Knowing that..."

Nate nodded against her temple. "Yeah. Same. It doesn't fix everything, but—it helps. A lot."

She exhaled into his chest, her fingers curling slightly into the back of his shirt. "One less thing to worry about, for now at least."

They stood there for a moment, letting the quiet settle around them—until it didn't.

The buzzing started again. Persistent. Unrelenting.

His phone lit up on the table behind them.

Text after text. Call after call.

Amelia nudged his shoulder playfully. "You should probably talk to Cassidy."

"I know." He kissed her cheek. "Mike, too."

"Go. Handle your Hollywood life." She smiled, trying to keep the tone light. "I'll be here, holding down the Colorado fort."

* * *

RONNIE ALWAYS HAD perfect timing—especially when caffeine and emotional triage were involved.

The front door creaked open, and her voice rang out like it belonged there.

"Hey! I come bearing pastries and moral support."

Amelia beamed as she walked in, holding a paper bag and two to-go cups. "Perfect timing."

"I wanted to get here sooner," Ronnie said, setting everything down. "Luke told me what happened. Are you okay? I've been freaking out all morning."

"I'm okay." Amelia hugged her tightly. "It was a lot, but I'm okay."

Nate greeted Ronnie with a quick hug of his own. "I'm going to call Mike and Cassidy. You two catch up."

"Take your time," Ronnie said with a knowing grin.

When the door closed behind him, Ronnie turned back to Amelia with her signature raised eyebrow. "Okay, so—really, how are you?"

Amelia sank onto the couch. "It was terrifying, Ronnie. I thought something happened to him. I thought I was going to lose him."

Ronnie sat beside her, her expression softening. "I know. Luke told me it got pretty bad. He is shook up, too."

"Really?" Amelia asked, surprised.

"Yeah. He said he's ramping up security quickly. He's already pulled in two more guards. Luke doesn't take this lightly."

Amelia smiled faintly. "He's good at what he does."

"He is," Ronnie agreed. "And apparently... pretty easy on the eyes."

Amelia grinned. "Oh? Something you want to share?"

Ronnie waved her off, but a pink flush crept up her neck. "I mean, he's nice. And smart. And probably impossible since he lives in LA."

"You know you sound exactly like me, right?" Amelia teased.

Ronnie rolled her eyes, stealing a pastry. "Don't turn this around on me."

"No, seriously," Amelia pushed, her smile growing. "What's going on with you two?"

Ronnie shrugged, but didn't deny it. "There's... something. I don't know. It's easy when we're together. He makes me laugh. And I kind of like that he's a little intense."

Amelia raised an eyebrow. "You like intense now?"

"I might," Ronnie admitted, laughing.

Their ease was so natural, so familiar, that Amelia finally exhaled the weight of the past twenty-four hours.

Ronnie's gaze softened. "And you?"

"I told him I love him," Amelia said, her voice quieter now, more settled. "And I do. I do."

Ronnie's smile bloomed wide. "Wow. That's beautiful."

"I know it probably seems fast," Amelia admitted. "But it doesn't feel that way to me. Every moment with him feels... real. Honest. Like I've known him longer than I have."

Ronnie nodded, her expression full of something deeper than surprise. "Love doesn't work on a timeline, Lane. It's not about how long—it's about how true. And you wouldn't say it if you didn't mean it."

Amelia felt her throat tighten, the truth of it sitting warm in her chest.

"I've been so afraid to say it," she murmured. "As if it meant I was letting go of Grace. But... I think I'm understanding that love isn't limited. It's not a fixed thing. It grows. It includes. Nate's not replacing anything. He's part of the next chapter. At least I hope so."

Ronnie reached for her hand and gave it a squeeze. "Then hold the pen, babe. Write it how you want.”

“Grace would want that for you.”

Amelia nodded, tears brimming. “I think so, too.”

Ronnie playfully nudged her. “Now, seriously. When’s the last time you showered? You smell like sleep and trauma.”

Amelia laughed, wiping her eyes. “Thanks for the support.”

“Come on,” Ronnie grinned, pulling her up. “We’re going to make you human again.”

Upstairs, Amelia turned on the shower while Ronnie perched on the closed toilet lid, scrolling through her phone. The door stayed open; the steam rising as Amelia stepped inside.

From behind the curtain, Amelia called out, “So, Luke, huh? You sure there’s nothing more there?”

“I didn’t say there was nothing,” Ronnie called back, smirking. “It’s complicated.”

“Sounds familiar.”

“Oh, shut up.”

They both laughed, the sound light and easy.

As Amelia rinsed the conditioner from her hair, she let herself feel the comfort of this—her best friend upstairs, the man she loved downstairs, her house still standing.

Maybe life didn’t have to be either-or.

Maybe she could have this.

Maybe she already did.

When she emerged, wrapped in a towel, Ronnie was still scrolling through her phone.

“Anything interesting?”

“Only Luke texting me to make sure you’re okay.”

Amelia’s eyebrows lifted. “Oh?”

Ronnie shrugged, trying to look unaffected. “He’s being thorough.”

“Sure he is,” Amelia teased, bumping her shoulder.

They grinned at each other, holding a secret no one else knew.

By the time Amelia changed and they went back downstairs, Nate was off the phone and waiting with fresh cups of coffee.

He stood, pulling Amelia close the second she reached him, pressing a kiss to her hair. "Everything's handled for now."

She melted into him, letting the solid weight of him soak through her skin. "Thank you."

"For what?"

"For loving me like this."

He kissed her again, behind her ear. "It's the easiest thing I've ever done."

Ronnie groaned playfully. "Okay, I'm leaving. Too much sweetness in the air."

"You love it," Amelia called after her as Ronnie grabbed her bag.

"I do," Ronnie agreed, grinning as she slipped out the door. "See you two lovebirds later."

* * *

WHEN THE DOOR clicked shut, Nate and Amelia settled into the couch, their fingers laced together, their pulses finally slowing.

"Everything okay?" she asked, sliding her feet into his lap.

"Mostly." He ran his hand over her shin, slow and absent. "I talked to Mike. He's doing what he can to control the press side of this, but it's...messy. He's spinning it as a story about me lying low after a rough shoot, needing downtime. He's trying to keep you out of it, but it might be too late."

She bit her lip. "What about Cassidy?"

He let out a breath through his nose. "She's pissed. Not about us—well, maybe a little—but mostly because I've been ignoring her calls again. I told her I've got things to handle here, and she didn't argue after that. I think she gets it now."

Amelia's eyes softened. "That's progress, right?"

"Yeah, but..." He hesitated, his thumb brushing idle circles against her skin. "My mom called, too. She saw some photos online. She was worried at first, thinking I was in trouble or doing something reckless. But then—" his mouth tipped into a small, knowing smile—"she wanted to know who the pretty girl in all the pictures was."

Amelia's stomach flipped. "What did you tell her?"

His grin deepened. "I told her you're my girlfriend and I love you."

Her breath caught, warmth flooding her chest in a way she hadn't expected. "Girlfriend?"

"Yeah." His voice softened, sincere. "That you're more than someone I'm seeing. That you're the person who makes me feel like I can breathe. That you're someone I want to bring home. Someone who matters."

The weight of those words settled in her chest, both terrifying and thrilling.

"Your mom must think I'm nuts," Amelia said, trying to brush it off with a light laugh.

"She thinks you're exactly what I've needed." He squeezed her calf, his gaze steady. "She told me not to screw it up."

Amelia's heart stuttered, then kicked into overdrive. Everything around her kept moving, but this settled deep in her chest—undeniable and sure.

Nate shifted, reaching for his phone. "You haven't seen the pictures yet, have you?"

Her stomach turned at the thought. "I've seen enough of myself in hospital press releases to know I don't want to see whatever's floating around now."

But curiosity tugged at her ribs. It was her world they had stepped into. Her quiet coffee shop. Her sleepy streets. Her front porch.

"Show me," she said, bracing herself.

Nate pulled up a gallery of paparazzi shots, scrolling through carefully. "Okay, so this is the first one. We're at the coffee shop. This is you ordering for both of us. That barista looks like she's going to pass out."

Amelia groaned softly, half-embarrassed, half-fascinated. "Oh, my God."

"This one's us walking down Main Street. I love this one. You're laughing, and I'm staring at you, already a complete goner."

Her throat tightened as he flipped to the next image—a shot of her porch, of them eating dinner, of him reaching across the table to take her hand.

"They were this close?" she whispered, her chest hollowing. "They were in my backyard. On my street."

"I know," Nate said, his voice thickening with guilt. "And I hate that."

Her pulse thudded heavily, the layers of this pressing in. It was one thing to be seen with him in Denver, in public spaces. It was another to feel like the walls of her life were no longer hers.

"You're supposed to go back to L.A. in three days," she said quietly, her gaze fixed on the phone screen. "What happens then?"

His thumb brushed over the back of her hand. "I'll come back. I'll make time. But Luke's going to stay here for a while. I don't want you left without protection until things cool down."

Her heart clenched at the word *protection*. She wasn't used to needing that. But suddenly the idea of him leaving—of being in this house without him—felt impossibly heavy.

"Hey," he said, gently tilting her chin so she would look at him. "I know all of this is because of me. And I hate that. But I'm here, Amelia. Whatever this takes—I'm in."

Amelia swallowed hard, but the knot in her throat wouldn't budge. She was falling deeper than she'd ever thought possible—and the idea of losing him, even temporarily, made her chest ache.

"Okay," she whispered, leaning into his touch. "We'll figure it out."

# 19

## the socialite

AMELIA STARED AT herself in the bathroom mirror, fingertips braced against the cool porcelain of the sink.

Her reflection looked tired, with dark circles under her eyes, and her hair twisted into a loose bun she hadn't bothered to redo since waking up. She hadn't slept well.

Not because of anything Nate had done—he'd been perfect. Quiet. Protective.

The night before had ended softly, with Luke stopping by and delivering pizza—his version of a peace offering and a security directive rolled into one. He'd stood by the counter and declared, in no uncertain terms, that there would be no more unmonitored deliveries to the house. No more strangers on the porch. No more chances taken.

They'd eaten at the kitchen counter, the three of them, with Nate unusually quiet and Luke trying to fill the space with logistics—security rotations, car patrols, updates from the detective.

But the night had ended early. The exhaustion was too heavy. No one said it, but they all knew—this wasn't over.

And now, staring at her worn expression, Amelia couldn't shake the feeling that the worst was still coming.

She could smell the storm on the wind, even if it hadn't arrived. The danger hadn't ended—it had simply changed shape.

She exhaled slowly, pressing her palms flat against the countertop. Then she pushed away from the mirror and headed for her home office, determined to focus on the donor stewardship plans waiting in her inbox.

But the tension hovered right outside the door.

So did Nate.

Every so often, she'd catch him pacing the hallway quietly—looping past her office as if he was trying not to disturb her but also couldn't bring himself to sit still. Once, she saw him pause at the window and stare out across the backyard, his jaw tight, hands flexing like he was fighting some invisible urge.

Finally, she leaned out of her chair. "Hey," she called, lightening her voice deliberately. "Are you doing laps, or is this your way of training for a very slow marathon?"

Nate stopped and looked over at her, forcing a faint smile—but it was the kind that barely brushed the surface. His eyes gave him away.

"Just... walking," he said.

She tried again. "You're stressing me out. Come on. Let's eat some cold pizza. It's practically a rite of passage."

"Yeah," he murmured, his voice trailing off. "Pizza sounds good."

They made their way downstairs together. Nate pulled the box from the fridge and set it on the counter, flipping the lid open without a word. Four slices remained unevenly arranged and cold. He stared at them for a beat too long, as if they might answer a question he hadn't asked yet.

Amelia kept her eyes on him, a flicker of knowing settling in—he had something to say, and no idea how to begin.

She peeled a slice from the box—stiff and slightly curled at the edges—and grabbed a napkin from the drawer. "You know, there should be a dating app filter for people who still eat cold pizza without reheating it," she said. "It would weed out the amateurs."

Usually, that would've earned her a smirk or a quip. But Nate didn't bite.

He gave a distracted hum and reached for a slice of his own, his gaze already drifting.

Something in her tightened.

Amelia carried her pizza to the living room and flopped onto the couch, grabbing the remote from the coffee table. She started flipping through channels with no real intention of watching anything — trying to fill the room with noise. Movement. Something.

The silence felt too loud. And Nate's silence? Even louder.

She didn't ask what was on his mind.

Not yet.

But she could feel it pressing in around them, waiting.

The channels kept flicking—nature doc, sitcom rerun, commercial, something about antique cars. Her thumb moved without thought.

Then the logo for a Hollywood gossip show filled the screen.

She hesitated.

Her thumb hovered over the remote.

She should have changed it.

Should have kept flipping.

But she didn't.

The volume wasn't loud, but it was loud enough.

The host's glossy smile beamed across the screen as the segment began.

"Turn it off," Nate said suddenly, his voice tight. "Mils—please. I want to talk to you first. Please... turn it off."

But Amelia didn't move.

Couldn't.

She was frozen.

"Nate Carter's mystery woman spotted in Colorado! Who is she, and what does this mean for his L.A. girlfriend, Savannah Lord?"

The breath whooshed out of Amelia's lungs so fast she thought she might faint.

She felt the room tilt slightly, her pulse pounding in her throat.

*L.A. Girlfriend? Savannah Lord?*

Her heart slammed painfully against her ribs. Her fingers slackened on the remote.

Her voice barely formed the words.

"What girlfriend?" she asked, her voice barely a whisper, her throat tightening as she slowly turned to face him.

Nate's head snapped toward the screen, his eyes narrowing with intensity that could burn the whole segment to the ground.

"They've got it wrong," he said immediately, his voice tight. "There is no girlfriend."

The show continued. Now flashing photos.

Nate exiting a hotel in L.A., two days before flying to Denver.

The woman beside him—Savannah—turned slightly, her hand resting low on her stomach.

Her body language is unmistakable.

As if she were trying to signal something.

A pregnancy.

The host continued chirpily, 'Speculation is swirling online that the socialite may be pregnant—and Nate Carter is the rumored father. No official confirmation yet, but insiders close to the actress say they've "been spending time together again" after filming their latest project.'

Amelia's stomach twisted, nausea rising sharp and vicious.

"Nate," her voice cracked, splintering under the weight, "what is this? What is this?"

His hands flew up, a desperate attempt to keep everything from unraveling. "I had lunch with her. That's it. Just lunch."

He stepped closer, his panic bleeding through his voice. "She's not my girlfriend. She never was. Amelia, please, they're twisting this. It's what they do."

"She's your costar," Amelia whispered, every insecurity, every buried fear coming up in tidal waves. "You filmed an entire movie together. You're Nate Carter. She's a socialite. Of course, they think you're dating."

"We're not," he pressed, his voice breaking in all the wrong places. "We're not. I haven't dated her. I haven't been with her. I haven't—" He ran his hands through his hair as if he wanted to tear the whole moment apart. "She's struggling, Mils. Her recent breakup. Her mental health. I only wanted to be there for her as a friend."

But Amelia couldn't hear anything past the word "pregnant."

Pregnant.

Of course. Of course, that would be part of it.

And now—now she was the woman on the side? The mistake? The headline?

She felt sick. Trapped in the story she'd never want to be part of—one that could take everything from someone else.

She would never forgive herself for being part of tearing another woman's life apart.

She'd experienced unfathomable loss.

She would never cause it.

Her head spun as the thoughts crashed over her. It was too much. It was everything she'd feared. That this—whatever this was—was temporary. That she was temporary.

"It's true, isn't it?" she said, her voice hollow, barely holding itself together. She locked her arms around her torso, as if bracing against the fallout. "The photos. The timing. The way she's holding her stomach, already laying claim to the future—*your* future. You look every bit the guy who came to Colorado to hide out with his 'other' girl, and I look like the fool who never saw it coming."

"That's not what this is!" His voice snapped, then softened as quickly as it had risen. "I met her for lunch because she asked me to. I didn't think—"

"No. You didn't think." The tears stung, but she forced herself to blink them away. "You didn't think about me. About this. About how this would look."

"Mils, I thought you knew me better than this."

Her chest tightened, but she shook her head and stepped back, as if distance might dull the ache. "I thought I did, too."

He flinched—an involuntary jolt, as if her words had struck harder than any hand.

A beat of silence followed, thick and heavy.

Nate met her eyes, waiting—hoping—for her to return to him in some small way, to take it back, to say she didn't mean it. But she didn't. She couldn't.

Because that would mean pretending this didn't hurt. That it didn't confirm every fear she'd buried.The words hung between them, brittle and final.

Nate took a small step forward, but Amelia held her ground, her breath shallow and uneven. Everything inside her screamed to pull away—to retreat to safety before the weight of disappointment crushed her again.

She wrapped her arms around herself, trying to quiet the shaking.

He said the right things. He always did. But this wasn't about words anymore.

This was about what came after. What always came after.

"Nate, come on. You're supposed to go back to L.A. in two days. You expect me to believe you're going to walk away from that entire world? From her?"

She hated how bitter her voice sounded. Hated that it came from a place so wounded, it couldn't help but sting. But the words had sharp edges, and they flew out anyway, too fast to catch.

He was leaving whether he meant to or not.

The last time she'd heard those words—"I didn't mean to"—it had been Grant.

He'd stood in their old doorway, a duffel bag slung over his shoulder, his eyes hollow from grief. He'd promised to call and vowed to come back and talk when things weren't so heavy. But he never did.

She remembered sitting in the kitchen hours later, waiting for the sound of his keys in the lock and waiting for him to come back and choose her. He didn't.

The house emptied after that. Slowly. Piece by piece. Until Amelia was the only thing left.

And now she stood here again. A kitchen. A man with a packed bag. A conversation teetering at the edge of goodbye.

Somewhere deep in her chest, something snapped

Nate's eyes locked on hers, his chest rising fast with each breath.

"I would walk away from *everything* if it meant keeping you. I don't give a damn about the press, or premieres, or Savannah, or whatever story they're spinning."

His voice shook—not from anger, but from the weight of everything he hadn't been able to protect her from.

"I didn't come to Colorado to escape anything. I came here because of you. And I stayed because I wanted to. Because I needed to. Because you're the only thing that's felt real in a long time."

The words should have landed as an anchor—strong, steady, grounding. But they didn't.

Because she didn't feel real—not anymore. Not in this world of rumors and headlines and pictures she couldn't unsee.

Her legs wobbled under her. She wanted to believe him so badly.

God, she wanted to.

But her body had already decided.  She was folding in on herself and shutting doors before they slammed in her face. The doubt clawed its way up faster than she could reason with.

"I'm not built for this," she whispered, her voice shredding apart. "I can't be this girl, Nate. I'm a fool."

"You're not a fool," he said quickly, desperate.

"I am," she choked. "I thought I could do this. I thought we could...make this work. But I don't belong in your world. I don't think I ever did."

And if Savannah *was* pregnant—

If that possibility was even remotely real—

Then what was she?

A placeholder. A detour. A secret.

His body sagged, as if her words had knocked the wind out of him.

"Don't do this. Don't push me away."

"I'm not pushing you," she said, her voice shaking.  "I'm protecting myself."

And that was the truth. Brutal. Icy. Necessary.

The lump in her throat was suffocating. Her ribs ached from holding herself so tightly together.

She could already feel the walls rising, the lock clicking into place. It was always safer on the other side of the wall.

Her throat burned. "I think you should go."

"Mils, no. Please don't do this."

"You can call me when you're home," she added, her heart physically breaking in her chest. "But not now. Not today."

The moment she said it, she felt the break—clean and final. A cliff edge that didn't have a path back.

He stayed frozen, his breath coming fast and shallow, struggling to pull air through the panic rising in his chest.

His hands curled into fists at his sides, his whole body screaming that he wanted to fight for her, but something in his eyes said he knew he'd already lost.

"You're running," he said finally, the words thick with pain.

"And you're leaving." Her voice was cold now, her walls climbing fast and hard.

He stepped toward her, his movements careful, then pressed a soft kiss to her forehead.

"I'm not giving up on us."

She didn't answer. Couldn't.

She wanted to believe him. She wanted to scream that she loved him. That she wanted him to stay. But the voice in her head—sharp, familiar, brutal—whispered that she couldn't trust this.

Couldn't trust him.

Couldn't trust herself.

A thick silence pulsed between them.

"I need to pack," Nate said finally, his voice raw. "I'll—I'll grab my stuff."

She stayed silent and turned away while he moved past her, climbing the stairs with slow, heavy steps.

Amelia sank back onto the couch, her chest hollow, her arms wrapped tightly around herself as the sound of his footsteps faded. She sat there, staring blankly at the television, her body shaking as the tears came harder, faster, completely uncontrollable.

Upstairs, she could hear the distant rustling of drawers, the soft scrape of a zipper, the faint thump of his backpack hitting the floor. She pressed her palms against her face, trying to breathe, trying to steady herself, but it was impossible.

Minutes passed—she wasn't sure how many—before she heard his foot-steps on the stairs again. She slowly rose, wiping her tear-streaked face with the sleeve of her sweater, and crossed to the door. Her hand wrapped around the doorknob as Nate reached the entryway.

His duffel bag was slung over his shoulder, his face carved with frustration, pain, and something that looked dangerously close to heartbreak.

"Mils, please," he whispered, his voice fraying. "Please don't do this. I love you. You don't have to do this."

Her grip tightened on the doorknob, every muscle straining to hold back the scream clawing its way up.

"Goodbye, Nate."

His jaw tensed, ready to push, to fight—but he didn't. The tension drained from his shoulders, leaving him hollow. He stepped closer and pressed a final kiss to her forehead; the goodbye settling in his silence.

"I'm not giving up on us," he said quietly. "I'll wait."

She couldn't speak. Couldn't even nod. She turned the knob and slowly opened the door.

He paused for a heartbeat, eyes locked on hers, words hovering—but he turned, stepped through the doorway, and disappeared down the porch stairs.

Amelia shut the door, the soft click sounding louder than it should have.

And then she crumpled. Right there against the door, sliding down to the floor, her sobs cracking wide open, shaking through every inch of her. She clutched her knees to her chest and cried harder than she had in years; the grief coming in waves that wouldn't stop.

Not just for him.

For Grace.

For Grant.

For the life she thought she might finally be brave enough to start again.

Gone.

In a breath, in a blink.

Just like that.

Minutes blurred into hours. Her body eventually went still, her chest hollow, her tears long since dried.

When she finally forced herself to stand, the house was quiet in a way that felt unbearable.

She dragged herself up the stairs, each step heavier than the last. When she pushed open her bedroom door, she froze.

Nate's hoodie lay abandoned on the edge of the bed—the gray one that had become like a second skin to him, its sleeve still bearing the faint rust-colored mark from that frightful night.

Draped over it was a small, folded note.

Her fingers trembled as she picked it up and read the three simple words:

*I'll be here.*

The note slipped from her hand as she gripped the hoodie to her chest, breathing in the faint trace of him that still lingered in the fabric.

It smelled of warmth, of safety, of everything she had just released.

She climbed into bed without changing, without turning off the light, without thinking.

And the moment her body hit the mattress, the memories rushed in.

Every kiss. Every whisper. The way he had held her when she cried. The way he had made her laugh so hard she'd nearly fallen off this very bed.

The way he'd looked at her made it feel as if she were the only thing in the world worth staying for.

She curled around the hoodie and pulled it tighter, burying her face into the fabric, and a new lake of tears found its way out of her body.

Hot. Exhausting. Endless.

His weight was everywhere. And she wasn't sure how to carry it.

When Nate's name lit up her phone later that night, she didn't answer.

Not that night.

Not the next day.

Not the day after that.

Not even when his voicemails filled up her inbox.

The first one was soft, tentative.

"Mils, please. Call me. I can explain this better. I can fix this."

The second cracked in the middle.

"I hate that this is how we left it. I hate that I hurt you. I didn't mean to."

The third?

Hoarse, quiet, and broken.

"I love you, Mils. Please let me fix this. Please."

But she didn't pick up.

She couldn't.

Because somewhere inside, the belief had already rooted itself.

That she didn't belong in his life.

That maybe she never had.

That maybe love wasn't enough this time.

And that terrified her more than anything.

And no amount of "I love you" could fix that.

# 20

# radio silence

THE DAYS STRETCHED long.

Then longer.

Then they folded into each other until Amelia couldn't remember what day it was anymore. She stopped checking.

Stopped looking to see who was calling her phone. Stopped listening to Nate's voicemails.

Stopped trying to tell herself this would pass. It didn't seem that it would.

The second week had been the worst. Or maybe the third. She wasn't sure anymore. There wasn't a clean line between the beginning and the middle of this ache.

Just the fact that he was gone.

That he kept trying to call.

And that she wouldn't let herself answer.

The first few days, she'd stared at the screen when his name lit up, her chest constricting so tightly she thought it might snap her ribs clean in half. His voicemails came one after another. Some long. Some only his breathing before he'd quietly hang up.

Eventually, she stopped playing them.

But the voicemails didn't stop. They changed.

Some days, he called to tell her about his day. About what he was cooking, or that his mom had asked about her, or that he was still watching that dumb movie they'd started when she fell asleep on him.

Some were raw.

"Mils, please. I can't — I can't sleep. I keep looking for you and you're not there."

One cracked under the weight of itself. "It's me. I'm the problem. I didn't protect this the way I should have."

One was almost angry. "I hate that you won't answer. I hate that you don't believe me."

One came late at night. "I swear to you, I was never with Savannah. Not once. It's not my baby. It was never mine. And I hate I have to say this into a machine instead of to your face."

And one was soft but certain. "I'll walk away, Mils, from everything. I'll leave the movies, the press, LA—all of it. None of it makes sense without you. Nothing's worth losing you for."

Then it softened again. "I love you. That's all I know. That's all I'll ever know."

There were so many now that her mailbox filled up, then filled up again. She'd clear the inbox without listening. Without letting them in. Without letting him in. She couldn't bear to hear his voice anymore. Not when it made her knees weak, not when it made her want to run back to him.

One night, her phone buzzed slightly after midnight. She didn't recognize the number. She nearly declined it, but something in her gut told her to answer. When she did, Cassidy's voice filtered through.

"Amelia, hey. I—I didn't know if I should call you. I wasn't sure you'd even pick up."

Amelia's stomach flipped. "Cassidy?"

"Yeah. I'm sorry to call so late. It's…Nate's not doing great. I know we don't know each other very well, but I thought you'd want to know. He's— he's shutting down."

Amelia pressed her eyes shut, gripping the phone tighter. "Why are you telling me this?"

"Because he won't." Cassidy's voice was steady but soft. "He's too proud. But he's a mess, Amelia. He's not working. He's not eating right. He's just—he's waiting for you. And I think you're the only person who can fix this."

Amelia's throat closed. "I can't talk to him."

"I think you can," Cassidy said gently. "But if you can't, please...don't stop loving him."

Cassidy's voice softened. "He loves you. And... for what it's worth? I get it now. I didn't before. But I do now."

"And Amelia...I owe you an apology."

Amelia sat straighter, the rawness in Cassidy's tone catching her off guard.

"For leaving the hospital the way I did," Cassidy continued, her words breaking around the edges. "I shouldn't have slipped out without saying goodbye."

There was a pause, a faint breath in Amelia's ear as if Cassidy were trying to steady herself.

"That morning, before the hospital, I got a call about a family emergency," she said quietly. "It rattled me. And then...I saw you and Nate together."

Cassidy's voice softened further, threaded with something fragile. "I knew he was in good hands. It felt like the right time to step back and deal with my own world for a while."

Amelia's breath caught, surprised by the honesty. "Cassidy..."

"I don't say this often," Cassidy continued, a faint edge of her usual sharpness returning, "but I was wrong about you. You care about him. Maybe more than anyone else ever could. And that matters. So...thank you."

Emotion pressed tight in Amelia's chest. "Take care of yourself, Cassidy."

"I will. You too."

The call ended with a quiet click, and Amelia sat there on the edge of her bed, her chest caving in on itself. This time, she didn't delete Cassidy's number; she saved it.

The next morning, the flowers started appearing.

First roses.

Then wild bouquets in every shade of spring.

Then magnolias.

At first, she'd been home to turn the delivery drivers away. She'd barely opened the door, shaking her head, her voice so quiet it barely registered. "No. I don't want them."

When she wasn't home, she'd come back to find them waiting on her doorstep. Dozens of them. A new one every day.

She stopped bringing them inside.

But Luke and Tyler started collecting them, anyway. Quietly placing the bouquets on her kitchen counter when they knew she wouldn't fight them on it.

Sometimes she'd catch Luke glancing at her as if he wanted to say something. Maybe he thought she was being ridiculous. Or perhaps he felt she'd cave soon. But he never said a word. Just left the flowers there.

And the house slowly filled with them.

A garden of apology. A museum of regret.

She hated them. She hated that she loved them.

Sometimes she'd crush a petal between her fingers to remind herself it wasn't a dream.

Sometimes she'd stand in the middle of the kitchen, her heart pounding, wondering if Nate had picked any of them himself or if his manager had called a florist and said, "Whatever you've got, send it."

She told herself the magnolias were random, just another flower from another florist, but her chest tightened every time she saw them.

She kept her phone on silent now. Easier that way.

One night, while wandering downstairs in his pajamas, his name lit up her screen at 2:17 a.m. She stared at it, the blue light washing over her face in the darkness of her bedroom. Her finger trembled as it hovered over the answer button. The phone vibrated against her palm once, twice, three times.

"Mils, please," she whispered to herself, echoing what she knew he'd say.

Her thumb slipped. The screen went dark.

She slid down the wall until she hit the floor, knees pulled to her chest, and cried until her ribs felt bruised from the inside out.

* * *

SHE STOPPED WALKING by Grace's old house. She stopped visiting the cemetery.

They weren't sacred anymore. They'd become reminders of what else she'd lost.

Grace.

Nate.

Herself.

Even her walking routes changed. She used to weave through the familiar streets of Longmont without thinking—past the hospital, past the house she and Grant had bought, past the parks she and Grace had played in. Now she walked in the opposite direction.

Toward the unfamiliar. Toward streets she'd never explored. Toward a tiny convenience store three blocks further than she needed to go, to avoid the places that held his memory. To avoid the streets where the air still felt thick with him.

She went there to buy milk she didn't need. A pack of gum she'd never open. She needed somewhere to go that wasn't soaked in ghosts.

She turned corners for no reason at all, sometimes circling the same block twice. Forward no longer meant progress—it meant moving her feet until she could return home and sink back into the quiet.

One afternoon, while tracing a new route through a side street she'd never walked before, she glimpsed her reflection in a store window.

She barely recognized herself. Pale, small, shoulders drawn in as if she were going to fold into herself. She didn't stop. Just kept walking.

Kept moving.

The ache was steady now. A dull hum in her chest. It didn't burn anymore. It didn't twist. It just...was.

The only thing she still allowed was the sweatshirt.

She'd found it again days after he'd left, crumpled in the corner of her bedroom where she'd tossed it the day after he left.

She told herself she wouldn't pick it up.

But her fingers found the fabric, anyway.

She clutched it hard, a lifeline in her grasp—gripping it as if holding tight might keep her from falling apart.

Some nights she wore it. Some nights, she buried her face in it.

Most nights, she did both.

The house felt impossibly big now. Too many rooms. Too many walls. Too much space for the silence to echo in.

She stopped watching TV. Stopped sitting on the couch. Stopped looking at the DVD player.

Everything seemed to watch her, the air itself thick with attention.

Waiting for her to press play.

Waiting for her to let him back in.

She couldn't. She wouldn't.

She started spending more time in her home office, flipping mindlessly through quarterly giving campaigns she never finished. She would open her inbox, skim emails, and close her laptop. Then open it again. Sometimes she'd stare at the screen, the numbers blurring, the words dissolving before they could settle.

She didn't go back to the hospital.

Couldn't.

The halls felt tainted now. Every corner of that place had Nate's finger-prints on it. The staff had stopped asking when she'd be back. She'd made it clear she was working remotely. Indefinitely.

The coffee shop had lost its comfort, too.

She stepped inside once, the scent of croissant sandwiches dragging her back to a day that now lived in another lifetime.

She didn't sit. Didn't order her usual. Grabbed a chai latte and left, pretending not to notice the barista's flicker of recognition.

The girl behind the counter offered a soft, sympathetic smile—knowing, almost too knowing—as if the entire world had already decided what happened to the mystery woman who vanished as quickly as she appeared.

Ronnie's calls came on schedule, steady and unrelenting.

At first, they'd been playful. "Still alive in there? Blink twice if you've showered this week."

Then they'd turned exasperated.

"Okay, zombie girl, you need to get your ass up and move. Now."

Then quiet. Serious.

"Amelia, I'm worried about you."

Ronnie tried stopping by most days. Sometimes bringing food, sometimes dragging Amelia into conversations about everything except Nate.

But it was never far from either of their minds.

"Eat," Ronnie would scold gently, pushing a container of soup toward her. "Your body needs fuel. And if you don't, I'm calling your mother."

Amelia smirked weakly. "Joke's on you. She wouldn't answer."

Ronnie's face softened. "Okay, fair. But seriously, you need to get out of this house."

She'd sit with Amelia on the back porch, sometimes for hours, filling the space with updates about her life, her work, and the couple's hiking trip coming up.

"Thinking about inviting Luke," Ronnie mused one afternoon, sipping from a plastic cup. "But honestly, I don't want to leave you."

Amelia shook her head firmly. "You should go. You should definitely take Luke. Don't worry about me."

"Of course I'm gonna worry about you. You're my best friend."

"I'll be fine," Amelia lied.

Ronnie studied her carefully, then sighed. "Luke says Nate's not doing so hot."

The words stung. They always did.

"Says he barely leaves his apartment," Ronnie added softly. "He only goes to the studio when he absolutely has to. Spends most of his time at home. Alone."

A twist of nerves coiled low in Amelia's belly.

She picked at the sleeve of Nate's hoodie, her thumb tracing the rip in the fabric where he'd gotten cut.

"Still sending flowers?" she asked, her voice small.

Ronnie nodded. "Yeah. Luke says Nate's the one picking them out now. Every single one."

Amelia's throat tightened. "Doesn't matter."

"Doesn't it?" Ronnie pressed.

Amelia didn't answer.

Because it mattered, it mattered so much that she could barely breathe around it.

A few days later, when Ronnie dropped by, the usual rhythm between them cracked.

Ronnie snapped the moment Amelia brushed off lunch.

"You can't keep living like this," Ronnie said, her voice sharp, her patience finally thinning. "You think this is helping? You think this is strong?"

Amelia flinched, caught off guard by Ronnie's tone.

"This isn't strength, Lane. This is punishment. For you. For him. For everyone who's still trying to show up for you."

Amelia's throat burned. "I can't—"

"You can," Ronnie cut in. "You just won't."

The words hung there, electric and awful.

Ronnie's voice broke as she softened. "But don't pretend this is working. I can't keep watching you disappear piece by piece."

Amelia blinked fast, her chest tightening.

Ronnie shook her head, pulling her into a quick, fierce hug. "I love you. But you have to stop hiding."

Amelia didn't answer. Not with words.

She nodded into Ronnie's shoulder, even though she wasn't sure she agreed.

She wasn't hiding. She was surviving.

There was a difference—wasn't there?

The trouble was, she wasn't sure anymore.

When Ronnie finally left, the house felt even quieter than before.

Later that week, Luke stopped by to check on security. He lingered in the kitchen, watching Amelia silently as she fiddled with a chipped mug.

"You know he's not giving up on you, right?" Luke said, finally, his voice quiet but firm.

Amelia didn't look up. "I can't call him."

"You won't call him."

The correction landed with the weight of a stone—small but heavy, impossible to ignore.

"You think this is what he wanted?" Luke pressed. "For you to shut him out? For you to shut yourself down?"

She gripped her mug tighter.

"All you're doing is proving him right—that you don't believe in this. That you don't believe in him."

Her throat ached, the lump sitting heavy.

"I've seen him fight for things most people would walk away from," Luke added. "But even Nate Carter can't battle against what you refuse to let him confront."

He let the silence sit, then turned and left.

And Amelia stayed there, her knuckles white against the mug, her stomach knotted.

Because the awful part was—Luke was right.

She wasn't letting Nate touch the broken parts.

She wasn't letting anyone touch them.

One afternoon, when Ronnie caught Amelia wearing Nate's hoodie for the third day in a row, she finally dropped all the teasing.

"You're allowed to call him, you know," Ronnie said gently. "You don't have to keep punishing yourself. Or him. It's been two months now, and neither of you has moved on."

Amelia's throat worked hard to find words. "I'm afraid if I call, it'll all come rushing back. And I don't know if I can survive losing him twice."

Ronnie's expression softened in the quietest, saddest way. "But you've already lost him once. And look—you're surviving that. Barely. But you are."

The words hung there, heavy and honest, and neither of them filled the silence.

But if she said it out loud, she wouldn't survive it.

She knew that.

So she kept breathing.

Kept pretending the loss of him didn't completely hollow her out.

She caught Luke's eyes sometimes when he'd pass through for security updates. He never pushed. Never told her to call Nate again. But she saw it in his face.

He wanted her to.

She couldn't.

She told herself this was self-preservation, a sign of strength. But neither rang true.

It felt more like waiting for something that would never arrive—

The hollow ache of every loss she'd ever carried.

And the house—full of his flowers, full of his ghost—kept waiting for her to make a move.

But she didn't. She wouldn't.

Not yet. Maybe never.

But even as the lie formed, even as the ache settled deeper, she pressed the hoodie tighter to her chest and inhaled.

Because it still smelled like him.

And no matter what she told herself, she wasn't ready to let that go.

The next day, an email notification pinged on her screen while she was half-reading a donor report she'd opened out of habit, not focus. She ignored it at first. But when she glanced again and saw the subject line—"Final Grace Gala Coverage: Photos & Press Release"—a cold flutter passed through her.

If it hadn't been her job, she would've closed the laptop and walked away. But this was her foundation. Her name. Her responsibility.

So she clicked.

The press release was glowing. Of course it was. Full of praise for the gala, for the volunteers, for the families. But mostly—for Nate.

Nate Carter's visit lit up the hospital. His speech moved people to tears. His smile brightened the room. The release described him as a "humble force of light" and credited him with bringing national attention to the event. There was a line that said, "His presence reminded us all of the power of hope."

Amelia read every word.

Then came the photos.

She scrolled through image after image. Nate beaming from the stage, his shoulder brushing hers. Nate kneeling at the bedside in 417, his attention fixed on the small face before him. Nate with his arms wrapped around Nurse Jenna, both of them teary-eyed. Nate mid-speech, his gaze piercing the camera lens with something raw and wounded behind his smile.

Then she stopped scrolling.

There they were, caught in a dance. His fingers pressed into the curve of her waist, her chin tipped up, mouth open in genuine laughter. Ballroom lights cast halos around them while other guests blurred into watercolor shapes. In that frozen moment, they existed without complications or pain.

The kind of photograph that deserved a silver frame. The type that belonged on a nightstand, where it could be the last thing seen before sleep and the first thing touched at dawn.

She loved it. She hated it.

She wanted to delete it.

She wanted to save it forever.

It was everything she missed and everything she wasn't ready to face.

It made her want to shut her laptop.

It made her want to call him.

*Focus, Amelia.*

There were also other pictures of her. She barely remembered the flash of most of them being taken. But there they were—moments frozen in time where she and Nate stood so close it hurt to look at.

She reviewed every image. Every caption. Every sentence of copy. And when she reached the end, she clicked reply and typed: "Approved. Beautifully done. Thank you all for your incredible work."

Her fingers hovered over the keyboard for a moment longer. She considered forwarding the file to Cassidy herself—a quick note, a professional courtesy. But it felt too close to something else, too close to touching Nate.

So instead, she added one final line to the email:

'Please loop in Cassidy Mercer for final approval before publication.'

And just like that, it was done.

Delegated. Distant. A door quietly closed.

What she wanted to say was:

Please handle this without me. This time.

And in a way, she had.

Not directly. Not emotionally. But enough.

So she pressed Send, closed her laptop, and sat there in silence.

The silence pulsed around her, tender to the touch.

# 21

## all alone

RONNIE DEPARTED a day ahead of schedule for the couple's hiking getaway. Luke arrived to collect her in his black SUV, packed with hiking equipment and a weekend's supply of enthusiasm. Amelia had encouraged them to leave early, saying she'd be okay.

"You deserve it, both of you," she told Ronnie on the porch. "You never stop showing up for me. Go let someone show up for you."

Ronnie hesitated, looking back at her, eyes narrowed, suspicious of Amelia's sudden excitement. But eventually, she'd hugged her tightly and whispered, "You better eat and take showers while I'm gone."

"I will," Amelia lied against her shoulder.

Before she left, Ronnie had kicked into full older-sister mode—restocking Amelia's fridge with premade wraps, fresh fruit, hummus, soup, and three unnecessary flavors of ice cream. She filled the cabinets too, lining them with herbal teas, crackers, protein bars, and a giant tub of peanut butter pretzels.

"Just pretend I'm yelling at you every time you reach for coffee instead of real food," Ronnie said, stacking a final box of La Croix onto the shelf.

Luke chuckled in the doorway. "She's never stocked her kitchen with this much stuff."

Ronnie smirked. "That's because I work so much, so I'm never home!"

Luke gave Tyler a final run-through of security protocols, including a quiet but stern conversation Amelia couldn't fully hear. There was an odd comfort in that, knowing there were layers of eyes watching over her. She was still learning how to receive that kind of care.

They all stepped out of the front door and paused just before reaching the driveway. Tyler kept walking, offering Luke a brief nod and lifting his hand in a quick wave to Amelia as he passed.

To Amelia's surprise, Luke walked up to her and gave her a big hug. "Text, if you need anything, we will reply when we have cell service. Tyler is here for you, though."

"Thanks, Luke. For Everything."

Amelia waved them out of her driveway, the gesture too calm, too casual—more suited to parents leaving for a quiet weekend than security guards pulling away after an intruder scare.

But this felt different from the freedom that comes from a parentless weekend.

This was the total definition of being alone.

*Pathetic, Amelia*, she thought as she sauntered back inside her front door.

Tyler, barely twenty-four and all limbs and awkward silences, mainly stayed out of sight. Amelia appreciated the space, if not the solitude. The house was too quiet. Too tidy. She picked at Ronnie's grocery offerings but left most of them untouched. It was easier not to feel anything if she didn't give her body what it needed.

Days started blurring again. She went through the motions—barely.

Tyler would check in once or twice a day, never pressing, always polite.

She answered with a slight nod. Short replies. Forced half-smiles that never touched her eyes.

At night, she curled into the corners of the house, trying to disappear into the quiet.

She stayed small. Contained.

She kept expecting the quiet to feel like peace.

Instead, it felt like drowning.

Tyler offered to put on a movie once—something light and forgettable.

Amelia pretended she was tired.

He didn't ask again.

If nothing else, she had consistency.

She woke. She stared. She moved only when necessary.

There was a strange comfort in the numbness—a routine built from avoidance.

But the third night after they left, everything shifted.

She had barely turned off the hallway light when a flicker of movement caught her eye.

Not from the front yard. From the back.

The kitchen window. A flash. A shadow. Maybe a figure.

Her breath hitched as unease curled in her gut.

She didn't scream. Didn't move.

This time, it didn't disappear right away.

The man was standing on her back porch. Bold. Brazen. Close.

He stepped forward, right up to the sliding glass door.

Amelia turned to stone. The hardwood floor seemed to reach up through her bare feet, its chill climbing her legs until her entire body became a vessel for terror. Even the simple act of glancing down to check the door lock felt impossible, as if the slightest movement might shatter whatever fragile barrier stood between her and the man on her porch.

The man didn't knock. Didn't speak. Only stared directly at her.

He stood tall, leaner than Nate, but broader through the shoulders. His hood was up, but the dim porch light revealed enough stubble, a narrow nose, eyes that caught the light with a glint of river stone. Familiar. Unmistakably so.

Too familiar.

Her pulse roared in her ears.

Was he the man from that night? The night Nate got injured?

Everything inside her sank.

Then—without warning—he slammed one hand flat against the glass.

The sound split the silence—a sharp crack that tore through the air.

Amelia jumped, stumbling back a step as her heart vaulted into her throat. The glass vibrated from the impact, her entire body going cold.

It wasn't an attempt to break in.

It was a message.

He wanted her to see him.

To know he'd been that close.

To remind her—she wasn't unreachable.

As suddenly as he'd appeared, he turned. His head snapped to the side, reacting to a sound only he seemed to hear. A dog? A siren? Another presence?

Without hesitation, he ran.

He moved fast and silent, startled—gone in an instant, the way a deer vanishes mid-graze.

She collapsed to the ground only after he disappeared into the dark.

Shaking, she fumbled her phone out of her hoodie pocket and called Tyler.

By the time he arrived, flashlight in hand and jaw tight with concern, Amelia was still sitting with her back against the kitchen cabinets, eyes locked on the patio door.

"He was right there," she said hoarsely, pointing. "Just... standing there."

Tyler moved methodically, sweeping the perimeter, speaking into his radio. He checked the motion sensors—logs confirmed someone had been there, but it was too late to stop him. No one caught. No one stopped.

"I believe you," he said simply.

That helped—a little.

Still shaken, Amelia sent a text to Ronnie:

*Someone was here. I'm okay now.*

The message failed to send. "Undeliverable."

She tried again. Same result.

The silence was a knife to the gut.

She really was alone.

Tyler lingered after clearing the yard, sitting stiffly in the living room chair across from her. He was doing his best, but conversation wasn't his strong suit. The room felt heavy with things unsaid.

"Will Nate find out about this?" she asked finally, voice barely above a whisper.

Tyler hesitated. "Yeah. He will. He's the one paying for the surveillance reports."

Amelia stared at her hands. "Okay," she whispered.

But when Tyler looked away, she unlocked her phone and typed a message, anyway.

*I'm okay. I wanted you to hear it from me.*

She stared at it for a full minute before hitting send.

The reply came almost instantly.

*Please call me. What happened?*

She didn't answer.

Tyler's phone buzzed. He looked at it, then at her.

"It's Nate."

Amelia swallowed.

"I'll take it in the front," Tyler said, already moving down the hall.

She could hear muffled tones through the hallway—the unmistakable urgency in Nate's voice. Tyler's low responses. Then a long pause.

Footsteps returned.

Tyler stood awkwardly at the threshold, phone in hand, extending it in her direction. "Nate would like to talk to you."

Her stomach tightened as the whooshing sound in her ears returned. Her body resisted, but something within her broke open.

She reached for the phone and slowly placed it to her ear.

But no words came.

"Mils?" Nate's voice filled the silence. It was raw, worried, breaking through her shell. "Mils, are you there?"

A beat passed.

Then another.

"Mils, please tell me you're okay."

"I'm here," she whispered. "I'm... I'm okay."

She sat on the edge of the couch, curling inward, trying to disappear into herself. Tyler stepped out without a word.

"I'm so sorry," Nate said. "Jesus, I'm so mad I wasn't there."

"You can't be everywhere," she murmured.

"This guy—was he the same? Do you think it was one of them?"

"I don't know," Amelia said, her voice cracking. "He looked... familiar."

There was a pause, and when Nate spoke again, his voice shook with anger.

"I'm calling Luke the second we hang up. He never should've left."

"No," Amelia said quickly. "Don't blame him. He deserves time off. He's with Ronnie. I insisted. Besides, Tyler is here."

"But still—"

"Nate," she said, gently but firmly. "It's not his fault."

He exhaled hard. "Then let me come. I can be there tomorrow. I'll find the first flight."

She closed her eyes. Her body ached with the desire to say yes.

But her voice said, "No."

A long silence.

"Okay," Nate finally said, though his voice carried the weight of all the things he couldn't fix from miles away. "But promise me you'll text me tomorrow. Even just a few words. Let me know you're okay."

"I will," she said quietly.

"I love you, Mils."

She closed her eyes again. "I know."

"I'm still here," he whispered. "I'm still waiting."

"I'm sorry," she said. And meant it.

"So am I."

The call ended, but Amelia didn't move.

She stared at the dark sliding glass door for a long time. The image of the man's face burned into her memory like a photograph of someone else's life.

* * *

THE NEXT MORNING arrived in the slowest, most unwelcome way.

Amelia stirred under the covers, not because she'd rested well—she hadn't—but because the sun was pooling in her room, a silent invitation to rejoin the living. Her phone buzzed on the nightstand, the soft vibration too persistent to ignore.

It was Nate.

*Checking in. Did you sleep? How are you feeling?*

She stared at the message for a long time. The sun edged a little higher. The room remained still, save for the steady whisper of blades turning above and the distant sound of a garbage truck a few blocks away.

How *was* she feeling?

Not safe. Not settled. Not okay.

But he didn't need to know that.

She rolled onto her side, tugging the comforter higher over her chest, wrapping it around herself like armor. His voice from last night echoed in her mind—*I love you*, steady and sure, *I'm still waiting*, spoken like a vow.

Part of her ached to tell him everything. The rest didn't know how to put the chaos in her head into words.

She began typing:

*Made it through the night. Waking up now.*

She read it once. Then again. Then hit send.

It was enough. He'd know she was alive. But it didn't cost her more than she could give.

She left the bed an hour later, shuffled into the kitchen, and stood barefoot in front of the fridge that Ronnie had lovingly overstocked. She ate half a protein bar and dropped the wrapper on the counter, a small badge of survival—proof she'd at least tried.

By mid-afternoon, her phone rang.

**Ronnie Wells.**

Amelia nearly dropped it in her rush to answer.

"Ronnie?"

"Jesus, finally," Ronnie said in a rush. Her voice crackled as if the cell towers had only now returned to consciousness. "We finally hit a stretch with signal, and I saw your messages. Are you okay? Are you safe?"

"I'm okay," Amelia said, trying to sound stronger than she felt. "He's gone. Tyler checked everything and stayed with me for a while. Nothing since."

"I feel like crap for leaving you," Ronnie said. "Luke feels worse."

Amelia could hear Luke in the background, his voice low and agitated.

"What's he saying?" Amelia asked, pressing the phone tightly to her ear.

"He's on the phone with Nate. I think Nate's chewing him out."

There was something almost absurd about that—Nate yelling at Luke through the phone while Ronnie was still catching her breath from the descent. But part of Amelia expected it. Nate carried a fierce protective streak, and this had hit too close to a wound still raw beneath the surface.

"Well," Amelia said, exhaling, "tell him not to be too hard on Luke. This wasn't anyone's fault."

"I will. He's just worried. And pissed. And... Nate."

A pause stretched between them, heavy with everything Amelia hadn't said and Ronnie already understood.

"I'm coming over tomorrow," Ronnie said firmly. "First thing, once we're unpacked and human again. I mean it."

"Okay," Amelia said quietly. Then, after a breath, "Tyler's going to drive me to the police station in a couple of hours. Detective Mallory wants me to give a new statement."

"Oh, Lane," Ronnie breathed. "I'm so sorry I can't be there."

"It's okay. Really. I don't want you to worry. I'll be fine with Tyler."

"I hate that you have to do this alone."

"I'm not *totally* alone," Amelia said, trying to make it true. "And I know you'll be here tomorrow."

Ronnie said nothing at first, but Amelia could feel her presence through the line—solid, unwavering.

"Please let me know how it goes. The second you're home, text me. I'll be waiting."

"I will."

They lingered for another minute, the silence that only best friends could hold without rushing to fill.

When they finally hung up, Amelia set the phone on the counter and rubbed her temples with both hands. The kitchen was still bright, still stocked, still quiet.

A hollow pang hit her—she hadn't even asked how the trip went.

She'd been so caught in her storm, she hadn't thought to ask if Ronnie and Luke had found what they were looking for out there in the silence of the mountains.

God, I'm selfish, she thought. I didn't even ask if she had a good time.

But the truth was—she wasn't ready to make space for someone else's happiness.

Not today. Maybe tomorrow will have room.

She walked to the fridge, opened the door, and stared at all the new, endless culinary options.

After a long moment, she pulled out the soup.

She was still here.

She could start with that.

As the microwave hummed, her phone buzzed again on the counter beside her. It was Nate once again.

*I don't want to push. I need to know you're really okay. Even if it's one word.*

*Please, Mils. I'm still here.*

Amelia read the message once. Then again.

She didn't respond.

Not yet.

But she kept the phone close.

* * *

AMELIA DIDN'T ARGUE when Tyler said Detective Mallory wanted her to come into the station this time.

She nodded, her voice gone somewhere she couldn't reach. Luke and Ronnie were still in and out of range, and Tyler, ever steady, had already called the station to confirm they were on their way.

The car ride carried the same weight as a final step off a ledge—slow, inevitable, bracing.

Even with Tyler beside her—silent, respectful, unobtrusively protective—Amelia had never felt more alone. She watched the neighborhoods blur past her window, sunlight flickering through trees she didn't recognize, as people walked their dogs and cyclists zipped by. Life unbothered.

Her fingers twisted in her lap, restless and cold.

She'd never been to a police station before, not like this. The closest she'd come was the courthouse next door, where she sat in a hallway that smelled of old paper and disinfectant, waiting to finalize her divorce. Even then, she'd felt stripped bare.

But this?

This was worse.

The building loomed dull gray as they pulled in, the air thickening around it—oxygen itself seeming to pause at the door. She followed Tyler through the front entrance, her feet numb, her breath shallow. The interior matched its exterior—cold, sterile, humming faintly with flickering fluorescent lights overhead.

They approached the front desk.

A woman sat behind a sheet of bulletproof glass, her expression as impersonal as the wall of empty chairs lining the wall. Amelia stepped closer and cleared her throat.

"Amelia Lane, for Detective Roy Mallory. He's expecting me."

No response. Not even a nod.

Only a sidelong glance from the woman behind the glass, followed by a flat, "Have a seat."

Amelia turned toward the lobby. Shoved in the corner were three sad chairs against the far wall—gray, upholstered decades ago, metal armrests chipped and scratched. She sank into the middle seat; the cushion collapsing beneath her, weary in its own way.

*Even the chairs here are depressed,* she thought.

Tyler stayed standing beside her, hands loose at his sides, eyes scanning the room. Quiet, but not relaxed.

Across from them sat a vending machine with two flickering lights and barely any contents—crushed chips, candy bars no one wanted, and a suspicious bag of something green. Next to it, a bulletin board with faded flyers: missing persons, local PSAs, wanted posters whose edges curled with time.

This wasn't a place you came to for help.

It was where you went to give up.

Her thoughts drifted. Uninvited but unrelenting.

Her mother had been here. Well, somewhere similar here.

Too many times.

Drunk and disorderly. Disturbance calls. Public intoxication. Amelia had overheard it whispered, had watched the slurred apologies, the way her mother never really looked ashamed—only tired. Despite that, her father showed up—every time.

Cheryl Lane had died when Amelia was twenty, her liver already failing by then. Her father, John, still lived a couple of hours south in Monument, Colorado—but they hadn't spoken in years. Too many years of choosing the wrong things. The wrong people. Not showing up when it mattered.

Not for her concerts. Not for her spelling bee wins or middle school art show. But for Cheryl, shaking and weeping in a holding cell, he always came.

Did her mom feel like this?

Cold. Exposed. Small?

Did she sit on one of these awful chairs, heart in her throat, afraid of the next thing she couldn't control?

A voice cut through her thoughts.

"Ms. Lane?"

Amelia blinked, startled. Detective Mallory stood in the doorway to the right, holding it open as if he'd already called her name more than once.

She looked at Tyler.

"I'll be right here," he said gently, nodding.

She rose on unsteady legs and followed the detective, her boots clicking faintly on the linoleum. The hallway was too bright and still too cold, a strange combination that made her shiver. She folded her arms tightly across her chest as they passed nameless doors and blank walls until they stopped at one labeled **INTERROGATION ROOM 1**.

Of course. That made her feel worse.

Mallory opened the door and gestured her inside without a word.

The room held nothing dramatic—a small table, two chairs, no windows, a vent pulsing overhead. Still, it pressed in around her, more cage than space.

They sat across from each other.

"Let's get started," he said, flipping open a slim file. His voice came sharp, all business—no smile, no warmth. All work.

Amelia described everything: the sound, the figure at the door, the hand slamming against the glass, how he turned. How he ran. How close he'd been.

"Do you believe it's the same individual from the previous incident?" he asked, pen poised.

"I... I don't know," she admitted. "I didn't see the men's faces last time. I can't say."

He made a note, then leaned back slightly.

"Well, considering Mr. Carter was involved in that first incident, I'd wager you wouldn't be dealing with any of this if he hadn't come to town."

Amelia blinked.

Was that supposed to be a joke?

She opened her mouth to respond, but nothing came out. She didn't ask for this. Didn't deserve this. But her body was too tired to fight the narrative.

Mallory didn't seem to notice. Or care.

He jotted another note, then stood.

"I need to go check something. I'll be right back. You want anything to drink?"

She shook her head.

"No, thank you."

She could hardly swallow past the dryness in her mouth. A drink wouldn't help—it would only tighten the feeling, make her choke on it.

Alone again, the vibration of the vent filled the silence. She dropped her gaze to her hands, the faint tremble still there. Her mind drifted—to the print on her glass door. To how close he'd been. To the way her heart had slammed against her ribs, a warning she hadn't wanted to hear. Maybe she could ask Tyler to wipe it off. She didn't want to see it anymore.

The door opened again.

Mallory returned and dropped back into his seat.

"Alright. I've got everything I need. We haven't located the guy—yet—but be extra diligent, Ms. Lane."

She nodded faintly, bracing for what came next.

"Lucky you've got security, right?" he added, almost too casually.

Another jab.

She didn't flinch this time—only stood as he motioned toward the door.

He didn't walk her out.

Tyler saw her before she reached the lobby.

"Let's go," he said softly.

He opened the passenger door for her, helped her in, then shut it carefully before walking around to the driver's side.

The ride back was quiet.

No questions. No pressure. A soft vibration filled the cabin as the car cruised along, light shifting across the dashboard in quiet intervals.

When they pulled into her driveway, she hesitated.

Her home stood unchanged, solid and warm against the fading light of the afternoon. And for the first time in a long time, she was grateful for it. Even empty, it was kinder than that station.

Warmer than the judgment she'd sat across from moments earlier.

She slipped inside, letting the silence fall around her like a blanket.

No harsh lights.

No sharp voices.

Only the small comfort of closing the door and keeping the world out.

# 22

# the key

AMELIA HADN'T SLEPT, not really—drifting in and out of restless thoughts until morning finally arrived.

After closing the door behind her the day before, she'd stood in the quiet for a long time, unsure what to do next. She'd eaten half a bowl of cereal, stared blankly at the TV, paced the living room, then walked upstairs and crawled into bed without ever changing clothes. Her body had curled toward the edge of the mattress out of habit, but her mind refused to settle. Even now, she had only moved a little—still in the same familiar oversized sweatshirt, her hair a tangled mess, her skin bare of anything but exhaustion.

The house was dim, early morning light merely beginning to stretch its fingers through the curtains, when she heard it—a gentle knock at the front door.

She padded down the stairs, heart rising slightly as she opened it.

Ronnie stood there, framed by the soft gray light, holding a bouquet of white magnolias.

"Don't be mad at me," Ronnie said before Amelia could even form a greeting.

Amelia blinked. "What did you do?"

Ronnie stepped inside without waiting for an invitation. "I brought you something. Well, technically, Nate did. But Luke and I helped."

Amelia's eyes narrowed. "Ronnie."

"They're not the usual ones," Ronnie said, placing the flowers carefully on the kitchen counter. "These are different. They come with... more."

Amelia crossed her arms. "More?"

Ronnie turned and scanned Amelia from head to toe before saying another word. "Okay, hang on. I need to check you out first," she said gently, stepping closer.

Amelia blinked, too distracted by the flowers to process it. "What—why?"

"Because I wasn't here. Because I should've been. Because I've been picturing a dozen different versions of you since I got that text."

"I'm fine," Amelia said quickly. "Really."

Ronnie raised an eyebrow. "That's a lie. But I'll let it slide—for now."

Amelia sighed and tried to redirect. "So... how was the hiking trip?"

Ronnie gave her a look. "Not important right now. I'll tell you all about it later, I promise."

She nodded toward the bouquet. Tied with a pale ribbon was a notecard and a silver key.

Amelia stepped forward, drawn to the subtle shift in energy. "What is this?"

Ronnie looked almost nervous now. "Nate wanted to be the one to give this to you. He did. But with everything that's happened, he thought you should have it now. It came while I was out hiking with Luke, so this is the first chance I've had to get it to you."

"Give me what?" Amelia asked, voice sharper than intended.

"Lane," Ronnie said softly, using the nickname only she could. "Promise me this won't break you. This is a good thing. A healing thing. Okay?"

Amelia took a breath, her pulse loud in her ears. "Give me what?"

Ronnie didn't answer with words. She simply untied the ribbon, placed the notecard and key into Amelia's hand, and stepped back.

The notecard was flat, not folded—a simple rectangle tied through a small punch hole at the top. Amelia turned it over.

The handwriting was unmistakable. In Nate's handwriting, she read:

*You Are Here*

Confusion rose for a beat—then clarity cut through, fast and blinding. She looked at the key again, really looked at it.

And the breath left her body.

She knew this key. She knew it in her bones.

It belonged to Grace's old house—the one she hadn't set foot in since everything fell apart.

Her knees weakened, and she reached for the edge of the counter.

"Ronnie..." she whispered. "Is this real?"

Ronnie nodded. "It's real."

Everything inside her sank.

She looked at Ronnie. "Where is he?"

"Still in LA," Ronnie said softly. "He wanted to come. He was ready to get on a plane the second I told him I was coming over. But I told him to wait. To give you some time."

Amelia looked down at the key again. It felt heavier than it should have.

Ronnie stepped closer. "Come on," she said quietly. "Let's get you cleaned up a little before we go."

Amelia looked up, her voice barely steady. "Where's Luke?"

"He's outside," Ronnie said gently. "He wanted to give us a moment. But he's ready to drive you when you're ready."

Amelia didn't speak. She couldn't. The words stayed lodged in her throat.

Trying to stay aware, she moved on cue, following Ronnie upstairs. She sat on the edge of her bed while Ronnie gently worked through tangles, pulling her hair back into a loose braid. She changed into jeans and a soft sweater that Ronnie handed her, barely registering the fabric against her skin.

Nothing felt real, each second slipping past as though it belonged to another life.

She could hear Ronnie's voice—kind, firm, familiar- but it reached her from somewhere far away.

"Let's brush your teeth."

"Rinse."

"Okay, good. One step at a time."

Amelia nodded, though she wasn't sure if she'd actually heard the words or just knew what they'd be.

By the time they came back downstairs, the light had shifted—brighter, but not warmer.

Ronnie reached for her bag, then paused, glancing back at the kitchen counter.

"The key," she murmured.

She stepped over, picked it up along with the note, and turned to Amelia. Without a word, she placed the cool metal in her hand, then the notecard, curling Amelia's fingers gently around both. Then she gathered the bouquet with her free arm and held it close.

"There," she said, almost whispering. "Now we're ready."

She double-checked that Amelia had everything, then opened the door with quiet care.

The air outside was crisp—the kind that would usually wake Amelia up. But today, it barely touched her.

She stepped outside slowly, her body moving on instinct more than intention.

Luke stood beside the SUV, waiting, his expression unreadable but calm. He opened the back passenger door without a word.

She moved as if underwater, sliding into the seat and fastening her belt by muscle memory. Luke said something meant to soothe, but her brain translated it into static—unfocused, unreachable.

She held the key and paper in her hand.

She didn't let go.

* * *

THE DRIVE TO the house felt impossibly short. The stringed key and note lay in Amelia's lap, her fingers returning to them over and over, as if touch alone could make sense of them. Her posture remained locked, her spine straight and unmoving.

Ronnie sat beside her, the magnolia bouquet tucked in her lap, arms wrapped around it with quiet tenderness. She held it close, the way you hold something that matters. Neither of them spoke.

As Luke turned onto the familiar street, Ronnie reached over with her free hand and rested it gently on Amelia's leg.

"We're almost there," she said softly.

Amelia didn't reply. She couldn't.

When Luke turned into the driveway, her chest constricted.

She'd seen the house plenty of times since she sold it—the outside hadn't surprised her in years. But now, knowing what was inside—knowing it was hers again—it hit differently. The same stained glass window above the kitchen sink. Same uneven walkway to the porch. Same slightly crooked mailbox that Grant had sworn he'd fix and never did.

Only now... it wasn't someone else's. Not anymore.

"Are you sure?" Amelia asked to no one in particular.

Luke parked and turned off the engine. "Take as long as you need. I'll be right here."

Amelia nodded but didn't move.

Ronnie touched her hand gently. "I'll come with you. I'll stay out of the way."

That was all Amelia needed to hear. Her legs moved on their own. She climbed the porch steps, Luke holding the screen door open behind them but staying outside as they crossed the threshold.

The key turned easily. The door opened, and the air gripped her, dragging the past into the present with a force she couldn't stop. Amelia stepped inside and walked straight into memory.

Ronnie stepped in behind her, quiet as a shadow, and walked the bouquet to the kitchen. She set it gently on the counter beneath the old kitchen window, where the light was always soft in the morning.

* * *

THE LIVING ROOM was just as she had left it.

The walls remained a soft cream. The hardwood floor still bore the scuffs of toy strollers, blocks, and countless dance-party socks. On the fireplace mantle, faint outlines marked where picture frames had once stood. The couch was gone now, but its absence left behind a sun-bleached square on the floor—a ghost of presence, still lingering.

Amelia tiptoed, her fingers brushing over the built-in bookshelves. She paused at a small notch in the wall—the one Grace had made years ago, flinging a toy pony with Olympic-level force. The memory struck hard, sharp, and immediately.

Ronnie followed silently, close but not crowding. She didn't speak. Didn't need to. She was simply there.

Amelia moved room by room, her breath catching at each doorway.

In the kitchen, the ceramic tile she used to hate was still there, chipped in one corner. She could almost see Grace sliding across it in her socks, arms stretched wide in flight.

She stepped into the hallway—just wide enough for baby gates, then tricycles. A faint discoloration on the wall stopped her. She reached out, fingertips grazing the spot where the height chart had once been taped. The marks were barely visible now, but unmistakable.

The bathroom—the one where she'd rocked Grace through a fever so bad she thought her own heart might give out.

And then... Grace's room.

She had saved it for last. Of course she had.

It sat at the front of the house, where sunlight continuously poured in—bright and constant, almost like a blessing. Her hand hovered at the doorframe for a moment. Then, quietly, she stepped inside.

The same soft pink walls greeted her. The identical twinkling star decals clung to the ceiling, some peeling now at the edges. The white built-in dresser still stood beneath the window, drawers long emptied, but Amelia could almost see Grace tugging them open, hunting for pajamas covered in owls or princesses.

The air smelled faintly of old wood and lavender—the kind Grace used to splash all over herself when pretending to have a 'spa day.'

Amelia stepped further inside and slowly opened the closet door.

And there, in uneven purple crayon, were the words:

*I love Mommy.*

Her breath broke.

The sound of it startled even her.

Amelia dropped to her knees.

The tears came without warning. Great, heaving sobs. She pressed her forehead to the carpet and cried until her ribs ached and her throat went raw. Her hands clenched the rug's fibers, the only thing between her and the rising flood within.

She didn't know what she was saying—if she was saying anything at all—but the grief poured out, summoned by the moment, the floor, the angle of morning light.

Ronnie stood in the hallway, watching. Her eyes shimmered, but she didn't move. She didn't speak or step forward. She leaned quietly against the doorframe, steady and still, keeping vigil.

Time blurred, lost its shape.

Eventually, when the sobs had dulled to tremors and the pain had burned itself hollow, Amelia shifted. Still shaking, she crawled to the center of the room and sat cross-legged on the floor.

She stayed there.

For minutes. Maybe hours.

No one disturbed her.

Luke never knocked.

And Ronnie never left.

* * *

WHEN AMELIA FINALLY stood—legs stiff, throat raw, and heart cracked wide open—Ronnie walked with her through the rest of the house. They said little. There wasn't much to say.

They returned to the living room, where the afternoon sunlight filtered in like honey across the hardwood floors.

Ronnie studied Amelia's face carefully. Then, with no need to ask, she said,

"You're not leaving tonight, are you?"

Amelia hesitated, her throat tightening. "I don't think I can."

"You don't have to," Ronnie said, already reaching for her handbag. "I'll go back to your place, grab a few things. And I'll bring the air mattress Luke and I used on the hike. It's in the back of the SUV."

"You don't have to do that."

"I know. But I want to." Ronnie squeezed her hand. "You need to be here. That's what matters."

Amelia glanced around again, the weight of it settling in. "This was Nate?"

Ronnie gave her a knowing smile. "He started asking questions before he left Colorado. Quiet ones—to me, to Luke. But once he got back to LA, he pushed harder."

Amelia blinked, stunned. "But... I... I didn't know it was for sale."

"It wasn't. Nate made it happen. He made them an offer they couldn't refuse," Ronnie said. "Complicated, but not impossible. When you're ready, we'll start the paperwork to transfer it into your name. No strings. No pressure."

Amelia leaned against the long dining room wall, holding the notecard again.

Her voice was quiet but confident. "Normally, I would never accept a gift this big... I don't even know what to call it."

Ronnie didn't interrupt.

"But this?" Amelia looked around. "This isn't something I can return."

Ronnie nodded, her voice soft. "I know. And he does, too."

Ronnie looked at her, not unkindly. "You could... maybe call him. To say thank you. Or more, if you're ready. I know he's waiting. I also know he's not perfect—but he's not going anywhere unless you tell him to."

Amelia didn't respond right away. But she didn't shut it down, either.

"I'll think about it," she said.

"Good enough for me." Ronnie gave her a soft smile, then glanced at her watch. "I'll be back in an hour."

"Thank you."

"You're welcome. And for what it's worth..." Ronnie nodded toward

Grace's bedroom down the hall. "She'd be proud of you."

Amelia swallowed hard, blinking fast.

After she left, Amelia moved slowly through the house, touching the walls as if she were tracing the edges of an old dream.

She wandered back into the kitchen, maybe for comfort, maybe for air. Her hands gripped the edge of the sink as she looked out the window.

The magnolia trees were still there in the backyard. The same ones that had bloomed every spring when Grace was little. Beautiful and steady.

She looked down at the new bouquet resting quietly beside her, petals full and white and alive in the filtered light.

The past and present—side by side.

She didn't cry. But something inside her cracked again, slightly. And this time, it wasn't breaking—it was opening.

Ronnie returned as promised, quietly bringing in a tote bag, the rolled-up air mattress, and a few essentials.

She held out one last item as she stepped into the kitchen—a soft pink throw blanket, neatly folded in her arms.

"This was on your couch," Ronnie said gently. "I figured you'd want it."

Amelia's breath caught. The blanket had once belonged to Grace—it had rested at the foot of her hospital bed, then later on Amelia's sofa, a quiet testament to what had been.

She took it wordlessly, clutching it to her chest. No one said a word. No one had to.

Ronnie helped Amelia inflate the mattress and set it up in Grace's room. The pink blanket was the final touch—gentle and reverent in its return.

Before she left, Ronnie reached into her bag and pulled out a single folded sheet of paper. She placed it quietly on the kitchen counter beside the magnolia bouquet.

"One last thing," she said. "It's a printed article. A press release that came out yesterday from Savannah Lord."

Amelia tensed, but Ronnie's voice stayed calm.

"You don't have to read it now. Or even tonight. But... when you're ready, it's there. I think it'll give you something you've needed."

Ronnie pulled her into another hug, murmured, "Call me if you need anything," and stepped into the hallway where Luke stood on watch.

Neither of them pushed Amelia to leave with them or change her mind.

Luke lingered in the doorway for a moment, his voice low and steady. "I'll be outside all night. You're safe here, Amelia. Focus on getting some rest."

She nodded, his words wrapping around her like armor—not burdensome, but steadying. Enough to let her breathe again.

The house hummed with a silence that wasn't lonely. It was sacred.

As the sun disappeared behind the trees and the rooms grew quiet, Amelia returned to the kitchen. The flowers still sat untouched, their petals glowing in the dim light. The folded article lay beside it.

She picked it up and slowly unfolded the page. It was a press release. The headline made her stomach twitch.

*SAVANNAH LORD ISSUES PUBLIC APOLOGY FOR MISLEADING MEDIA*

"I would like to apologize for the confusion and distress caused by recent media coverage linking Nate Carter to my pregnancy. I take full responsibility for misleading the press, and for allowing a personal moment of vulnerability to spiral into something far more harmful. Nate is not the father of my child, nor was he ever involved beyond the professional and kind-hearted support he offered me as a colleague and friend."

"I exploited his compassion, and for that, I am deeply sorry. I offer this apology not only to him, but to anyone I hurt by my actions."

Amelia stared at the words. She read them twice. Three times.

This was it—the proof she had needed—not for the world, but for her heart.

That Nate hadn't lied about not being the father of someone else's child.

Her breath shook as she folded the paper neatly again, pressing her palm over it. Not to hide it—but to hold it. To steady herself.

For the first time in weeks, something inside her exhaled.

# 23

# never alone

AMELIA DIDN'T REMEMBER falling asleep—only that her body had stopped fighting.

The air mattress whispered beneath her as she shifted. The pink throw blanket Ronnie had brought back clung to her legs, warm from hours of stillness, a tether she hadn't realized she needed. Grace's room seemed to hold its breath. Above her, the glow-in-the-dark stars scattered across the ceiling faded into the early dawn, dimming one by one, blinking out like fireflies.

The silence was unlike any she'd known in a long time.

Not hospital silence.

Not her too-quiet house silence.

This was something else entirely—like being underwater, not drowning, but held in quiet suspension.

She could still smell Grace's old shampoo on the closet doorframe. She could still feel the whisper of her daughter's laughter in the corners. She'd slept here with Grace many times, curled in the tiny twin bed when fevers spiked, when sleep was elusive and storybooks ran out of pages.

Now she lay alone in a house full of ghosts and dust motes.

And yet...

She didn't feel alone.

Not in the way she expected.

Because it wasn't only Grace who lingered in the corners, it was Nate, too.

The curve of his voice. The warmth of his hands. The way he looked at her as if she were still whole, even though she knew she wasn't.

He hadn't lied. He wasn't having a baby with another woman.

And Savannah's apology—God, that strange, printed proof—had cracked something wide open in her.

It wasn't only relief. It wasn't simply vindication.

It was hope.

She didn't know exactly how she would move forward, but for the first time since everything fell apart, at last she might want to. Love wasn't something she had lost, but something she still deserved.

And maybe... Nate had seen that in her all along.

Even when she couldn't.

Her eyes slipped closed slowly, and her lips formed the words before she even realized they'd risen:

"I'm still with you."

She didn't know who she meant the words for—Grace, Nate, or the version of herself that had nearly vanished beneath the weight of grief.

She didn't hear a reply. But something inside her softened. Her body surrendered to sleep—and the dreams came, not gently, but with the weight of memory breaking through.

* * *

THE LIGHT HIT her first—warm and golden—spilling across the kitchen, melting over the walls, kissing the countertops, and turning the ceramic tile floor into a river of morning.

The scent of cinnamon and sun-warmed apples filled the air—joy left simmering too long on the stove, rich and lingering, but not yet burned.

She stood barefoot on that floor, her feet damp with the memory of spilled orange juice.

It was sticky-slick under her toes, the way it always was when Grace got too excited opening her own juice box.

She was in the house—this house—but different. Brighter. Unburdened.

No echoes of grief in the corners. No silence draped in sorrow. Only light, motion, and sound.

And then—

Grace.

She burst into the room, a small comet, wearing footie pajamas two sizes too big and a frilly purple tutu over the top. Her curls were half-brushed, wild and buoyant.

She clutched a plastic mixing bowl in one hand and a rubber spatula in the other, waving both as if they were parade flags.

"Mommy!" she shrieked. "You're just in time! The soup is ready!"

Her voice rang out in the center of the room—pure, high, whole. It filled every corner with something Amelia hadn't felt in years: aliveness.

Amelia blinked. Her body no longer felt real, more memory than flesh— something fragile wrapped in skin.

She was weightless and heavy all at once—grateful and breaking.

She knelt slowly, instinctively, her knees finding the exact place on the tile where she used to sit. The cool floor met her touch with familiar ease. Her palms flattened on the tile, grounding her to the moment.

Grace plopped the bowl in front of her with a clatter.

"It's carrot-peanut butter-chocolate," Grace declared. "It's my new recipe."

Amelia laughed. Not any laugh—one from deep in her gut, the kind she hadn't made in years.

"That sounds disgusting," she said, grinning.

Grace gasped, eyes wide in teasing offense. "It's not disgusting. It's delicious."

Amelia reached beside her and picked up the worn giraffe plush from the floor, brushing off imaginary crumbs. She held it out, and Grace's whole face lit up as she took it into her arms.

She dropped a kiss on Amelia's cheek, sticky and sweet. "Eat it. You have to."

Amelia pretended to take a big slurp. "Mmm. Best soup I've ever had."

Grace beamed and hugged the giraffe tightly to her chest. Her curls bounced with the movement, and for a moment, the world seemed to glow.

There was sunlight on every surface. The spoon in Grace's hand shimmered gold. The kitchen window opened to a backyard filled with soft wind and magnolia blooms.

The air felt thick with love.

But then, the sunlight dimmed.

Not abruptly. A flicker—a long, lingering blink that failed to return.

The corners of the kitchen dulled. The smell of chocolate and apple juice vanished.

"Mommy?" Grace asked, her voice suddenly smaller.

Amelia looked up, but Grace was no longer in front of her.

Only the empty bowl remained.

And the silence was back.

It came rushing in—a tide of feeling. Familiar. Heavy. Brutal.

Then, faintly, a whisper through a wall—Grace's voice again: "Where did you go, Mommy?"

A question, not a scolding. But it pierced Amelia to the marrow.

She opened her mouth, but no words came out. Her throat closed against the ache.

The tile floor faded. Her breath caught. And the hallway pulled her in.

*  *  *

AMELIA TURNED A corner she didn't remember walking toward and found herself in a long, endless hallway.

It was too quiet.

The air was sharp with antiseptic. Underneath it, she caught the stale scent of old coffee and overused hand sanitizer—an odor she hadn't smelled in years but recognized instantly. Her stomach clenched.

The floors were polished linoleum, gleaming and sterile, the overhead lights casting sharp white pools every few steps. She knew these floors—she had walked them for months. Every square foot held some version of her panic, her pleading, her breathless waiting.

Somewhere ahead, she heard the squeak of worn rubber soles, and then—Grant.

He walked past her, his shoulders hunched in defeat, a single white paper in his hand, his face pale and tight. His eyes were glassy, distant. He didn't see her. Didn't even glance her way.

But as he passed, Amelia glimpsed the paper he clutched—crumpled and soft corners. It was a drawing. Crayon lines. Big, bold colors. A blue sky. A stick figure with curls. A tree bent slightly in the wind. Her chest ached at the sight of it.

Amelia turned slightly, wanting to call out, but her throat locked.

She heard the beep of machines, muffled and distant.

Doors lined the corridor, all closed.

Except one.

Room 316.

Her knees weakened at the sight of it.

The number jumped off the door, as if written in a different ink. Back then, that room never stayed closed—doctors rushed in, nurses checked vitals, visitors whispered prayers.

But now it stood only slightly ajar.

Amelia approached it, each footstep echoing louder than the last.

She didn't want to open it. She wasn't sure she could.

But something inside her pulled forward.

She reached for the handle, and the moment her fingers touched the cool metal, the door opened by itself.

Inside, the room was dark.

But someone was sitting on the edge of the bed.

Amelia froze.

It was Grace.

Older.

No longer a toddler, not quite a teenager—maybe ten, maybe twelve. Her face was the same and different all at once, with longer hair and deeper eyes. She wore a white hospital gown with stars drawn on it in marker.

In her lap was a notebook.

"Mommy," she said without looking up. "You came back."

Amelia's mouth went dry. "I never left."

Grace smiled, turning the page in her book. "I knew you'd say that."

"What are you drawing?"

Grace shrugged. "Places I want to go. With you."

Amelia stepped forward. "Where?"

Grace tilted the book. There were trees thick with green leaves—one had a rope swing. Mountains with snowy peaks. A carousel with tiny lights. A garden full of lavender. A pier over a vast, still lake. The bench under a tree had a small plaque that read *You Are Here.* On one corner of the page, Grace had drawn the Eiffel Tower and a small dog wearing sunglasses, reminiscent of a travel poster. And a beach. The kind Amelia had once promised to take her to—the one with the pink shells.

Tears filled Amelia's eyes. "That's beautiful."

She pointed to the bench drawing, blinking slowly. "Where did you hear that? *You Are Here?*"

Grace smiled, as if it were obvious. "From Nate, silly. I heard him say it."

Amelia's breath hitched. "You... did?"

Grace nodded, the gesture effortless and sure. "He says it a lot. I like it."

"I'm not scared here," Grace said softly. "Not if you're with me."

Amelia opened her mouth to answer—

But then Grace coughed. A soft sound at first. Barely a hiccup.

Then again.

She reached for a tissue from the bedside table—Amelia hadn't noticed it was there-and pressed it to her mouth. When she lowered it, a faint smear of red appeared.

Amelia froze.

Grace kept flipping through the drawings, unbothered. "It's okay," she whispered, sensing her mother's panic without looking up. "It's just a little."

Amelia stepped forward. "Grace, what's happening?"

Grace tilted her head, her curls brushing her cheeks. "Don't worry, Mommy. I'm okay. I just wanted you to see."

The beeping returned—slow at first, a heartbeat struggling to steady itself. But it grew louder. Sharper. Grace's hands stilled over the notebook. Her eyes lifted to Amelia. Calm. Steady.

"Do you remember the pink shells?" she asked.

"Yes," Amelia said, her voice cracking. "Yes, baby, I do."

"I want to go there," Grace said, her voice a little fainter. "Someday."

The machine behind her gave a sharp warning tone.

Amelia stepped closer, heart pounding. "No—don't go. Don't—"

Grace reached out and squeezed her hand. Her grip was warm, soft, firm.

"Don't be afraid," she whispered. "I'm not."

The light in the room dimmed. The sound escalated—alarms, monitors, footsteps approaching from nowhere. The notebook papers on Grace's lap fluttered in a breeze that wasn't there.

And then Grace leaned forward, her voice a whisper that reached straight to Amelia's soul.

"Don't forget, okay?"

Her smile never wavered.

Then everything slowly vanished.

First, her hand. Then the notebook. Then the outline of her shoulders.

Until only her voice remained.

The hospital room dissolved, and Amelia tumbled backward into warmth and grass.

* * *

THE AIR WAS now warm and fresh again.

Crickets sang in the distance.

Amelia stood barefoot in the grass, the familiar uneven patches of their old backyard cushioning her feet. She knew this exact spot—it was the place she used to sit with Grace on late summer nights, wrapped in blankets, watching fireflies and naming constellations they couldn't quite find.

The magnolia trees stood tall in the corners, branches still, their pink and white blooms glowing under the moonlight.

Someone had already spread a blanket across the grass.

Grace sat with her legs crisscrossed, gripping the flashlight with quiet authority—a tiny queen in her own world.

Amelia moved toward her but paused—someone else was sitting beside Grace.

A man.

Nate.

He wore a hoodie and jeans, his hair tousled, his posture relaxed in a way Amelia had never seen. He handed Grace a marshmallow from a little bag. She squished it between her fingers with a laugh.

Amelia stepped closer.

"Is this real?" she asked aloud.

Neither of them looked up. But Nate said, "You always used to ask that."

Grace giggled, then turned toward him. "She doesn't get it yet, does she?"

Nate shrugged with a soft smile. "She will. Takes her a little longer to believe the good stuff."

Grace looked at Amelia now, beaming. "Mommy, come sit. You're missing the best part."

Amelia knelt beside them. Her hand brushed Nate's shoulder. He didn't vanish.

"You're here," she whispered.

Nate smiled, eyes locked on the stars. "Always."

Grace lifted the flashlight again and pointed it toward the sky. "That one's Orion. He's the strongest."

Nate chuckled. "I heard he moonlights as a superhero."

Grace gave him a knowing look. "He does more than that."

Amelia glanced between them, heart caught between wonder and ache. "You two are acting like old friends."

Grace shrugged and reached for another marshmallow. "We talk sometimes. In dreams. In hearts. That kind of thing."

A breeze swept through the trees then, lifting the edges of the blanket and carrying their laughter into the magnolia-scented air.

Without warning, Grace climbed into Nate's lap with a familiar curl Amelia had loved. She cupped a hand to his ear.

"I have a secret," she whispered.

Nate leaned in, nodding solemnly. But his eyes flicked to Amelia. Whatever this was, it wasn't really a secret. They meant for her to hear it.

Grace's words were soft but clear. "Take care of Mommy for me."

Nate wrapped his arms around her tiny form and pressed a kiss to the top of her head. "Forever."

Amelia blinked, tears thick in her lashes. "Grace…" she whispered, but the breeze grew louder, pulling at the blanket, tugging at her edges.

The stars above them shimmered—then fell inward.

Grace looked at her one last time, her voice trailing through the wind: "You're almost ready."

And Amelia fell with the stars, the laughter in the air giving way to frosting and candlelight.

* * *

THERE WAS MUSIC this time.

A soft hum of laughter and low voices. The smell of frosting and the faint sweetness of strawberries.

Amelia stood in the doorway of a small dining room—their dining room, exactly how it had looked when Grace turned four.

The party had been tiny—only the three of them. She remembered it now. Grant had been traveling for weeks, and Grace had barely returned home from an extended hospital stay. Her immune system was still too fragile for a big celebration. So Amelia had gone all out in secret. Handmade decorations, a princess tablecloth, a stack of pink paper crowns, and a strawberry-frosted cake with too much food coloring.

Grace had danced barefoot on the chairs, grinning even though the chemo had taken her curls. Her angelic giggles had echoed in the walls. She had insisted the frosting be "swirly, not flat."

Amelia stepped forward.

There she was again.

Grace sat at the head of the table, her cheeks full, her grin wide. Her head was bare now, her skin more delicate. But her eyes—those were still fierce, still shining.

And across the table sat someone Amelia didn't expect.

Nate, again.

He wasn't supposed to be there.

He hadn't even existed in their world then.

But in this dream, he belonged—entirely.

He leaned across the table and said with quiet confidence, "Make a big wish, okay?"

Grace looked at him thoughtfully, then at Amelia. "Make one too."

Amelia smiled, but it trembled. "Always."

Grace nodded once and looked at the candle. The flame danced in the soft light.

That's when Amelia felt movement behind her. A presence. She turned.

Grant.

He stepped into the room, a shadow resolving into color. His features were tired but kind, as if carrying the weight of a goodbye too long. He looked the way he had the last time she saw him—coat half-buttoned, eyes heavy, the exact moment he left the house for the last time.

"Hi, Ames," he said softly.

Amelia's breath caught. "Grant..."

He nodded toward Grace. "You did good."

Her voice cracked. "I didn't do enough."

He stepped closer and reached out, brushing a strand of hair that wasn't there. "You did everything."

Then, finally, he looked at Nate. A long, unreadable glance passed between them. Grant gave the faintest smile. Not forced. Not jealous. Just... peaceful.

"He loves you," Grant said. "You can see that, right?"

Amelia didn't respond, but she didn't look away either.

Then Grant turned to Nate, steady and clear. "Take care of her."

Nate met his eyes. "I will."

Grace rolled her eyes dramatically. "She still doesn't get it?"

Amelia tilted her head, more impatient this time. "Get what?"

Grace giggled and swiped a finger through the thick swirl of pink frosting, leaving a tiny trail behind as the candle's flame flickered above, steady, hopeful, and waiting.

"It's okay," Grant said. "She'll figure it out."

For a moment, everything paused. The lights, the laughter, the warmth—it all hovered on the edge of forever.

Then Grace looked at the candle again.

The moment stretched impossibly long.

And then she blew it out.

The flame went out, and the sky turned a grayish hue.

* * *

A SOFT, ENDLESS gray light spread over a landscape unfamiliar to Amelia. It wasn't cold or devoid of color—just serene. It felt like a subdued memory, one you hesitate to disturb. She remained motionless, listening intently. The silence wasn't void; it was anticipatory. It felt as though the world paused, observing her.

The sky stretched overhead in a soft pewter wash, as if someone had sketched the scene in pencil but never inked it in. There was no sun, but everything glowed faintly, as if lit from within.

The ground held onto the mist, as if cradling a forgotten memory.

She stood motionless, unsure of how she'd arrived here.

She wore her softest jeans, a navy sweater with the sleeves pushed up, and worn sneakers caked with memory and mud. Her hair was down, slightly wind-tossed, clinging faintly to her cheeks. A thin veil of mist settled on her skin, delicate as breath pressed to glass.

The silence pressed in from all sides, a muffled ache that made her chest feel tight.

Then—movement.

In the distance, two figures ambled away.

Grace.

And Nate.

Hand in hand.

Their outlines were blurry at first, like a photo before it comes into focus. But Amelia would know them anywhere. The way Nate's shoulders tilted when he walked. The swing of Grace's arm as she skipped ahead. It was them.

She opened her mouth to call out—but no sound came.

Panic rose in her throat. Her voice, her power, felt swallowed by the dream.

She tried again. "Grace!"

Nothing.

"Nate!"

Still nothing.

She walked toward them, then faster, then faster—until the landscape stretched and pulled, rubbery and unyielding, as if trying to hold her back, refusing to let her follow.

Still, she pushed forward.

She could see them more clearly now.

Grace's hair bounced with each step. She was older again, closer to how she might have looked at ten or eleven years old. Confident. Calm. She wore a lilac tank top and jean shorts, her legs tan and strong, the way they might've been if she'd grown up without IV poles and hospital gowns.

Alive in a way Amelia hadn't let herself imagine.

Her eyes sparkled even from a distance, and her gait was light, as if she belonged to the mist and gravity couldn't touch her.

Nate glanced back once.

His expression wasn't sad.

It was steadfast, a gaze that watched over her—unshaken, sure this wasn't the end.

He didn't speak—but his eyes held something. A knowing. A quiet love. The kind that didn't beg or plead. It waited. Trusted.

Grace turned, too.

She didn't speak at first. She only raised her hand in the air—fingers stretched wide, palm facing her mother—and held it there. Not a wave. A beacon. A message.

Amelia took another hesitant step. Then another.

"Please," she whispered, finally able to hear her own voice, hoarse and thin. "Don't go. I'm not ready."

But the mist thickened. The wind picked up, curling around her legs, pulling her backward.

Still, she kept going.

"Grace," she cried again. "Nate—please—don't leave."

But neither turned again.

Not fully.

Not yet.

Grace paused at the top of the hill before the horizon faded them into shadow. She looked back; her face was full of something ancient and young all at once. The eyes of a child who had seen too much. The wisdom of a soul that still loved, anyway.

And then, as the wind seemed to quiet, Grace's voice came—clear, delicate, and piercing as glass:

"You're not alone."

The words echoed through the mist, sharp and clear as a bell.

Amelia dropped to her knees—not from defeat, but because the wall inside her had finally split wide open. Pain bloomed in her chest. Her breaths turned shallow. And then—suddenly—her heart kicked into a sprint.

It pounded once.

Then again.

Then again, faster.

Too fast.

As if it had stopped for a moment... and now was racing to make up for lost time. She clutched at her chest, panicked, her pulse thundering in her ears.

The surrounding air thickened. Mist crawled higher—up her arms, her neck—pressing in like a second skin.

Her heartbeat turned into a drum—wild, erratic, consuming.

She gasped—

And woke up.

* * *

HER EYES FLEW open, lungs burning, sweat damp on her back and temples. Her pulse still galloped beneath her skin, her body trembling as if she had run through something enormous and unseen.

The room was still. Unbothered by what it had witnessed. Unfazed by the journey Amelia had just taken within its walls. It was unchanged.

But everything was different now.

She blinked against the stillness, half-expecting the mist to rise again, for Grace's voice to call her back.

But the dream had let her go, and the morning light had touched the corners of the room.

Amelia clutched the pink blanket to her chest, her breath ragged and uneven.

*In and out,* she told herself. *Breathe.*

She closed her eyes again, for a second, half hoping the dream might return. That if she willed it hard enough, she could fall backward into that world and see them again.

Grace.

Nate.

Together.

The pull was strong. She could still feel it in her chest—the echo of Grace's voice, the press of Nate's steady presence, the warm air of a world she didn't want to leave.

But slowly, the hum of morning came back.

The creak of the house settling.

The soft rustle of trees outside the window.

The weight of her breath, still her own.

The room was nearly bare—no toys, no photos, no books on the shelves: only shadows and light and the softness of an old carpet worn down by small feet.

And yet, it felt full. Not haunted. Not empty. Complete.

Amelia sat up slowly, pressing a hand to her chest. The ache was still there, but softer now. Not a wound. A tether.

"I heard you," she whispered. "I remember."

She didn't know what came next.

But for the first time in a long time, she wasn't afraid to find out.

# 24

## i am here

L IGHT FILTERED SOFTLY through the kitchen windows, catching on the glass and warming the tile beneath Amelia's bare feet. She moved with an ease she hadn't felt in weeks—no tightness in her chest, no invisible weight on her shoulders. Even her breath came freely, unforced. Something inside her rested.

She reached for the phone, already knowing what she'd find. A message from Ronnie.

> *Coming by this afternoon. Please shower.*
> *There's a change of clothes and your toiletries on the counter—no excuses. XO.*

Amelia gave a quiet laugh. The text was bossy, blunt, and full of love—typical of Ronnie.

She wandered into the kitchen and opened the fridge. She picked at a few grapes, half an egg roll, and a container of pineapple chunks—leftovers Ronnie had tucked in the night before. She wasn't hungry, but it gave her something to do.

Around ten, a soft knock came at the back sliding door.

Tyler stepped in with a to-go cup and a small paper bag.

"Thought you might want this," he said, holding them out. "Still warm."

Amelia accepted them, surprised to find herself smiling. "Thanks."

"Ronnie's orders," he added with a wink, already backing toward the deck. "I figured."

But before he stepped back outside, Tyler paused. His expression shifted slightly—still casual, but not as light.

"Detective Mallory and his team are still dragging their feet, but we've been running our parallel check. Reviewing street cams, neighbor feeds, combing for a match."

"Okay," she mumbled, surprised by the news.

"We aren't letting up. And for what it's worth, I've been doing this a long time, Amelia. That guy wasn't there to rob you."

"Then what did he want?" she asked softly.

Tyler hesitated. "That's what worries me."

She told herself not to dwell on it, but the chill in Tyler's voice made her stomach turn.

Her face tensed with worry, but Tyler's voice softened. "You're going to be okay. Nate's already agreed to keep security on you until we're absolutely sure there's no more threat. No expiration date."

Amelia swallowed, the gratitude catching in her throat. "He did?"

Tyler nodded once. "Said it wasn't up for discussion." He gave her a slight nod, turned, and stepped back outside, resuming his quiet sweep of the yard.

As he walked the perimeter, Amelia stood still, the scent of cinnamon rising from the paper bag—softening the fear that had flared. She sipped the coffee and took a bite of the sugary roll, warmth spreading through her like sunlight through glass.

She didn't say it out loud, but she knew what this was—Ronnie making sure she didn't disappear again.

She was more than grateful. Ronnie wasn't only a friend—she was a lifeline.

After breakfast, Amelia moved toward the bathroom and finally did what Ronnie had asked. She showered, letting the hot water loosen everything still clinging to her. Then she pulled on the clean, folded clothes left on the counter—leggings, a soft tee, and socks that didn't match but made her smile.

It felt cleansing—shedding the last fragments of the night before.

By early afternoon, the house was quiet again, filled only with the soft buzz of the refrigerator and the faint, sweet scent of hope. Amelia caught sight of the white blossoms near the kitchen window—still full, still standing tall in the vase they were in.

She walked over and gently touched one of the petals.

They were soft. Resilient.

The very image of the man who'd chosen them.

The memory of Nate—his steady voice, the warmth in his eyes, the way he always waited for her to decide—rose in her chest, light and unshakable.

It wasn't longing. Not exactly.

It was a reminder. Of who he was, of what he'd offered.

And of the truth, she hadn't been ready to face.

She still needed to do something about Nate.

She *wanted* to do something about Nate.

Breaking her away from her daydream, a light knock came at the front door. It was soft and familiar. Ronnie never announced herself. She just showed up.

Amelia opened the door and found her standing there with two hands full of takeout bags. The comforting scent of garlic and soy sauce drifted in with her.

"You didn't have to—" Amelia began.

"I did," Ronnie said, stepping inside. "You were probably about to eat a jar of olives and a stale protein bar."

"That was only *one* time," Amelia giggled.

Ronnie grinned and set the takeout bags on the counter, then lifted a separate grocery sack from her arm and placed it beside them.

"What's all that?" Amelia asked, eyeing the grocery bag with suspicion.

"Just a few things," Ronnie said breezily as she started unpacking the takeout. "Orange juice, bagels, cream cheese, fresh berries, and some utensils."

"I still have stuff left from what you brought yesterday," Amelia said. "Are you restocking me for the apocalypse?"

Ronnie didn't look up. "Trust me—you're going to need it."

Amelia frowned. "Why? What's happening?"

Ronnie shot her a quick, knowing smile. "Nothing. Yet."

Amelia rolled her eyes. "That's comforting."

"Eat," Ronnie said, unbothered. "I brought enough to feed three versions of you."

Amelia gave her a look. "I don't even have a table."

"Then stand here and sulk like a normal person," Ronnie replied, handing over chopsticks and opening cartons across the kitchen island.

They stood side by side, quietly sorting through lo mein, dumplings, and packets of soy sauce.

"Did you sleep okay last night?" Ronnie asked gently.

Amelia hesitated, then slowly nodded. "I had dreams last night."

Ronnie looked up, her eyes narrowing slightly. "What dreams?"

"All of them," Amelia said softly. "One after another. Grace was there. She was older. Talking. Drawing. In one of them, even Grant was there. In another dream, Grace was talking to Nate."

Ronnie stilled, hand hovering over the lo mein. "Wait—Nate?"

Amelia nodded, her voice barely above a whisper. "She told him to take care of me."

Ronnie's expression shifted, her voice low and careful. "She said that?"

"It felt like I was really there, Ronnie. Inside a moment that never happened. But should have."

Ronnie was quiet for a beat. "Then maybe it wasn't a dream."

Amelia blinked. "What?"

"I mean, maybe it was, and maybe it wasn't. Who gets to say what's real with things like that?"

Amelia swallowed, her hands curling around the edge of the counter. "It felt so big, like I'd been holding my breath for four years and didn't even know it."

Ronnie reached for her hand. "You don't have to explain it. You just have to feel it. Let it matter."

"I think it already does."

She paused, her voice barely a whisper again. "I realized something in the middle of it all... that losing Grace didn't mean I lost all the love I had to give—or all the love I may receive. Nate—he's shown me that there's still more. More to feel. More to hope for. And somehow... none of it takes away from her. There's still space in my heart. All the space in the world. Grace will always be there."

A quiet moment passed between them.

Then Ronnie said softly, "Nate told Luke... that he talks to Grace sometimes. On the nights he can't sleep. He asks her to get through to you."

Amelia's eyes widened. "He does?"

"I think part of him believes she is still with you. With both of you."

Amelia's breath hitched. She reached for a napkin and wiped at the corners of her eyes.

"Did you read the article?" Ronnie asked. "The press release from Savannah?"

Amelia nodded. "Yeah, I read it last night."

Ronnie tilted her head. "Is that what you needed? To understand? To forgive him?"

Amelia hesitated, her voice low. "Yes... But I don't know what to do."

"I'm standing on this edge, and I don't know if stepping forward will feel like flying or falling."

Ronnie gave her hand another squeeze. "Then don't look down. Decide what's worth the jump."

Amelia looked at her, eyes glassy but clear.

"I'm scared it's too late," she whispered. "That I pushed him too far away."

Ronnie shook her head. "You didn't. People don't break that easily when they're your person."

She grabbed the grocery bag and slid her purse over her shoulder. "I'm going to go. Let you sit with all this."

Amelia protested, but Ronnie waved her off.

"But before I go—hear me out, okay, Amelia?"

"Uh oh, you only use my first name when I'm in trouble," Amelia replied.

"You deserve love, Lane. More than healing. Love. Grace would want that. Grant would want that. I want that. And you already know who your person is. You've always known."

A single tear traced its way down Amelia's face.

Ronnie leaned in and hugged her tightly. "Whatever comes next... accept it. Don't fight it this time."

She paused at the door, her hand on the knob. "And maybe... brush your teeth again. Something tells me tonight's not the night to wear ugly pajamas to bed."

Amelia stared at her. "Wait—what does that mean?"

But Ronnie only smiled, tugged the door open, and disappeared down the front steps.

And when the door finally closed behind her, the silence that followed didn't feel heavy anymore.

It was breath, caught just before the first word—the stillness between decision and transformation.

* * *

THE KITCHEN STILL carried traces of dinner—garlic and sesame oil hanging in the air like an invisible fog. Amelia scrubbed her toothbrush back and forth, watching foam gather at the corners of her mouth. She wasn't following Ronnie's instructions; she told herself. She just couldn't stand the thought of falling asleep with the lingering taste of takeout on her tongue.

When she finished, she rinsed, toweled off her face, and glimpsed herself in the mirror. There was no grand transformation staring back at her—only a woman still standing. "That's good enough," she muttered to her reflection.

She moved into the living room, phone in hand, her bare feet quiet against the floor.

The magnolias by the kitchen window caught her eye again. Their petals were softening slightly, but still holding their shape, open and white and brave. A reminder—one she hadn't quite unpacked yet.

Ronnie's voice came back to her, clear as if she were still in the room.

*"Something tells me tonight's not the night to wear ugly pajamas to bed."*

Amelia paced once, twice, then circled back to the kitchen. She leaned on the counter, then stood up again. The nerves weren't panic—they were a possibility. And she did not know what to do with that.

She'd known she'd end up holding her phone. The question was what she'd do with it.

*Just text him.*

Two words. One tap.

She opened a message. Her thumbs hovered.

**Thank you.**

Delete. Too short.

**I'm sorry. I was wrong.**

Delete. Too vague.

She tried again.

**Thank you for the house, for Grace, for everything you gave me—even when I didn't know how to receive it.**

Too long. Too stiff. Too incomplete.

The cursor blinked in the empty message box, as if daring her to be brave. But there weren't enough words. Not for this.

Not for *him.*

Nate had given her more than a home. He'd given her memories she didn't know she was allowed to make again. He'd held her hand through the heartbreak she thought would never heal. He'd waited.

He had been her quiet, patient miracle.

She took a breath and started again—

When her phone lit up.

**Incoming Call: Nate Carter**

Butterflies stirred, unexpected and wild.

She froze.

Then she tapped Accept.

"Nate..." she whispered.

His voice came through, low and reverent. "Mils, you answered."

"I-I don't know what to say," she stammered, the words snagging in her throat as emotion swelled, fast and unstoppable.

"It's okay, Mils," he said softly. "You don't have to say anything. Just know that I love you."

She closed her eyes, pressing the phone tighter to her ear, willing it to hold her together.

"Thank you," she managed, voice shaking. "For the house... for not giving up on me... for loving Grace."

His breath caught audibly on the other end. "She's easy to love. Like her mom."

Amelia let out a soft, broken sound that wasn't quite a laugh, wasn't quite a sob.

"I was so scared," she whispered. "I pushed you away because I thought I didn't deserve it. Any of it. You, the house, a second chance..."

"You do," Nate said. "You always did."

The floodgates opened. All the emotions she had been suppressing—grief, fear, the pain of losing him—came rushing out uncontrollably. For a brief moment, neither of them uttered a word. Her breathing was harsh and uneven, met by the calm strength of his silence.

Then—

A sound outside. The creak of a floorboard.

Her ears caught it before her mind understood. Not through the phone— but close. Real.

Her breath hitched as she turned toward the front door, drawn by an instinct deeper than thought.

"Nate..." The name escaped her lips like a prayer. "Where are you?"

His voice came through the phone, but somehow filled the room around her, too. "I'm here, Mils."

The truth of those words crashed against her ribs like waves.

She looked down at her phone, then toward the front of the house. *Here.*

Her feet carried her across the living room before her thoughts could form. Three heartbeats later, her hand was on the doorknob, pulling it open with such force that the hinges protested.

And there he was.

The impossible made flesh on her doorstep.

*He came back for me.*

Nate stood on her porch, his hair messy from the journey, eyes filled with a mix of hope, exhaustion, and something more profound—steady, unwavering love. A duffel bag rested at his feet. He wore a soft long-sleeve shirt with the sleeves rolled up to his elbows and jeans still carrying traces of airport dust. It was his expression that took her breath away—open, raw, and relieved. He looked like a man returning from a long battle, one he fought on his own.

A single tear slid down his cheek.

Not because he was broken.

Because she had answered, and he didn't have to fight alone anymore.

A sound left her before she could form words: a cry, a squeal—something in between—as she rushed into his arms.

He caught her instantly, buried his face in her hair, and pulled her close, releasing a hug he'd been holding in for far too long.

Amelia sobbed into his chest. "Thank you," she gasped. "I'm so sorry. I love you."

His hand cradled the back of her head. "Shhh. I've got you. You're okay."

"I didn't know how to fix it," she whispered. "I didn't know how to come back."

"You didn't have to. I never left."

They stayed there, tangled together in the doorway, the night quiet around them, the moment too full to speak.

Then, as her tears finally slowed and her breath came easier, Nate leaned down, brushed his lips to her ear, and whispered—

"It's okay, Mils. It's okay."

He held her a little tighter.

"I am here."

# About the Author

Charlotte E. Bassett is a storyteller at heart who finally put her imagination on paper when one idea refused to let go. Her debut novel, *You Are Here*, is the first step in a writing journey she hopes will grow to include romance, memoir, and children's literature.

Originally from Colorado, Charlotte now calls Florida home, happily trading snow boots for sunshine and sandals. She describes herself as witty, driven, and dependable — qualities her family sees in both her life and her work. On weekends, she can often be found cooking with her daughters, watching Court TV, or discussing her characters as if they were old friends.

Charlotte lives with her husband and their four daughters, who inspire her daily and remind her why stories matter. Her greatest hope as an author is simple: that finishing one of her books leaves readers eager to pick up the next, whether it's hers or another waiting on their shelf.